THE
COMPANION

THE
COMPANION

· A NOVEL BY ·
GORDON T. ALLRED

BOOKCRAFT
Salt Lake City, Utah

Library of Congress Catalog Card Number: 92-72654
ISBN 0-88494-832-3

First Printing, 1992

Printed in the United States of America

1

P resident Linford?" I pressed the receiver to my ear, listening with mingled anticipation and nervousness.

"Yes?" A single word, yet it somehow conveyed confidence. Perhaps it was the tone, deep and resonant, but it seemed to emanate from a man well-prepared for anything—which, come to think of it, might be a basic part of the job description for any mission president.

"President Linford," I said, "my name is Nathan Connors, and I'm calling from Ogden, Utah. Our son Darren is one of your missionaries down there in Phoenix . . . well, Glendale at the moment, I guess."

"Oh, *yes*, Elder Connors!" This time the yes also contained a note of pleasure, possibly even a trace of amusement. "Dare's a great missionary. What can we do for you?"

I was a bit surprised that he would refer to one of his missionaries by first name (nickname, in fact) since the title *Elder* is rigidly adhered to in most cases for Latter-day Saint males throughout their two-year missions. His reference to my son suggested, therefore, that I might be dealing with a man who wasn't too strictly bound by the rules of orthodoxy.

"Well, I have a request," I said. "It's rather different,

so please don't feel obligated in any way. If you have to say no, I'll certainly understand."

"Fair enough—fire away."

I then stated my case, explaining first that I had recently served as a stake mission president and had long ago been a full-time missionary to Eastern Canada. I also mentioned that Darren was my fifth son to serve in that latter capacity, with number six, the last, preparing to leave before long. Finally, I told him that I was a professor of English who spent much of his so-called spare time writing.

"What I'd dearly love to do, if it's at all possible," I said, "is to come down there to the Arizona Phoenix Mission and spend about three weeks working with my son and his companion to gather material for a novel on the subject. I definitely wouldn't want to interfere with the work, just participate in any way that might prove helpful."

For a moment he didn't reply. That made me nervous. "I realize, of course, that visits by family members are normally verboten, so please don't be afraid to say no if I'm out of line. I'll certainly understand."

The good president gave a faint chuckle. "Oh, I won't be afraid, but . . . weelll . . . this sounds like an interesting proposition. Hmmmm . . . might just be a fine arrangement, and accomplish a lot of good." He paused. "In fact . . . this all seems pretty fortuitous the more I ponder it, the ideal time." I was definitely "all ears," or maybe I should say "all ear," since my hearing was gone in the left one. "Your son just happens to be without a companion at the moment."

"Oh, really?" I said. The statement piqued my curiosity, since missionaries these days are virtually linked together like Siamese twins. "How did that happen?"

"Well, it's an interesting story. I guess you knew his latest companion was a Navajo—Elder Begay?"

"Yes, that's what Dare said in one of his letters. Really enjoys working with him."

"Right. Unfortunately, Elder Begay's father died

recently, and the young man's back on the reservation attending the funeral. He may not return for some time; in fact, Navajo custom being what it is, not until after a suitable period of mourning and so on."

"I see—sad, but interesting."

"Yes, the Navajo are a fascinating people. One of these days, if we're not careful, most of that culture—language included—may be gone."

"I'm afraid so," I said.

"Anyway, it came so unexpectedly that your fine young son was left empty-handed."

"So he's all on his own now," I observed.

"Well, not exactly. Two of our Elders who live about a block down the street are staying with him. There's more room in his apartment than theirs. The three of them are working together. Once you arrive, though, the other two can head back home. By the way," he added suddenly, "how soon are you planning to leave?"

I hesitated, feeling a sense of disbelief and excitement. Already it had become a fait accompli. Then I took the leap. "Probably early Monday morning, about six o'clock." It was now Saturday afternoon, two days after Thanksgiving.

"Sounds good. Planning to fly?"

"Drive," I replied. "Straight through. I thought I'd bring along my sleeping bag and air mattress. That way, hopefully, I won't discommode anybody or end up on the couch if our young Navajo returns right away."

"Good idea," the president said.

"And having my own car would give me some mobility."

"Perfect—sounds like a winner. I'll call your son right away and give him the glad news."

"Wonderful!" I enthused. The excitement was welling. "I really appreciate—"

"On second thought . . . " President Linford interrupted and paused musingly, long enough that I feared he might be having a change of heart. "Why don't I just tell

Dare . . . " His words were measured, calculating. Suddenly I realized, with near-certainty, what he had in mind. I could almost see, almost feel, the half-mischievous frown, imagine the squint in one eye. "Why don't I just tell Elder Connors," he added, correcting himself, "that I'm sending him a temporary companion—a slightly *older* fellow, say?"

"Ha!" The idea brought me sheer delight. "Tremendous!"

"Normally I wouldn't do that." The words were mellow, slightly mirthful. "But your son's quite a character, as you know—quite the joker in his own right. Might be fun to turn the tables on him in a good cause."

"Absolutely. Maybe you could say his new, *old* companion has his own car and will be arriving around six or seven Monday evening." I hesitated. "Of course, he may not fall for it because I told him some time back that I might check with you on the possibility of going to Arizona."

"Well, let's give it a whirl," the president said. "One way or another, he'll be one happy young man."

That was how our conversation ended and the way my unforgettable mission began.

2

And that was why, about four in the afternoon two days later, I found myself trundling across the Arizona desert in our little red Chevette, the plutocrat school teacher special. I had taken the long route from Ogden toward Phoenix past Las Vegas rather than the more direct one through Page on the southern Utah border. It was almost December, and I was a bit apprehensive about the snowy, mountainous regions of Flagstaff beyond.

Now, however, I was beginning to regret the decision, or at least to have mixed feelings about it. The journey to Vegas had been a piece of cake, even though the cake itself was rather stale. Nice freeway cruising, but gray skies and increasingly drab landscape relieved only by an occasional flight of birds or sporadic snow flurries.

From then on, the highway had become narrow and poorly marked. The traffic, widely interspersed before, had backed up to a crawling, sinuous caravan as it crossed Hoover Dam with its mighty metallic skeletons of electrical installations that looked like characters from some science fiction movie, special effects by Salvador Dali.

Then it was onward into the desert, a rather hazardous odyssey with much road construction and narrow, winding highways marked along the way by a variety of creative, if morbid, warning signs. Most of them depicted cars or trucks in collision, usually crashing head-on thanks to drivers who drink, speed, or fall asleep at the wheel. At times, I told myself, safety might be better served if the visitor also had a few more signs to indicate where he was going. Much of that, apparently, is left to personal revelation.

Near Kingman, an hour's drive beyond Lake Mead and the great dam, I passed a road veering off to the left and a sign reading, "East to Flagstaff." An instant later, a huge semi thundered by on my right under a full head of diesel, so close it nearly flung me from the highway with a horn like the blast of a freight train and a buffeting wind like the gust from a hurricane.

Shaken and indignant, I continued my dubious course, having encountered no other signs for many miles. Incredible! The abominable vehicle seemed to have sprung from nowhere and been upon me like some awesome juggernaut. Indignation evolved into anger—anger at the stupid driver for his total disregard of the speed limit and for human life, anger at myself for somehow being so unaware.

A minute or two later I pulled off the road, well out of the line of fire, to check my map. Yes, happily, I was still headed the right way. I continued onward, and, within an hour, I was only a hundred miles from my destination, having recently passed the thriving metropolis of Wikieup—aptly named, since the entire town was apparently not much larger than the old-time Indian shelters by that name.

It was only five o'clock, but already the sun was setting, fading into muted, slightly smoggy tones of orange and peach across the darkening desert. "The lone and level sands," in the words of Shelley, "stretched far away," leaving nothing but the mesquite digesting into shadow and the silhouettes of saguaro cacti—gigantic spiney pickles with stubby upturned arms that lent them a human quality as well, half amusing, half forlorn.

Somehow, I had imagined that the daylight would last

much longer in those warmer climes even though it was the end of November, but not so. Far off in the hazy west the sun hovered furtively on the horizon then vanished as though through a trap door. Within minutes the land was enveloped in gray, and already the headlights of cars traveling the opposite direction were flashing on. I turned my own lights on, adjusting the same little black knob simultaneously to light the instrument panel, and discovered something else even more disquieting.

My gas indicator had almost reached the red mark. Just ahead in the gathering dusk, I spotted a sign that read, "Wickenburg–60 Miles." For the moment I felt only faint uneasiness. Surely there would be a chance to refill the tank before long; there almost always had been before. The stretch from Ogden to Vegas, with its frequent rest stops and signs promising food and gas at some of the most remote outposts, had made me complacent.

Now, as the road unravelled before me, darkness rushed backward in a tidal wave, and I flipped on the high beam. Again I spotted a warning sign: another incongruously humorous cartoon of two cars in a head-on bash thanks to the blessings of alcohol. A wise reminder for many, no doubt. But again I thought irritably of the dearth of other road signs. It would be nice, I mused if the scarcity of gas stations had been indicated some twenty-five miles back at the last one.

It was a growing dilemma. If I returned to the previous stop it would mean fifty extra miles of driving, almost another hour added to an already long trip. By now I was beginning to feel somewhat frazzled and didn't relish the prospect of arriving late in Glendale to search for my son's address in a mass of apartments on some obscure back street.

"The best thing to do," I told myself, "is to stop right now, find some place well off to the side, and use your brain a little. Take time to think this out." And yet . . . For some perverse reason, I pressed onward. Without quite realizing it at first, I began driving faster and faster under the foolish impression that in so doing I might reach another gas station before my fuel ran out! The whole idea was ludicrous; my mind admitted it, but my foot remained heavy. Meanwhile, the fuel indicator seemed to be entering the ominous red zone with diabolical speed. It was, in fact, fluctuating erratically now with every dip and rise in the road.

At best, I decided, I might have a gallon left, enough for another thirty miles or so, and it was now apparent that I had reached the point of no return. There was nothing left to do but keep driving and pray the prayer of a fool. In the very process, though, I had visions of myself abandoning ship there amid the desert wastes, a wayfarer in the fell clutch of circumstance, dependent upon his legs and a hopeful thumb.

I became more despondent with each passing mile and was beginning to feel a childish urge to cry a little, when the miracle occurred. About two-hundred yards ahead and off to the left there appeared to be a store of some kind, one so dimly lit that under normal circumstances I might have failed to notice it and passed right on by. There in front—my heart did little back flips, and I scarcely dared believe—were two faded yellow gas pumps! For a few seconds they seemed to hover mirage-like, part of a dream, too wondrous to be real.

The station, as I pulled in, looked like a fire-scarred chicken coop. A sign over the door read "T'aint Much," but to me it was Shangri-la. The attendant appeared promptly, a wiry, simian specimen with frizzly, brindle-colored hair that reached his shoulders. "Welcome to Nothing!" he proclaimed jovially.

"Friend," I replied, "you may not realize it, but right now this is *everything*."

At that he gave a knowing cackle as though I hadn't been his only visitor in such a predicament. "Gettin' a mite low on the old petrol, were you?"

I nodded emphatically, grinning like an idiot. "Running on fumes alone." By now I was feeling rather jubilant.

"Well, we can rectify that problem," he assured me, and cranked the antiquated tank to zeroes with a handle on the side that might have belonged to the door of an old Ford. Moments later, the pump was grinding rustily away as if at any instant it might lose a few cogs, but nothing had ever sounded more melodious—except for the accompanying flow of gasoline swilling into the famished belly of my little Chevette.

My benefactor wore thick-lensed glasses and, despite the hour, dark green sun shades, the clip-on variety. He sported a sleeveless leather vest that exposed a hairy, cadaverous chest, and his arms were tattooed as though he might have been the prototype for Bradbury's Illustrated Man. "And now, kind sir," he said amiably, "it appears that I must liberate you from some of your hard-earned income to the tune of eight dollars and thirty-five cents."

"Gladly," I replied and presented him a ten. "Keep the change." He was truly an angel in disguise.

3

An hour and a half later I reached Glendale, but having arrived, I had not arrived. No one had ever heard of the street, or so it seemed. "West Eugie?" Dubious frowns, slightly suspicious glances as if perhaps I'd made it up, a few grins.

Eventually, however, I obtained a map of the city at a service station, where the attendant also discovered the street name I longed for. Physically and temperamentally he was the exact opposite of my hippiesque rescuer back in the wastes. His face and bald head were inflamed and characterless like a chunk of boiled frankfurter, and he wheezed with each grudging word. But then, I wasn't looking for charm school, merely West Eugie, a name that by now was beginning to sound like an animation from the Saturday morning cartoons.

Yet even after I had pinpointed West Eugie and was headed west along a large thoroughfare, supposedly in the right direction, I was having my troubles. Long sections of the road were undergoing reconstruction, pitted by tractor treads, potholed, and separated down the middle by blinking yellow flasher lights. The night air swam with dust that obscured the street signs. At times, I slowed, craning my neck and squinting to no avail, merely exciting honks from the impatient procession behind.

Eventually I arrived at a major thoroughfare, having apparently left little Eugie back somewhere in the dust. By now it was eight o'clock, though it seemed closer to midnight, and I found myself alone in the parking lot of a nearly deserted shopping mall. The entire place seemed to have been abandoned at first, almost as though evacuated under the threat of war. Abandoned, that is, except for a large furniture store cascading a small universe of fluorescent light.

I entered. The light was almost consuming, the store immense and filled with furnishings of nearly every kind from lamps to couches, arm chairs, expensive dining room sets and beds. There were also handsome stereo cabinets and TV's, some with thirty-inch screens, still playing with the volume turned low. The only human occupants were two salesmen, or perhaps managers, conversing together at the far end near a glass-partitioned office. Both wore ties and white shirts and glanced at me with a kind of mild expectancy, a bit as if they had been awaiting my arrival.

For a moment I felt a strong sense of déjà vu. Even though this was my first trip to the Phoenix area, it seemed as if I had been in that very place before under the same circumstances. One of the men looked Hispanic with thick, dark hair, a bristling moustache, and a pock-marked face. Both were trim, but the other man was older, rather gnome-like with a silver widow's peak and the beginnings of a pot belly. "Yes sir—what can we do for you?" he inquired.

"Gentlemen," I said, "I'm lost."

At that, the gnome-type tossed his head knowingly, a little to one side, accentuating a nose so large and hooked it seemed to throw his entire body off balance. His chuckle was asthmatic. "Aren't we all!"

Laughing, I felt the déjà vu increase. The Hispanic gentleman simply grinned faintly, steadily. It was as if they both knew something about me that I didn't, or at least something that, from a rational standpoint, they normally couldn't. Had they somehow tuned in on my foolish error back there in the desert? Crazy! Of course not.

Ironically, however, it was the knowing gnome with his laconic allusion to the general state of mankind who managed to orient me fully at last and inform me as to the exact location of W. Eugie. It was four blocks back the way I had come. "First one past Thunderbird Road," he promised. "Just hang a right and keep going about three hundred yards. That'll put you about 5185."

Thanking them earnestly, I went on my way, happy once again. Yet even then, it wasn't all that simple. The apartment complex was far larger and, indeed, more *complex* than I had supposed. For several minutes I wandered along a labyrinth of little walkways, flowers, and cactus gardens, twice encountering the same swimming pool, brightly glowing underwater lights, an inviting cerulean blue there in the Arizona night.

"I'll know the apartment," I assured myself, "before I ever see the address because I'll spot a couple of bicycles either on the front porch or through one of the windows." And at that precise moment—I'd swear to it were I a swearing man—I spotted what I was seeking. Well, not two bikes, but I did see one. That, in fact, was *all* I could see; it was leaning against a living room wall, visible through a slight separation in a drawn pair of window curtains.

Yes, that definitely had to be the place. A glance at the address confirmed the fact, though it wasn't really necessary. Immediately I felt my pulse rate increase, spirit brimming with warmth at the prospect of seeing my son after a separation of almost two years. My now twenty-one-year-old kid, Darren S. Connors. I pressed the doorbell, feeling my face brim with a doting fatherly smile. There was no way I could have disguised it even if I had wanted to.

Then the door opened, and there he was. I'm tempted to say "big as life," but that's trite, and besides, he was *bigger* than life. Still lean and a bit fox-like, but about two

12

inches taller than when I'd last seen him—a good six-feet four or maybe five. For a moment his face was a total blank, as though I were someone he had never seen before. "Hello there, young man," I said and extended my hand. "I's your new junior companion."

His eyebrows leapt, full of sudden, delighted mischief; and his eyes welled wide with disbelief, then recognition and the old rapport—green and brown, the color of my own, of *my* father's also. "Pop!" There were faint lines on each side of his mouth that I hadn't seen before. His grin was now so wide it exposed the gums and the slot from his missing molar on the upper left side. His face contained a few zits, from poor eating habits probably. Simultaneously, he looked quite handsome. There was a special light in his eyes, something in his bearing that told me he was no longer just my kid, that he had become a man.

All these impressions blended within a mere second or two. Then we were hugging each other unabashed, slapping backs amid exclamations of amused wonderment and rejoicing. "Hey, Pop, what's goin' on? Man, I can't believe it!" During our months of separation, his nose and chin had become more prominent, and he had acquired a more distinct beard, strong five o'clock shadow.

"Neither can I," I laughed. It was all so real, yet somehow part of a dream. "By the way, this place is not the easiest to find in the world. For a while there I actually wondered whether I'd make it. Ever since Las Vegas, in fact."

His eyebrows vaulted again. "Vegas? You came that way?"

I nodded. "Right—afraid I'd hit too much winter up there in the mountains of Flagstaff."

Dare tossed his head. "Oh, yeah—pretty bad up that way about now." Then he did a kind of double-take. "But, Pop, what's goin' on—what are ya doing here?!"

I shrugged, offering my most enigmatic grin. "Oh, just heard you were without a companion and couldn't be trusted on your own any longer." I grabbed his shoulder and gave it a shake. "No, I'm down here to do a little research and work with you for a while. Okayed it all with President Linford."

He blinked in slight astonishment, tucked in his chin. "That book deal you wrote me about a while back, huh?" I nodded, enjoying myself immensely. "Ha! I should have figured it out when the pres said he was sending me an older comp with his own car. But you haven't said anything about it for a real long time," he shrugged, tossing out his hands. "Sort of figured you'd bagged the idea."

I laughed. "Well, it's *in* the bag now."

Dare kept shaking his head and grinning. "Hey, this is out of sight! I can't believe the pres. Had us all snowed to the nose!" Until then I had barely been aware of the other two missionaries. One was in the adjoining kitchenette with the fridge door half open. The other had emerged from a bathroom somewhere, clutching a toothbrush, his mouth agape and still foamy. He was short, very stocky, with nut-cracker nose and chin. His shirt sleeves were rolled up to the elbows revealing heavily tattooed forearms, much like the friendly proprietor of "T'ain't Much."

"Hey, guys, check this out," Dare persisted. The Elder at the fridge was big all around, almost hulking, even taller than Dare, with close-cropped carrot-colored hair, and freckles. "This is the companion Pres said he was gonna send me, that *older* dude he was talking about." We were all laughing a little, sharing one grand, collective grin. "My own *pop*!"

4

At midnight I was still awake, lying there on the twin bed, in my fluorescent, lime-green pajamas, reflecting upon all that had happened since my departure from Ogden the morning before. Dare was snoring away in the other bed. His companions had gone to their apartment in the next block soon after my arrival, leaving father and son to their own devices.

We had shared some time-hardened neopolitan ice cream we'd found clinging to the corners of a battered carton in the fridge and downed some chocolate chip cookies I had brought along, his favorites, lovingly provided by his mom and kid sister Lori. Later we had "kicked back on our sacks" and "rapped" (if you want the missionary lingo) about whatever happened to surface—family, friends, hunting, and fishing. We recalled with much amusement the time years ago when he had become so agitated over the loss of a large rainbow trout that he flung his pole into the Ogden River.

And we spoke of his mission, including his days of "deep res." (short for deep reservation) among the Navajo near Window Rock. The old man there who, upon being asked if he was baptized, replied, "Oh yes, many times; it makes those young uldahs (elders) so happy." The good sister who had come to love and treat Dare as though he were her own son, wept many tears on that fateful Tuesday transfer day when word came that he'd be off to Gallup, N. M., on the morrow. She had lost a son his same age a few years before from a truck roll-over on one of the reservation's winding backroads.

Lying there now, strangely wakeful, I pondered these things, as a pleasant, moonlit breeze entered the open window, lilting the curtains. I felt sorrow for the Navajo sister in her loss, gladness and appreciation for the presence of my own son sprawled there on the bed a mere arm's reach from mine. He bested me in height now by two or three inches, but inside him somewhere were all the younger sons he had once been.

I had but a general idea as to what lay ahead, all that might happen in the next three weeks or so before I returned home for Christmas, but I knew that it was a unique opportunity. Unique in the sense that precious few family members, except for married couples, ever have such experiences together. Yet there was more to it than that. With each faint lilt of the curtains, I felt a kind of prescience: whatever lay ahead would not merely be different but somehow extraordinary. Or was it merely my imagination, wishful thinking?

The past eighteen hours or so, in fact, had certainly been different. For a while I lay there, still feeling the momentum of my little red Chevette, hearing the purr of the motor, the hum of the tires, while places and events flowed through my mind much as though recorded on video. At times it would pause, back-track briefly, often fast-forward, consuming vast distances, but much of it was very vivid. More than ever, I realized that nothing is ever forgotten, not in terms of being annihilated, merely filed away somewhere beyond immediate recall awaiting the right stimulus—the suggestion of a hypnotist, an electrode touching a certain area of the brain, a nostalgic melody or memorable odor, a voice, a face . . . or the putting of words on paper.

16

"So nothing is ever forgotten, Nate old boy," I told myself. My son stirred in his sleep, rolled onto his side, and stopped snoring. I hadn't even minded the snoring; it had extended the sense of closeness and reunion. "No, nothing really forgotten. Perhaps, in fact, no sound, act, or deed is ever lost. Everything simply hovering there somewhere in a kind of fourth dimension."

Momentarily, I thought about accounts I had read of people who had died, then returned to mortality. Some of them had described encounters with a "Being of Light" who in certain cases asked a loving yet disconcerting question: "What have you learned?"

"Well, Nate, all right," my own mind inquired. "So what have *you* learned, this very past day or so?" Hmmmm . . . maybe that journeys are often symbolical of life. Hardly a new thought, of course, the theme in countless works of literature, yet not to be lightly esteemed because of its commonality. New context and perspective can always add insight. "Anyway," I reflected wryly, "you've learned something about keeping your gas tank filled nearer the top, especially on the long haul when you don't quite know where you're going." Symbolical? Possibly. Virtually anything can be if you truly want it to be. "Well, hopefully, in any event, you've learned more about not overlooking those 'trivial little details' that may have profound, even disastrous, consequences if left unattended.

My wife, Sally, had once maintained that I was the ultimate absent-minded professor. "You *might* actually *qualify* for heaven," she laughed, "but may not get in anyway."

"Oh?" I replied, regarding her with doting amusement. "Why not?"

"You'll have lost the requisition. Either that, or you won't have your computer code number."

5

I awakened to the faint bleeping of an alarm—an urgent little series of SOS's—feeling groggy, as if I had finally been carried down into the very dregs of sleep, dragged right through the mattress and springs. It was something that didn't happen very often. Generally, I'm a light and rather restless sleeper, but the cumulative effect of my fourteen-hour drive and scant four hours in bed was having quite an impact. I felt drugged, and sleep graced by a flower-fragrant breeze was extraordinarily beguiling, especially now that the bleeping had ended.

I could hear Dare stirring, yawning, the springs squeaking as he sat up and stretched. His shoulders popped, along with two or three vertebrae.

"Hey, Pop!" His voice was muffled with sleep, a bit dry and cracked. He yawned prodigiously. "Man, I still can't believe it. I mean, this is really *unreal!*"

"Morning, Merry Sunshine," I managed. My own voice sounded even worse than my son's, a bit like someone feeling the first twists of the rack. "What makes you shine so bright?" I lay there, left forearm across my brow, regarding him covertly. But even then, I was feeling the gladness of reunion, that inexplicable sense of having a kid you're proud of, one who amuses you, whom you not only love but also like.

"Hey, Dad . . . " Rubbing his eyes. Sometimes it was "Dad" as well as "Pop," occasionally even "Father," when he was having a little fun being formal, sometimes "Nate." It didn't matter, I enjoyed them all. "I'm gonna hit the scriptures, but maybe you'll want to stay in the sack for a while, what with the big trip, getting to bed so late, and all."

It was a tempting thought. For a moment I nearly succumbed. Then he arose, blond hair disheveled, reminding me a bit of windblown straw, and headed for the bathroom in his bright yellow pj's. His mother, I recalled, had stayed up late sewing them for him, special material he had requested, the night before he left for the MTC in Provo. His twenty-four-hour beard was surprisingly heavy, blue-black, something I had never noticed before his mission. "Yeah, well . . . " I groaned, lolling in the embrace of temptation, but responsibility prevailed. It would be a short stay, three weeks or so at best, and I wanted to live the role of missionary as much as possible, also to follow his example. It would be important to start out right, I told myself, read the scriptures together, and all the rest. "I'll be up in a sec," I called, "soon as you're through in there."

Already his electric razor was buzzing away, agonizing a little over the denser areas of his beard. I could hear it muted through the closed door, and the very mutedness was intensely soporific.

I awakened with a surge of chagrin in a room so full of sunlight that it hurt my eyes. I squinted at my watch incredulously; it was almost nine o'clock. There were voices in the front room, something I couldn't quite make out, but I seemed to hear a wisecrack or two directed at me. That and a unique sort of snuffling chortle with which I was still unfamiliar.

Dare entered the room a moment later wearing a freshly ironed, white shirt and a silk tie of shimmering

19

teal-wing blue. He grinned knowingly. "Hey, Pop, let's get with it. The Elders are here, and we're going to celebrate your arrival with some good, old-time tracting."

"Wow!" I exclaimed, "what hit me?"

"Well," Dare said consolingly, "you needed your beauty rest, but now it's time to go for it. How does the tracting bit grab ya? Game?"

"Sure I'm game," I replied, and did a quick job of making my bed. "But I may not be in season."

"Well, let's get *with* it, my man!" The grin broadened, exposing the gap in his molars, making it even more mischievous. "We'll soon find out."

It was the grin, I suddenly realized, not only of youth but also of an "old pro" missionary who had about run the course. Run it well but hung loose. Fought the good fight but kept it mellow. The other Elders, MacDougall and Huddleston, had joined him in the bedroom entrance, their grins expanding with his own and all that sunshine.

"Right, absolutely," I said, laughing. I managed to effect a stiff little trot to the bathroom and gave them a combination wave-salute—parody of the good old boy who is "spry for his age." Or was it mere parody? The thought flitted moth-like through my mind. "Give me five minutes."

True to my word, I emerged showered and shaven, even toothbrushed, in five minutes. I was donning my suit pants, a navy blue polyester offering somewhat past its prime, when Dare interrupted. "Hey, Dad, feast your orbs on *these* duds." It too was a suit, of sorts. The trousers were slightly tapered, with old-time cuffs; the coat sporting narrow lapels. It was light cotton, a trifle wrinkled, and a dull yellow-gold with broad, rust-colored crosshatching. "Got this at the thrift store for five bucks."

"Hey there," I replied, uncertain for once whether the boy was serious or joking. "That's really something!" For an instant, I was reminded of the man who managed to avoid insulting the proud parents of a rather homely infant. "Say now, that really *is* a baby!"

"Try it on, Pop. I've been wearin' it, but it's too big around the bod."

"Yeah, well . . ." I was trying hard to sound appreciative, yet somehow find an out.

"*Wear* it, Pop! You'll look cool. I was planning to bring it home to ya—late Christmas present or something, but you might as well get some use out of it right away."

In terms of style the suit appeared to have been about forty years old, though it was in pretty good condition. Obviously, however, it had become the right item—something that, for complex and mysterious reasons even youth itself may not comprehend, was now "in." To my deep regret, it fit almost perfectly, except for a little bagginess in the rear. "Hey, all right! Cool!" *Coolness*—that was the grand secret. Whatever was cool would change the world for good or for evil. "Now try the coat." It fit too, perfectly. "Hey, Elders, get a load of my old man!"

More *all right's* and *cool's*. Elder MacDougall, the short, stocky lad, gave a little chortle of delight, and responded in what I now realized was a thick, Scottish brogue. "Hey, nou—thaht's bahd!" *Bad*, in fact, was even better than cool. "Gotta louve it!" Meaning, I surmised, gotta *love* it. And with approbation like that, what more could a fifty-nine-year-old greenie, junior companion do but wear the thing and like it. *Louve* it, yet!

6

Shortly thereafter, we were sauntering through a nearby suburb, one of the ritzier areas, with ranch-style homes of redwood or brick and stone or sometimes a lot of white stucco that almost dazzled the eye. Many of the yards contained coarse sand in place of lawn, or even crushed, dark red lava rock. There were also cactus gardens ranging from the giant saguaro to squat little specimens like sea urchins, bristling with ferocious spines. There it was, the first day of December, possibly snowing at home, but dry and arid in Glendale, and about eighty degrees at only 9:30 A.M.

Elders MacDougall and Huddleston (Mac and Hud, as Dare sometimes called them) took one side of the street while my son and I took the other. And suddenly I was feeling strange yet familiar sensations. It was that sense of déjà vu again that I had known at the furniture store the night before, yet this time less elusive. As we approached our first door, in fact, it became full recollection. All in an instant, I was transported back through space and time nearly forty years and several thousand miles to my first tracting door in Welland, Ontario, near Niagara Falls. I was there with my senior companion, Elder B. J. Nelson, feeling some of the same panic, the gray matter in my mind turned to pabulum, my tongue like a slab of Roquefort cheese. "Well, Elder," my companion had said. His blue eyes were full of mischief. "You want the first one?"

"Are you kidding?" My voice had broken like an early adolescent's. Elder Nelson hadn't given me the slightest briefing on how to begin. It was strictly on-the-job training, sink or swim. "Not on your life—not till I see how it's done." But my senior companion had been a very persuasive young man, and I had experienced the good or bad fortune of having the door slam in my face before I could stammer out the first sentence.

"Well, Elder . . ." my son said. For an instant the two missionaries had become one, registering the same sly, vulpine grin. Had Elder B. James Nelson also been missing that upper, leftside molar? Yes, I could visualize it clearly now, an odd and preoccupying coincidence indeed. "She's all yours."

I chuckled uncomfortably. I had stood before classes for years as an alleged professional, given countless talks in church, taught my share and more of priesthood and Sunday School lessons, but now I was just as tongue-locked, or nearly, as I had been that memorable day four decades earlier in Welland. "No," I said, "go ahead—youth before beauty. Let's see your modus operandi."

"My what?" He waggled his eyebrows as if I'd said something risque. Then he shrugged and faked a patronizing smile, punching the doorbell with a kind of flourish. We waited expectantly, not only for tell-tale sounds within but also for that elusive feeling, sixth sense, maybe, that conveys an awareness of presence or absence. I remembered that, too, from my own day. Again he pressed the bell, adding a forthright knock. Maybe a bit too forthright, I thought. The sunlight gathered, simmering, reflected from the white door. In the center, chin high, was a tiny peephole, and eventually Dare stopped, hunching and craning his long, angular body, squinting in on it as if the thing were a gun sight. "If somebody's in thar a-lookin' out," he muttered, "we'll be right down eyeball to eyeball, won't

23

we?" Only he said it with a Texas accent like Elder Huddleston: "*Aw-bowl* to *aw-bowl.*" Why? Simply because he was slightly crazy like everyone else in the family. He was also a natural mimic.

"So then what happens?" I laughed.

"Then, man, aw like hypnotizes 'em! They's at mah *muhcy*. 'You *will* answer . . . you *will* open this *doah* . . . you *will* buh-*lieve* . . . you *will* go *Dow*-un!'" Meaning by the last comment, I assumed, under the water.

"Not permanently, I hope." I watched for his response.

"Well, no—not necessarily." He held up a warning finger and shook it at me. "Only if they ain't fully repented."

But there was no answer. That was my first tracting experience since Canada and "nobody kept answering."

The second door was no different. The only sound from within was a constant, muffled yipping. In my mind's eye I saw a chihuahua, one of those frenetic little creatures that could scarcely qualify as canine, with the bulging eyes of an antelope and looking as if it had just been skinned.

On the third door, Dare pressed his thumb over the peephole. "Another of my tricks," he explained. "That way they don't know who's there, but their curiosity always gets the best of 'em."

"Ah so!" I was still feeling uneasy, but a little more relaxed. Then the door was unlatching, drawing open with a vacuum-like suction as Dare deftly withdrew his hand to avoid incrimination. The woman who answered wore a brightly flowered dress with a very low neckline, flame pinks and pomegranate reds on a violet background, and large, silver, pendant earrings. She might have been a model except for the thick-lensed glasses that greatly magnified the size of her eyes and lashes.

"Good morning, ma'am," my young companion said affably. "How are you today?"

"I'm feeling fine," came the reply, "but I'm just leaving, and frankly, I'm not the *least* interested." Her smile was twisted and disdainful, almost a snarl. She was wearing a henna-colored wig that looked very heavy and hot.

24

Dare nodded courteously. "Certainly, we understand. Thanks very much for your—" The door didn't quite slam, but it closed swiftly and firmly. "Your time," his voice trailed off wryly, the words seeming to stretch from the corner of his mouth. "Keen interest, extreme courtesy, and . . ."

"Wild getup," I added, and we both laughed. Already, a lot of it was coming back—the ambivalence, for one thing, the honest desire to do well and convey a vital message, but also the defensive cynicism in response to a rude rejection.

"All right, Pop," Dare said as we approached the next door. "Your turn—can't do any worse than I did."

I laughed again, raising my eyebrows. "You call that last one a turn?"

"Why, sure!" He clapped my shoulder.

"Doesn't give me much to go on."

"No *problema*, that's normally as far as we get. Tracting ain't too easy around these parts. Practically all our investigators, in fact, come from member referrals—that's where we get the real action. But . . ." Dare shrugged. "Once in a while something crops up this way, and it's always a good initiation for a real greenie."

He gave my shoulder a playful shake, throwing me slightly off-balance. "No doubt," I said. "But I still think I'd better watch you operate a little. After all, it's been a spell since your dear old dad engaged in this sort of thing. Besides, I have an idea our approach may have been quite a bit different way back when. We used lots of tracts, for one thing."

"Yeah?" He shot me a glance. "What are tracts?"

For a moment I thought he was putting me on, but no, he really didn't know the word. "Pamphlets," I said. "*Joseph Smith Story*, *The Apostasy*, *One True Church*, and so on."

"Oh, yeah, right." He nodded. "We got a batch of 'em back at the pad. Just don't use them all that much."

"Well, back in *my* day . . ."

"Back when they were still settling Utah, right?"

I laughed and nudged him with my elbow. "Somewhere back then—'long about the time of Jim Bridger actually. But anyway, back on my mission, we passed out tracts to practically anybody who'd take one. We'd ask people to read them, then let us return in a few days to see what they thought."

"Did it work?"

"Sometimes," I said, "some places." We had reached the next door, and even though it was framed in Christmas lights, I felt a certain anxiety. The spacious window to our right was similarly decorated, and the whole thing seemed highly incongruous. The day itself, in fact, seemed a lot more like the Fourth of July. Well, Labor Day, anyway. Dare punched the button, and after a long wait we were greeted by a large, rotund fellow who appeared to be Arabic. He was swarthy, with a prominent jaw and an imposing, hooked nose. Though balding on top, much like myself, he managed to overcompensate elsewhere. Coarse, black hair matted his forearms like spun glass in a furnace filter, covered his hands, even the space between his knuckles. It sprouted from his shirt front so thickly that momentarily I began to wonder if Darwin didn't have it right after all.

"Sorry, gentlemen," he said affably enough, "but whatever it is, I'm not buying."

"Well actually," I began, "we're not selling. We're representatives of—"

"Yeah, I know, I know," he replied, "but you're pushing something—right? Whether it's insurance, Amway, or religion—right?" He looked amused, self-assured, as though he had just completed a shrewd checkmate maneuver. "The only people ever dropped by this place since I moved in here and weren't selling something were a couple of characters from the FBI. Thought I was a mafioso!" One furry eyebrow arched like an inchworm, as though it had been a fine joke on them, and we all had a friendly chuckle. "Thought I was one of the 'brotherhood.' Actually, I'm a

Palestinian–was, that is, before I took out U. S. citizenship. But that doesn't mean I'm crazy in love with Arafat."

"Well," I said, beginning to catch my stride a little, "we're a part of the brotherhood ourselves."

"Really?" He drew back a little, feigning shocked surprise, and tucked in his chin, making it puff out double. Both chins, even though closely shaven, appeared to have been rubbed with ashes.

"A different kind, though," Dare said, "out of Salt Lake City."

"Ah–aha! Yeah, now I get it–the Mormons." He stroked his chins with a furred and pudgy hand. "My sister-in-law's married to one of them–whole bit, in their temple and everything. But I'm still not buying."

"Fair enough," I replied, "and believe it or not, we aren't out here arm-twisting, just telling anyone who wants to listen what makes us so different." He refused to take the bait. "How long since you left your homeland?"

He rolled his dark eyes eloquently. "What homeland?" Then, after a pause. "Anyway, I've been here over twenty years. Left following an interesting little historic event known as the Six Day War."

I nodded, smiling. "Yes, I seem to recall. Things haven't quite been the same there since, have they?"

Again the eye roll, even more theatrically. I decided he'd make a great character actor given the chance, maybe a Tevye for openers in *Fiddler on the Roof*. He had a deep, resonant voice, but his laughter was hoarse and phlegmy, wafting a faint gust of whiskey and nicotine. "Well, nice meeting you fellows. Maybe you'll have better luck on down the line."

It was definitely good-bye time. "At least he's friendly," Dare observed as we headed down the walk. "That's more than you can say for most of them."

"Yes," I said, "quite the genial fellow." We had reached the sidewalk and were passing a parked pickup truck when I glimpsed two people walking toward us. Simultaneously, I realized that I was seeing our reflection in the truck's large, sideview mirror. The good Elders Connors, Sr. and Jr., though which was which depended upon your point of view. I was obviously senior in age but, in effect, the junior companion.

I had momentarily forgotten my splendid missionary attire. In the brightness of that Arizona morning the image coming at me with its garish suit and amber sunglasses, the graying, brindle-colored hair winging up a bit on each side of my balding, freckled dome . . . Hmmm, what *did* I look like? More like a barker at some old-time carnival than an Elder of Israel. The thought made me laugh.

"What's the joke?" Dare inquired.

"Oh, nothing," I said. "Just life."

A second or two later we spotted our two cohorts across the street and a short distance ahead. They were just emerging from an open doorway, nodding, smiling, waving farewell to someone within. As the door closed, Dare called out. "Hey, hey—you actually got inside."

Grinning, they raised their fists, then strolled across the street to join us. "Told them they'd just won six million dollars," Elder Mac chortled.

"Naw," Elder Hud said. Each time I looked at him he seemed bigger. "The daughter invited us in for a glass of orange juice. Right sweet young lady." His Texas drawl was enjoyably pronounced, quite a contrast to his companion's brogue. "But then her gramma or somebody come along and gave us the boot." It was hard imagining anyone, especially someone's grandmother, giving Elder Huddleston the boot. In the words of my son, he was "one big dude," about six-six and two hundred and forty pounds. His face was freckled, very boyish, and utterly guileless. It was also the face of an athlete, with a broad brow and slightly curved nose. The prominent cheekbones and chin, with its distinct cleft, seemed to be emerging through a waning layer of baby fat.

We were standing there on the sidewalk in the frail shade of a young lemon tree. "Well, too bad," Elder Mac-Dougall said. "Grandma told us we weren't Christians."

Dare waggled his eyebrows and stroked the point of his chin. "Now, where have I heard that one before?"

I merely shook my head a little and smiled, knowing full well the temperament of such people, and what it all implied. "'Saved todayer'—right?"

"Right on," Elder Huddleston drawled. "Exactly."

"We had quite a few back on my own mission," I said, "back when lots of people actually thought Mormons didn't believe in Christ."

"Lots of people still think that," Dare said.

I nodded. "True, but not nearly as many. Now most of them say we aren't Christian because we supposedly teach false doctrine about the Godhead."

"Because . . ." Elder Mac shook his missionary quad at me—the four standard works in one—"We have the audacity to teach the God of the Bible." *Hahv thee ohdahcity ta titch thee God of thee Bable.* That was how it sounded. That, too, I enjoyed, having long felt it would be a great pity if we all spoke with the same accent.

By now it was unquestionably shirt-sleeve weather, the sun burning down at well over eighty degrees, and we returned to the car to shed our coats. "You heard what happened a while back with the 'saved todayers' in Salt Lake, didn't you?" I asked.

Dare flicked me a glance. "You mean that big old march on the temple grounds?"

I nodded. "A group came out there from somewhere, back East I guess, with a petition that supposedly contained about twenty-seven thousand names. They were going to present it to the Brethren and ask them to recant their beliefs."

"Twenty-seven *thousand*?" Elder Mac looked amazed.

"Pretty sure," I said.

A dog trotted by, a powerful, dun-colored pit bull, grizzled and battle-scarred. "Nice doggie," Dare soothed.

"So *did* they?" Elder Hud asked.

"The *Brethren*?" I laughed. "*Recant*?" A car went down the street, its occupants casting curious glances our way. "Actually, they never even got the chance. Turns out it was the Twenty-fourth of July, big parade day. The Church's offices were closed."

Suddenly we were all laughing almost raucously. "Gotta louve it!" Elder Mac slapped his thigh chortling, and Elder Hud gave a delighted little yelp as if his team had just scored a critical point.

Later that morning I unwittingly found myself drawn into a debate with just such a person, someone who undoubtedly would have joined the twenty-seven thousand given the slightest opportunity. It was another front porch conversation with a young mother of three who clearly considered herself the final authority on the scriptures. The old grace vs. works issue, one in which she argued that salvation not only came through grace alone but also from the mere acknowledgement that Jesus is indeed the Savior.

Saved? I challenged. Oh, but definitely! Saved from what? From the clutches of the devil, of course, from the awfulness of hell. But what of those who had never heard of Christ or would not have the opportunity? No matter, down they went, there to stay in a veritable Dante's Inferno of fire and brimstone. It was then, despite myself, that I succumbed to temptation, engaging in one of those scriptural dogfights that rarely if ever wins a convert to either side, no matter who emerges on top.

Somehow, during my long absence from the field, I had come to assume that such extreme beliefs had gradually faded, a bit like a bad odor after sufficient weathering; but not so. Here it was, manifest full force, personified in the form of a young woman with a surprisingly sweet, heart-shaped face and dark hair. A girl who might have been one of my own daughters, who might have walked Sunday morning into any LDS Relief Society room and appeared entirely at home. And yet . . . there she stood, a female version of good old Jonathan Edwards.

"You say you believe in a kind and loving God," I concluded, feeling both compassion and vexation. "Is that correct?"

"Of course," she replied. Her expression and tone implied strongly that the question was impertinent.

"And yet . . ." I looked at her beseechingly. "And yet, in the next breath you tell me he can thrust his own children down to endless torment, to burn in hell forever, simply because they haven't confessed Jesus is their Savior. Many who have never even *heard* of him, including helpless innocent infants. How can a thing like that make the slightest sense whatever? How can you ever reconcile such utter cruelty with the concept of a just and loving God?"

For an instant I felt her waver, the faintest stirring of indecision, like a dried leaf briefly displaced by the weight of an ant. Perhaps for that instant she had felt my sincerity, the honest desire for an answer that extended beyond the old, egoistic need to confound, fresh off the college debate team back in my early Canadian mission days.

Then, however, the fanatical gleam returned to her eyes with something bordering on sadism. Somehow in the short discussion that followed—though I could never detect the slightest trace of logic—the justice of God required it. "Justice," such as it was, clearly outweighed love and mercy, and that was that.

Throughout the entire engagement my son had offered little input, but I could sense his watchful amusement. The knowing, relaxed way he had lounged against the porch rail, arms loosely folded, head tilted forward, fighting a bit to keep his lips from curling up at the corners. Obviously, he had been through it many times before, to no avail, and was simply monitoring the situation to see how old Dad might handle it.

Later, as we returned with our two companions for lunch at the apartment, Dare announced: "Guess what? Pop got into a good old Bible bash with this cute young saved lady. Really dusted her!" He actually sounded rather proud, and our two cohorts laughed appreciatively, Elder Hud giving another of his little yelps. "Check that out!" he enthused. It was the missionary equivalent, I gathered, of "How about that?" Back in my own day it pertained solely to good-looking girls, but now it had acquired wider application.

During the hot afternoon to follow, we discovered that the entire street had been taken over by "saved todayers," none of whom would concede for an instant that in *addition* to the universal salvation through the Atonement, one might also need to engage in good works. It was strictly a matter of grace and a single confession that Jesus is one's personal Savior. Yesterday I was a sinner, today I'm saved.

7

At nine o'clock that night Dare and I were back in our "pad" as he called it. We had just attended a correlation meeting with Elders Mac and Hud and several stake missionaries in a nearby LDS chapel off Thunderbird Road. Now we were having a late meal, canned beef chunky stew with plenty of ketchup, and rolls that also came ready-made from a can.

Afterward I rinsed off a small pile of dishes in the sink and placed them in the dishwasher. Then I seated myself at the table in our tiny living room for a bit of journal writing. I wanted, in fact, to record my entire experience over the next three weeks in great detail for future reference in writing my novel. Dare was lounging nearby on a florid couch of sweat-stained yellow and orange, punching the phone's buttons for a call to one of his former companions, from Peoria, now located within the zone over which he presided. He had shucked his shoes and the shimmering tie of teal-wing blue, draping it over the handlebar of his bicycle.

"Hey, my man," he exclaimed, holding the receiver to his ear, "what's happenin'?" There was a brief pause. "Sis. Whitesides? Hey-hey, all right! Really coming through on the referrals, huh? Hey, great, that's cool!" Another pause.

"Well, sounds like you and the Batman are getting in lots of MCDs. Right–way to go . . . yeah, just goes to show how well I trained you." He grinned, throwing back his head, and gave a quiet, relaxed little laugh. I had discovered earlier that "Batman" was Elder Blackman and had learned long before from my stake missionary experience that MCD meant "member commitment discussions." During MCDs missionaries visited the homes of Church members and asked for the names of prospective investigators, "referrals," or encouraged the members to set a date, then pray for likely prospects during the interim.

"Yeah, Brother W's an all right guy, too," Dare was saying. "Still takes you boys out for chow at Bob's and stuff?" A pause. "All *right!*"

Stacked on one corner of the table where I sat were a variety of forms: baptismal records to be filled out in quadruplicate, sheets titled "Convert Baptism Checklist," designed for follow-up by ward bishops and ward mission leaders to ensure that new members are properly fellowshipped and integrated into the Church program. And . . . I sleuthed a bit further . . . a pile of missionary weekly planner forms. They were made of stiff, blue material the size of typewriter paper and scheduled each half-hour of the day from 6:30 A.M. to 9:30 P.M. Dare and all the other Elders carried one everywhere they went, often folded in thirds and, in some cases, projecting a little too prominently from their front shirt pockets.

On the table also were several familiar-looking envelopes, including a soft pink one from his girlfriend, Cindy Stewart, the girl who was waiting for him. Two others were from yours truly, and I began to peruse one of them for a moment, wondering irrationally if I had the right to read my son's "private mail."

He was still engrossed in his conversation, however. "Made you a birthday cake, huh? Hey, all right! She's a terrific lady. Yeah, true . . . well congratulations, you old twenty-onester. How's it feel?" A pause. A low chuckle. "Yep, now you're old enough to vote–just not smart enough." He gave another relaxed chuckle. "Hey, d'I tell ya who my new comp is?" He flicked me a sly glance and half a wink. "Oh, already heard from Mac and Hud, huh? Yeah, no kiddin', my old man. He's writing a book about missionary life or somethin' and got permission from the Pres. Yeah, unreal. I still can't put it together."

He then began discussing plans for a zone conference the mission president had scheduled for the near future. Unable to concentrate on my journal-writing for the time being, I continued to shuffle through various items on the table. Now I came across two or three packets of colored photos, some from home a few months ago, a few dating back to his days at the MTC in Provo, still others from the time he'd been among the Navajo. There he was, standing with a former missionary companion and an ancient Lamanite couple beside a shabby little dwelling that looked like a chicken coop. The two oldsters had shovels, and the young elders had hoes. There was a field of stunted corn in the background. Another photo showed the mobile home Dare had lived in during his stay in a little spot called Greasewood. Three truck tires held down the roof, as he had explained in a letter, to keep it from "takin' off in a high wind." The front yard, so-called, was sparse pasture grazed to the nub, sprinkled with stunted clumps of rabbit-brush. A gaunt Hereford was captured forever in the act of chewing its cud.

There were plenty of other shots. One was of missionaries, at a district meeting possibly, seated in a Relief Society room, sunlight streaming through the windows. An attractive blond-haired sister missionary was displaying a visual aid that said "Baptismal Goals for November." Another of Dare and several other Elders, including Mac and Hud, on "P-Day"—Preparation Day. They were decked out in raggle-taggle basketball attire, hamming it up like the kids they often still were.

Dare was still chatting about his missionary dad. "Remember those duds I got from the thrift shop for only five bucks? Well, they fit my pop just perfect. I gave 'em to him. Yeah, looks pretty cool, especially when he puts on his orange shades." Chuckles. "Sort of like the Godfather." I grinned, and for some reason my eyes strayed to the opposite side of the table, to a photo I had glimpsed the night before but not really noticed.

I squinted, frowning. It appeared now to be the photographic reproduction of a painting and is still almost impossible to describe. For one thing it was highly abstract. For another, the mood it conveyed was one, I suddenly realized, of intense negativism, perhaps even evil. It looked, in fact, as if it might have been rendered with a palette knife and something rather viscous, like hot tar, on a rough plaster background.

I continued to peer at it, feeling my frown deepen. In actuality, it now seemed to be several faces, perhaps many, literally evolving before my eyes. Some of them merely appeared a bit strange, disproportionate; others were ugly, from some angles even hideous and corpse-like. The picture seemed to contain many eyes, or what *might* have been eyes; again, hard to be certain. One or two appeared heavy-lidded, like mussel shells, one with a puffy, drooping pouch beneath, another in a badly scarred socket, or perhaps it was completely socketless. Simultaneously, the entire rendering also seemed to represent a single main countenance and contained what looked like a mouth, but one in which the upper lip was either mutilated or in a ghastly leer. One side of that main countenance appeared to be draped in long, frazzled hair reaching to the shoulders. Encircling the other side and surmounting the top of the cranium was something resembling a feathered Indian headdress, an Indian possibly from the Florida Everglades.

Or so it struck me. Everything was "might be," constantly swirling in form and mass, and the effect, though far more complex, was somewhat like one of those inkblot Rorschach tests which psychologists administer to determine certain things about their patients' mental outlook. The neck might have been a spiral staircase on the verge of collapse or possibly a column of oddly shaped, badly misplaced building blocks about ready to topple. Below were shoulders and possibly breasts that simultaneously were like birds' nests or swirling vortices leading down to nowhere.

When Dare emerged from his conversation a few minutes later I was still scrutinizing the thing, half-mesmerized, feeling quite perplexed and uncomfortable. "And where," I asked, "did you ever come across *this*?"

He grinned and shook his head, shrugging. "Really weird, isn't it?"

"Weird is putting it mildly," I replied, still peering, turning it this way and that. Now it seemed that two of the eyes were quite natural, the same for a nose slightly off the center of the painting. The nose actually appeared rather delicate and refined, feminine, with slightly flaring nostrils. It was as if these and possibly other appealing features had been smothered in a facade of ugliness. For a moment I experienced some highly ambivalent emotions that were impossible to articulate.

"Notice what's on the back?" Dare asked. His expression was half amused, half serious.

"No, what?" Turning it over, I read the following: "DEATH AND DAMNATION TO ALL MMs." For a moment we simply stared at each other. "Do the initials MM mean what I think they do?"

Dare shrugged, holding out his palms. "Mormon Missionaries?" I shrugged the same way. "I reckon," he said. "Or maybe it means M and Ms," he grinned. "Somebody's got it in for those little chocolate-covered candies."

I laughed. "So where did it come from?"

"Search me—came in the mail last week. Figured at first it came from Erlichmann. Remember that Elder I wrote home about—the one who was my comp about a year ago?"

"The one who kept taking off for home on his bike all the time, the one who was such a big character?"

He laughed, nodding vigorously. "Exactly. It looks like he's back here to stay now, incidentally—gonna make a go

37

of it most likely. He's over in Phoenix and not too thrilled with his companion, but hangin' in."

"Good." I nodded, stretching and yawning. I still hadn't recovered from "Chevette lag," as we had laughingly referred to it earlier.

"It's just the kind of thing old Erlich Boy would do," Dare mused, "he's such a crazy joker. I mean, you never know one minute to the next what he'll come up with. But he swears on the whole standard works he didn't do it."

I glanced at it again. "Some weird joke, if that's what it's supposed to be. It looks like somebody's nightmare reincarnated."

8

By now I had decided it was time either for bed or for a workout to liven me up a little. I opted for the latter—isotonics, combined with leg exercises such as squats and lunges with a little karate tossed in. Son Dare had his own exercise routine and had adjusted to his father's unorthodox antics long ago, generally taking scant notice of them. We, along with several of his brothers, had studied the martial arts together over the years, and we frequently made pseudo-belligerent passes at each other just for the fun of it. All in the spirit of camaraderie.

As I continued my exercise, Darren continued to reflect aloud about various of his former companions, including the notorious Elder E. "Old Erlichmann . . ." He yawned, leaning back, hands laced behind his head. "Quite the sturgeon." How we ever began using the word *sturgeon* for colorful, somewhat roguish characters, I don't know. It went back a long time, in any case, something I had probably invented myself. I had always enjoyed giving people strange names, myself included, and my kids had inherited the same propensity.

"You're quite the sturgeon yourself," I said, puffing slightly from my exertions, "when it comes right down to it."

"True, but old Elder E., he's really somethin' else. I ever tell you about how he calls different Elders up and pretends to be the pres?"

I nodded. "I seem to remember your mentioning it in one of your letters."

"'Elder, this is President Linford, and I'm calling up to check on certain irregularities regarding your missionary work.'" Dare sounded very much like the good president himself, only a little caricatured, and he grinned at me, on the verge of laughter. "He'd really shake 'em up sometimes. Remember that one comp I wrote home about, name of Espie?"

"The little, timid one who looks as if he's about sixteen years old?"

"Yeah, that's him. Always terrified he might break a rule. Well, he gets this call one night, and all of a sudden I hear his voice start to quaver. 'Yes, sir, President Linford . . . Why, no President. Well . . . yes, I guess I did call home that one time without getting permission, and I'm real sorry.'" Dare chuckled. "Poor little Espie; he even confessed to waking up a half hour late one morning because he wasn't sleeping too well. Then he started telling about the time he went out to buy a pizza at the supermarket and left his companion alone before he remembered it was against the rules."

"And all the time it was only Erlichmann?"

Dare nodded, face wreathing with impish humor. "Old Erlichmann even had him promising he'd never eat any more pizza on his mission just to remind him of the wicked mistake he'd made. And funny thing about it, Pres Linford isn't like that at all. I mean, he has his standards and doesn't ever compromise when he figures it's wrong, but he's flexible, a real mellow dude."

"I'd pretty well gathered that," I said. I was merely trotting in place at the moment, a poor man's aerobic dance.

"But Erlichmann could imitate darned near anybody and con people into thinking whatever he wanted. Like

40

sometimes when we were out tracting and people wouldn't answer the door, he'd start singing like Elvis Presley. I'm not kiddin'—he could sound exactly like old Elvis, and sometimes people would come to the door just to find out what was going on."

I laughed. "Crazy!"

"Really!" He shook his head. "Then they'd see this character who looks like an ostrich or somethin'. Sometimes he'd tell them he was Elvis's cousin Emmett, or some name like that, and ask if he could come in and sing a few gospel hymns."

"Did it ever work?"

"Once in a rare while. This one family even started discussions with us, just because they thought he was such a big laugh. At least, that's how it was to begin with. Then they really caught fire and ended up getting baptized."

"Amazing," I said. "Whatever works, I guess."

"Another of Erlichmann's tricks was to hit people up on the street and ask 'em if they'd ever heard of the Church. Then he'd say he already knew who they were, that he'd been assigned back in pre-earth life to come down and hunt 'em out."

"Character!" I puffed. "If some of them thought Mormons were weird before, I wonder what they thought when your pal got through with them."

"Yeah, I worried about that myself, kept tryin' to tone the guy down a little. But like I say, some people got a real blast out of him. He's got this far out kind of personality . . . what d' ya call it—sort of draws people like a magnet."

"Charisma?"

"Right, and lots of times it really worked. But every so often he'd hit these lows and decide he couldn't hack it any longer. The minute my back was turned, he'd hop on his bike and go cruisin' off into the sunset. Headed home for Kanab, Utah."

"All the way home?" I blinked in disbelief. "On his bike?" The whole thing sounded pretty incredible, but so did Elder E.

41

"Well, not always. Sometimes he'd change his mind out there on the road a ways. I guess the long hills and hot sun would start getting to him; I don't know. But home wasn't all that far away, really, least not up north there in Flagstaff. Couple of times he made it all the way home, hung around for a few days, then back he'd come."

"Most interesting," I said. My exertions were having their effect now. I could feel the sweat popping out as if I'd taken a flit from a warm spray bottle all along my vanishing hairline. That was about the end of the workout for now.

"But finally Pres Linford got tired of the whole business and told him to make up his mind once and for all. Shape up and stay or ship out and stay out. That was when old E. finally came around and got his act together. He's mellowed out a lot now."

"Well, good for Elder Erlichmann," I said. "Let's hope he can really hang in."

"Aw, he will now. I'm darned near positive," Dare said. "He's made it over the big hump, celebrated his first year in the field last week."

I finished my workout, then showered, flossed, and brushed my slightly jagged teeth. Then, having said our nightly prayers together, we switched off the lights and climbed into bed. Again we reminisced on days past, recalling his football experiences at Ogden High. Back then he had been so small he had scored several touchdowns in part because the opposing team members hardly noticed him. For a time, in fact, it had looked as if he was going to be the "shrimp" of the family. Then, miraculously, the hormones went to work, and he literally sprouted nearly a foot taller within about two years.

We also recalled an incident that occurred at the time of his fifth birthday. He had constructed a paper target with a red magic marker and asked one of his little pals to shoot at the bull's-eye with a BB gun. Unfortunately, young Dare had been holding the target in front of his own mid-section, the bull's-eye centered directly over his navel! Loud and wild were the shrieks—a most unhappy moment in the midst of a happy birthday.

Throughout the night, however, my mind was filled with the amusing personality of Elder E. and his capricious comings and goings. I was also preoccupied with the bizarre photograph. Gradually the thing became a kind of incubus that refused to be dismissed. Finally, half awake, half asleep, I was struck by a strange impression, a feeling somewhat akin to the one I had experienced in the furniture store a short while before. It wasn't actually déjà vu, but it seemed extrasensory and was highly disconcerting. The original painting from which that photograph had been derived was not only a woman, it was also . . . The realization welled like a chemical in the bloodstream. It was also a portrait!

For some time I lay there, pondering the thought, wondering if my writer's imagination was running away with me, seizing upon some far-fetched idea for mere dramatic effect. Yet the more I attempted to explain it away logically, the more convinced I became of my original conclusion. I had indeed been looking at a portrait.

I remained semiconscious for perhaps another hour, unable to escape my own brooding. I could vaguely sense the glowing moonlight outside our window, a pleasant breeze frilling the half-drawn curtains and scented with an increasingly familiar odor. Magnolias, maybe. And within the surrounding maple trees, countless little winged seeds stirred. At times, surfacing toward complete wakefulness, I could even hear them winging down in endless little whirlygigs to whisper and sift along the walkways.

Finally I arose. My throat was dry, and I needed a drink, preferably a glass of orange juice from the fridge if any remained. Long ago, in my early boyhood, I had developed a habit of getting up at night to raid the fridge. Once married with a large family of my own, however, I found it a fruitless effort, literally and otherwise. Various of my eleven children had inevitably been there ahead of me. The fridge, like Old Mother Hubbard's cupboard, was almost always bare.

At the moment, though, things were different. There were only two of us, and I had brought along quite a supply. Yes, still more than a quart of orange juice and half a pumpkin pie. I poured myself a glass of juice and sipped meditatively, encircled in the dim light of the open fridge. My shadow was gigantic and distorted against the opposite wall, and it made the hair, tufted slightly on both sides of my head, look like stubby horns.

For a moment I was tempted to try a wedge of pie as well. The can of shake-and-spray whipped cream was especially appealing. Then I decided against it. The combination of pumpkin pie, whipped cream, and orange juice didn't seem quite right, at least not at that late hour. Besides, I'd been growing more concerned about the dangers of cholesterol lately.

Instead, almost unconsciously, I entered the adjoining room and went to the study table with its missionary forms, letters, and photos. For a moment I didn't quite realize what I was looking for, my right brain not knowing what the left brain dideth. But my hand knew what it was doing. Reaching out, virtually of its own volition, it picked up that weird and awesome photograph.

The grotesqueness fairly sprang from it, a symbolical wreathing of evil, darkness, and despair. It was only after I had returned to my bed, however, that the final realization came. The thing I had been staring at, almost morbidly, obviously revealed a remarkable talent, and it was not only a portrait; it was also a *self* portrait!

The chemical sensation surged through my veins again, more strongly than ever, along with a prickling that began in my forearms then spread in a mounting wave throughout my chest and entire body. Steadily now, that pleasant, inoffensive room seemed to roil in darkness, and for some time I lay there hearing my son's oblivious snoring, feeling very alone, wishing that he was awake.

44

I wished it so strongly that he stirred, turning on his opposite side. Or was it mere coincidence? If so, even greater coincidence that he was actually now awake. I could tell by the way he breathed and adjusted his pillow.

"Pop?"

"Yeah."

"What's goin' on?"

I exhaled in a long poof, like a half-hearted attempt to blow out the candles on a birthday cake. "I'm not sure, son." Simultaneously I realized that I only referred to my boys as *son* in rather serious moments. "You . . . ah, *feel* anything?" I asked, not wishing to influence his reaction. "Anything different?" Maybe, after all, I was just suffering from a case of lively imagination—like that of little kids who insist there are monsters or boogeymen in the room.

The wait for an answer was so long that I wondered if he had heard me or merely drifted off. "Yeah," he said at last. "Maybe we should say another prayer."

9

With the return of dawn, all was back to normal. The sense of oppression from the night before seemed unreal now. Birds outside were celebrating the morn, and I silently thanked the Lord for another day. Not that I had supposed it would fail to come; I simply feel increasingly that each new day in this mortal probation is a gift. I am reminded, incidentally, of the old-timer who was asked upon his hundredth birthday how he had managed to survive so long. "Just keep waking up every morning," he replied.

In all seriousness, though, I was steadily coming to realize the preciousness, even sacredness, of time, and how vital it is to learn from the past, plan for the future, but live for today. I knew that my three-week mission with my son would be over all too swiftly, that I had been granted a special dispensation that should be lived to the full.

Already our days were assuming a certain necessary pattern in order to fulfill that ambition. It had been that way in general for Dare, in fact, for nearly two years. At six-thirty we arose for half an hour of reading and discussing the Book of Mormon. We then listened to cassettes of various Church leaders and scholars as we did our exercises. After that, breakfast, before showering and dressing

46

in preparation for some morning proselyting. The daily regimen wasn't much different than it had been forty years ago on my mission to Canada, and already I was slipping back into it with surprising ease. Far more tracting back then, more prayers (almost every time we turned around), but essentially the same.

The morning following our strange experience we traded companions—Elder MacDougall and Darren cycling off to an investigator lesson a few blocks away, Elder Huddleston and I taking the car to call back on several people who had previously accepted copies of the Book of Mormon. As the morning progressed, we received one rejection after another. None of those who had agreed to examine the book had done so, and in two cases it was virtually flung in our faces by disgruntled husbands who had not been there during the first visit.

"Sometimes ya wonder," Elder Hud said following the second one. He was looking a bit angry and downcast.

We were walking toward the car now, and I glanced at him quizzically. "Wonder what?"

"Oh . . ." he sighed a little. "If it's really worth the struggle. If I wouldn't be doing a lot more good somewhere else." Despite his size, rugged appearance, and casual Texas manner, Elder Hud had undergone some difficult trials on his mission. Called initially to Korea, he had never adapted to the new culture or made much progress with the language. He had arrived in the Arizona Phoenix Mission two months before I met him, after a long and trying year. Dare had shared that information with me the night of my arrival, explaining that our friend's outlook had improved considerably since his arrival in the Phoenix mission two months earlier. Nevertheless, he still had some rather deep lows at times.

"Sometimes, I think I'd be a whole lot better off back in school, or maybe just holdin' down a job," he continued.

I nodded. "I know that feeling," I said. "Sometimes you *do* wonder. Practically every missionary who goes out has at least a *few* doubts at one time or another. They may not admit it in their letters home, and rarely in that big homecoming talk in sacrament meeting. But it's there; it slips out in little ways eventually. Sometimes, in one great big unburdening."

Elder Hud regarded me with what seemed to be slight surprise. "I can remember when I was a missionary in Montreal," I continued, "going tracting one winter day for about nine hours straight with only thirty minutes or so out for a bowl of soup at some greasy spoon." It was all coming back with remarkable clarity. "A gray day in more ways than one, and that damp kind of cold that penetrates right down to the marrow no matter how much clothing you put on."

For a moment I smiled, thinking about my companion. "I had this missionary companion named Cecil Charlesworth who came from sunny California, and the poor guy never *could* get warm, even on days when it wasn't that bad. Thermal underwear, long-sleeved shirt, vest, sweater, suit coat, scarf . . . heavy wool overcoat!" Elder Hud began to laugh. "Ear muffs! Fleece-lined gloves, big calf-length galoshes." I shook my head. "Poor beggar could barely move, and he was *still* freezing! Of course, some places in the world you have to dress that way."

"Hardly the problem here," Elder Hud said.

"Right, especially in the summer. I hear it hits about one-fifteen part of the time."

"Yeah, that's what I hear—even one-twenty." We had returned to the car now and were driving down the street past a school yard, shrill and lively with children. "Anyway . . ." I continued. "I remember that one day in Montreal, especially. I wasn't feeling too well to begin with, and we kept getting one door slam after another. That day, in fact, I counted them—we tracted one-hundred and twenty-six homes, mainly apartments, and didn't get one invitation in. Nothing that even resembled a gospel conversation, not one kind word, literally."

"Wow!"

48

I smiled a bit wryly. "One old man who must have been about ninety began ranting and raving, said we were 'preachers of the devil' just because my companion asked whether he really believed in God. Then he began shouting for his daughter or someone to go call the police."

"Sounds like fun."

"Yes, great fun—a little amusing, actually, in the old man's case. But for the most part . . . well, that's when *I* got to wondering." The cries of the children fell behind, and from nearly a block away drifted the tantalizing odor of Harman's Kentucky Fried. "Get a whiff of that," I said.

Hud grinned. "I'm a-whiffin'!"

"And that wasn't the only time I felt down, believe me. In fact, it pretty much went that way for most of the next month—endless apathy, endless rejection, lots of hostility. It was tough. But . . ." I sighed, still feeling the weight of those days now, half a lifetime later. "Well, we kept slogging along, saying prayers we were sort of losing faith in. Then, one afternoon, on about the eighth floor of this old, weather-beaten apartment building, we knocked on a door and there was this lovely, dark-haired Jewish lady who invited us in almost before we had time to get a word out. I remember, in fact, that the first thing she said was, 'You're Mormon missionaries, aren't you?'"

Elder Hud tossed me a look of curiosity. "No kiddin'!"

"No kidding, and the next thing she said was—get *this*—'What took you so long? I've been looking all over for you!'"

"Ha!" A toss of the head. "*Unreal!*"

"Right, that's how it seemed to us. But two months later she was baptized along with her five children, and they turned out to be some of the strongest members in our branch."

"Fantastic! What about her husband?"

"Well, he dragged his heels for the next year or so, but he was a great guy, gave them all his blessing, so to speak, if that was what they really wanted." I chuckled. "She was a very determined, independent little lady. Probably would have thrown him out if he hadn't!" I braked for a stop sign and waited while an old man with a cane struggled across the intersection. He was hunched and tremulous but managed a fractured smile and slight wave of appreciation. "But finally we baptized the dad, too. After I was gone, actually. One of their teenage daughters sent me a special Christmas card with the happy news about a year after I'd returned home."

"Hey, that's *bad!*"

"Yeah . . ." I mused. "Unfortunately I've lost track of them. By now all the children are probably married and have families of their own. Some of the older ones may even have grandkids!" It was a strange thought because most of the time I still saw them as the youngsters they had been back about 1952. "And who knows? Maybe every single one of them all the way down the line is an active member of the Church." For an instant I felt a tingling that told me it was more than just a fond hope, not mere wishful thinking.

"Hmmm, fantastic!" Elder Hud's big hazel-colored eyes were growing warmer. "So it pays to hang in, is that your message?"

I laughed. "Just telling you I can relate, and how it went. I'll spare you the sermon."

We drove for a time in silence. "Well," he said quietly, "I've got some stuff to work through, but I'm real glad you told me, Brother Connors."

And with that encouragement, I did a little sermonizing after all. I guess you could call it that, but it was brief. "You ever play football?" I inquired. "*Sure* you did."

"Ah, yeah—played fullback in high school."

"Well, it's an oversimplification, but a mission really *is* like playing football in some ways. I mean, there's a lot of tough slugging, and training, bruises, disappointments. But, man, when you make that touchdown, or whatever—great pass, that first down after a big end run, that terrific tackle . . . Worth the whole effort, right? And besides that, you really come *away* with a lot."

"Yeah, I hear ya."

I longed to say more—about the magic formula my own mission president had given me: "work, study, prayer, and love." Especially the latter. That way, you always win in the end. I wanted to tell him about the imperishable sense of joy and triumph that comes from running the good race and fighting the good fight. But I resisted. Maybe later when the time was right.

Besides, not far ahead two familiar figures in white shirts had just straddled their bicycles and were heading our way.

"So how's it goin'?" Dare called as we pulled up.

"Oh, nothing spectacular," I said. "More of the same."

"Got two B. of M.'s chucked back at us," Elder Hud told them. "Lucky they were *soft*bound."

"And how was your morning?" I asked.

"Miserable," Elder Mac replied. "Up until"—he inspected the watch on his burly, tattooed forearm—"about forty minutes ago."

"But then," Dare added, "it was out of sight." He gestured with his thumb and a toss of the head. "House with the roses there just down the street." It was a ranch-style home, fairly unpretentious, brown brick and redwood with a trellis of yellow roses climbing the near side. "Fabulous little family."

"Husband home?"

"No, but his wife's really excited about hearing more, wants us to come back and show them *Together Forever* tomorrow."

"Claims she absolutely *knows* he'll be interested." Mac offered one of his gleeful little chortles.

"Hey-hey—sounds like a winner!" Hud exclaimed. True enthusiasm or manufactured? For real, yes; I could tell from the glow on his face.

"Wife's one fine lady," Dare continued, "and two grrreat little kids. Boy's about eight, and the girl's maybe a couple years older. You'll never believe how friendly they are till you meet 'em."

"Hope I can," I said. "We were just talking about a family like that, in fact, weren't we, elder?"

Hud smiled and nodded. "Yeah, we were. Quite a coincidence, actually."

"Well, they sound like a good bet for the video all right," I said. The *Together Forever* video had been released only a month or so earlier. I had viewed it for the first time with Sally and some of our kids on Thanksgiving, just a few days before my departure from Ogden. It was a series of brief, sensitive dramatizations stressing the importance of families and the Latter-day Saint belief that they can indeed be together forever. The final scenario, involving a young couple who had lost their daughter in a traffic accident, was exceptionally real and poignant.

As we were about to leave, the young boy to whom Dare had referred emerged from his house and waved at us, smiling. His big dark eyes were full of recognition as if we were already fast friends. "See there?" Elder Mac rejoiced. The "r" trilled with his Scottish burr. "Did-nae we *tell* ya noo?"

10

It is always dangerous to count one's chickens, as the old saying goes, but the good news was worth a celebration—lunch out, on Dad. We dined at Pancho's Mexican Restaurant, a brightly decorated place with fine south-of-the-border atmosphere, and went for the "All You Can Eat Buffet" at only $4.39 a plate.

It was a remarkable thing to see how much my young compañeros could stow away of everything—burritos, tacos, enchiladas, tamales, refried beans, Spanish rice, chile con queso, chalupa, guacamole—all without missing a word of lively, laughter-laden conversation. Unfortunately, however, old Nate himself became so caught up in the spirit of feasting that his belly rebelled. Halfway into the meal, I rushed in ignominy toward the nearest men's room.

I emerged several minutes later, hollow in the stomach and feeble in the knees, shaky, and pallid with a tinge of gray-green, appropriately chagrinned.

Back at our "pad" as the missionaries called it, I shed my tie, shoes, and socks and "flaked out" on the "sack." I could hear talk from the front room above the faint humming of the air conditioner. For a while there was reminiscing about events up north on the "res" and various Navajo customs.

Dare and Mac had been together for a time on the reservation, driving the backroads in a pickup and living in the little mobile home I had seen in the photograph, the one with tires weighting down the roof to keep it from sailing away on the desert winds. It leaked in several places during rainstorms, plinking then plopping into hastily arranged pots and pans. "Hey, remember that time," Dare's voice came, "when we were cruising along out there past Greasewood with Pres Linford?" It sounded mirthful, and Elder MacDougall chortled. "Remember that big, humongous wall of water about two feet high chargin' down that arroyo?" Dare persisted.

"Do I ever!" Elder Mac chortled again. "Floodin' like crazy across that little dirt road, but Pres Linford was never the type to stand around and wait. Insisted you gun the old pickup right on through to the other side."

"Yeah, and it wouldn't have been so bad, if the road was all that was flooded," Dare said. "But the water was spilling out like about fifty feet wide on both sides, and halfway through, the motor conked out. There we are, dead as a dinosaur, clear up past the hub caps in this wild, galavantin' flood the color of a chocolate shake."

"So good old Connors," Mac announced gleefully, "tells our mission pres. he's responsible and he'd better get out and push."

Dare tossed his head, laughing. "Pres actually believed me! Even started to take off his shoes and roll up his pants before I stopped him and said I was only kiddin'."

They were all laughing now, Elder Huddleston as well. I wondered momentarily about the scriptural injunction against loud laughter, and yet it had often seemed to me that hearty laughter–if not malicious or derisive–was good for the body as well as the soul. Certainly it seemed so in this case, especially for Elder H.

For a while I drifted on the quiet tides of a nap, gradually feeling better, and now I began to reflect upon Elder Mac's history and the remarkable sequence of events that brought him into the Church only two years earlier and to

54

the Phoenix mission a mere year or so after that. Dare had written about it in a letter home not long after they first became companions, impressed enough to elaborate in some detail. Most of his letters were masterpieces of brevity—laconic, often amusing, tidbits of information that required plenty of reading between the lines. Elder Mac's story, however, was another matter.

Half asleep, I began to recall some of the essentials and almost seemed to be living them. Bobby MacDougall, as he was known in his pre-Mormon days, had come from a broken home, one he had run away from several times. In his mid-teens he had joined a wild, booze-drinking, pot-smoking motorcycle gang—the Glasgow Devil Bikers, or in his own accent, "Divil Bakers." That accent had, in fact, left Dare badly confused initially. Bobby MacDougall had tattooed his arms and virtually all of his upper body with wild grotesqueries including the heads of snarling wolves and wildcats, and an old-time horned devil armed with a trident and riding a fire-breathing dragon. He and his cohorts carried brass knuckles and ball bats, and sometimes engaged in gang wars that landed them in jail.

He was, to all appearance, a highly unlikely candidate for the missionaries, especially the two Sister missionaries who called at his home one afternoon while he was recovering from a broken nose earned in a fracas the week before.

At first, of course, the young Sisters were badly taken aback, convinced that they had knocked on the ultimate wrong door. Nevertheless, one of them had been moved upon to explain their purpose, and for some reason—perhaps sheer curiosity, perhaps the fact that they were attractive young women—Bobby MacDougall had listened to their message and agreed to a return visit.

Even so, one of the Sisters had been reluctant to go back, fearful of the strange, fierce-looking young man with the long hair, dark glasses, tattoos, and bandaged nose. Fearful of the entire neighborhood. The visits had continued, however, with Bobby MacDougall hearing all the lessons and becoming a believer. At the time, though, he

55

had not qualified for baptism because of his inability to give up the bottle.

The Sisters had eventually been transferred, sorrowfully convinced that Bobby MacDougall would never make it into the waters, simply another "might have been," a name in their journals and letters home.

Thus it came as quite a surprise for one of them—the girl who had insisted upon teaching him—when a young man knocked upon her door nearly two years later in Provo, Utah. He was wearing a new suit, white shirt, and tie; he was clean-shaven, with hair so closely cropped he might have belonged to the military or maybe the FBI. "Good morning, Sister Myers," he said jovially. "Remember me?" The words contained a strong, familiar, Scottish accent.

The young woman had frowned, smiled uncertainly, wanting to appear hospitable but obviously confused. "You look familiar," she began, "but I'm afraid . . ."

The young man's grin broadened. "Elder Robert 'Bobby' MacDougall!" he announced. "Formerly of the Glasgow Divil Bakers—now of The Church of Jesus Christ of Latter-day Saints. Just thought I'd stop by and say hello on my way to the MTC!"

My reflections had gradually become a part of my dreams, and when I awakened, the apartment was silent. Arising, I strolled into the front room. There on the little study table in Dare's familiar, erratic scrawl was a note that said they had gone to visit two of the Sister missionaries in Dare's zone. "They just got one of those weird postcards with the same little hate message," the note said, "and some of the other Elders are getting them, too. Hope you're feeling better after all that gluttony. Thought we'd best let you sleep it off. XOX—Your Favorite Child—D." The signature was accompanied by a ludicrous self-portrait—a cartoon character with wild hair like a tumbleweed, crossed eyes, and a tongue projecting to a ridiculous length like that of a frog catching flies. One crazy kid. "P. S. We'll be dropping by to see the pres if he's not out in the boonies somewhere. Back before suppertime. Stay out of trouble."

That was the lighter, far-out side of my boy Dare. And yet, there was another important part of him—the maturing man and missionary that took his calling very seriously. It was not until the day after my arrival that I learned he had again been called as zone leader with the responsibility of supervising about twenty other missionaries in the Glendale area. I say "again" because he had held that same position earlier, on the reservation, before a brief stay in Gallup, N. M.

By now I was feeling so much better that I donned my purple swimsuit, the one I had brought along "just in case," and went for a dip in the apartment pool. The water was wonderfully refreshing, and I had been taking laps in its cool blue for about fifteen minutes when it struck me that maybe I was breaking mission rules. Swimming was verboten. But then . . . I told myself, I was in effect breaking rules simply by being alone without a companion. Furthermore, I was merely a visitor and certainly had not been called or set apart, so . . . probably no problem.

Returning to the apartment afterward, I showered and dressed in my casuals, then sat down at the study table to continue writing my combination letter-journal. In the midst of it all I glanced again at Dare's note, then rummaged about on the table top and discovered once more the abominable postcard. There, in the light of day with the curtains opened, it looked a little less sinister than before. At the moment it merely seemed a roily mass of black and gray, but it never appeared quite the same either. By turning the photo to one angle, I could see the eyes again, in one case what might have been a sly wink. At another angle, the mouths began to materialize, proliferate—railing, smirking, leering, voracious and fang-like.

I tossed the photo aside, shaking my head. Crazy! Surely no mere person, no matter how great (or diabolical?) the talent, could attain such artistic complexity. It *had* to be my own imagination, an almost hallucinatory reaction. I could feel my own features formulating a smile of odd surmise. So what did that really say about me? Was all that stuff and more actually latent there within my own soul? On the other hand—and this brought slight relief—if so, I apparently wasn't that different from everyone else. Every recipient of the blasted thing experienced the same general response.

And yet . . . I frowned, reflecting deeply. More than ever, underneath all that macabre facade, was something very human, pathetic, perhaps even beautiful. Maybe it was merely the one delicate, feminine nose with its sensitive, flaring nostrils, still uncovered by the writhing morass, valiantly emerging from it even. Maybe even one pleading eye, one wounded mouth tinged with reproach.

I was still ruminating over the matter, idly fluttering the photo between my fingers, when Darren and our two companion elders returned. "Look there!" Dare exclaimed and regarded me with his usual foxy grin. "Got Dad spooked along with the rest of us." Then, more seriously, "Pop, these things are cropping up all over the place—Peoria, Phoenix, Scottsdale, practically the whole area."

"Really?" I was astonished.

"Absolutely," Elder Hud replied. "Went to see the Sisters, and they claim practically everybody's gettin' the same thing."

"We phoned President Linford from their place," Elder Mac said. "He wasn't in, though—off making the rounds up north. But Sister Adamson said he's got wind of it."

"Who's Sister Adamson?" I asked.

"One of the mission secretaries—his right-hand gal."

"So what does the pres make of it?"

"Hasn't the foggiest, but he's trying to find out."

"Gotta be somebody who has access to our addresses," Dare said.

"Are you still convinced it's not your crazy old companion?" I asked.

"Erlichmann?"

I nodded.

Elder Mac gave his chortle. "Might just be. He's that kind of joker if there ever was one."

Dare squinted, tilted his head to one side as though reevaluating the possibility. "Naaah," he said at last. "I called him about it. Claims he's not the one, and I believe him. I can read the character pretty well by now. No, I figure it's probably some of those 'saved todayers.' They're always trying to hassle us one way or another."

11

That evening, Dare and I made more call-backs on people who had received copies of the Book of Mormon. Again, however, no luck. All, in the words of my son, were strictly "NI," not interested.

That is not to say, on the other hand, that all the people we visited were uninteresting. One of them, an ancient gentleman apparently nearing the century mark, assured us that he had no use for the book and took strong objection to what little he had heard at one time or another about the Word of Wisdom. "I once lived next door to a Mormon bishop," he wheezed. "Fellow was always bragging about how healthy he was. 'I don't drink, smoke, or chase around,' he'd tell me, 'and I'm one hundred percent fit!' Well, I got tired of that after a while, so one day I up and told him, 'I drink like a fish, smoke like a stovepipe, and chase women like a chicken after hoppers . . . and I'm *two* hundred percent fit!'"

At that we all began to chuckle, the old man bursting into a series of wheezing cackles that sounded more like death rattles. He had a bulbous, badly cratered, W. C. Field's proboscis that seemed to become redder by the moment. Pleased to have a responsive audience, he refused to relinquish us until he had recounted a little anecdote about the late John Barrymore. Seems Barrymore had led a lifestyle much like that of the old man himself but turned out less healthy and was eventually advised by his doctor that it was time to abandon wine, women, and song. "Well, Barrymore's not too happy over that," the old man observed, "as you might well imagine. So he up and asks the doc whether he's got to do it all at once. 'Why, no,' doc says, 'not necessarily, but it's time to start.' 'Well, good,' Barrymore tells him. 'In that case I'll give up *song* first.'"

The old man cackled raucously, one eye watering, and slapped me on the shoulder as though we were somehow involved in it all. "So there you have it," he said.

To this day I remain uncertain about the implication of those final words, but as we departed I made a last feeble attempt at returning to the subject. "I take it you haven't had a chance to read any of this then," I said.

His brow rippled upward to meet the few remaining strands of silver hair. "What's that—the Book of *Marmen*?"

I nodded.

"Oh, I read the thing all right, but frankly boys, it was quite a drag. Like Mark Twain says, 'chloroform in print.'" Another cackle and an affectionate paw at my shoulder that missed and threw him slightly off balance. I caught him gently by the elbow.

"He must have been referring to the book of Ether," Dare said. The old man nodded, grinning crookedly, but obviously missed the pun.

"So how did you like the part about Brigham Young and the pioneers?" Dare asked, as he tossed me a mischievous glance. It was the same question we had sometimes thrown at people back in my Canadian days.

"Well, now . . ." our friend replied and tugged at the dewlap beneath his chin with a tremulous, liver-spotted hand. "Tell the truth, that was the only good part about it."

I nodded, my son and I sneaking glances, trying to keep our faces straight. "Well, good," I managed, choking down the mirth. "Maybe one of these times we could tell you a bit about the pioneers and how they settled the West. It's a remarkable story."

The old man shook his head. "No, boys. I appreciate your dedication, but I'm too far down the road now to bother with it." For a moment I gained the strong impression that by "it" he actually meant religion in general, perhaps even life itself. "God and Old Scratch can fight it out for my soul, if they have a mind to, but it won't be much of a bargain for either of 'em."

Our remaining visits that evening were less entertaining and no more fruitful. There was, for instance, the surly, bearded fellow wearing a red swimsuit, sporting an impressive pot belly, and clutching a can of beer. "Not interested," he grunted and slammed the door. "Thank you, kind sir, for your remarkable cordiality," Dare chuckled as we headed down the walk.

"And touching magnanimity," I added.

Dare grinned. "And magnificent pot belly." I could not refrain from laughing. Missionary work, tracting, and call-backs especially, definitely required an ability to roll with the punches. For a moment Dare frowned. "His wife seemed like a nice person—very polite and everything. Acted pretty interested." He glanced my way. "How'd she ever get tied up with a guy like that?"

I shrugged. "It happens."

The next call was no better, worse in fact. We were nearly attacked by a savage German shepherd, barely restrained by its owner with the aid of a leash and choke collar. The owner, in fact, was a frail old woman who croaked raucously at the animal, or perhaps at us (it was hard to tell), and who hardly appeared up to the job.

"Talked to a guy there earlier; must have been her son," Dare said. We climbed into the car. "Not exactly the time for a gospel conversation right now though, was it?"

"Not really," I said. "That hound seemed rather argumentative." We rolled off down the street, seeing the glare of a red stop sign in the distance. "Praise be for choke collars," I mused.

Later that night we lay on our beds and talked for a while as usual, and once I glanced at the glowing amber numbers on his little, digital alarm—almost midnight. It was one of the birthday presents we had sent him the previous summer.

"You know," his voice drifted, "I keep thinking about what that old boy said about the Book of Mormon."

"*Marmen*," I corrected and laughed. "Real character—no question."

"Yeah, and that crazy bit about chloroform in print."

The amber numbers continued to change, magically. Sundials, hourglasses, water wheels, tick-tock clocks, and now the little digital lights of modern technology. No matter what the measuring device, though, the passage of time was inexorable. "Funny thing is," he finally added, "that's about the way I used to feel about it myself. All those names and places. And the wars! Seemed like they never stopped, and yet there's not that much description. Just all those 'behold's' and a million 'came to passes.'"

I gave a snort of amusement. "Yes, that was pretty much my own reaction the first time around." I remembered lying out on the old lounge in the backyard summer afternoons before my call had come, the rich burnt orange color of the pad that seemed to emanate added warmth, the comforting dry smell of its stuffing, the words of the book on the white page in the explosive sunlight: "I, Nephi, having been born of goodly parents, therefore I was taught somewhat in all the learning of my father; and having seen many afflictions in the course of my days, nevertheless, having been highly favored of the Lord in all my days; yea, having had a great knowledge of the goodness and the mysteries of God, therefore I make a record of my proceedings in my days."

I remembered the green of the surrounding lawn, the faint sighing of a breeze in a Russian olive tree, how the sunlight had blurred through my eyelashes and reflected upon those words. It seemed a strange way to begin a book, an odd style, dramatically unlike any of the prose that Joseph Smith himself laid claim to. Why the monotonous, rather distracting repetition, for example, of the phrase "in my days"?

Well, I had learned more about that since, long after my mission itself had drifted into the past: namely, that people wrote that way in *those* days in those lands. I had read the book at least a dozen times in its entirety since then and was beginning to read it again at the behest of a prophet living in *these* days. And now . . . it was incredible, absolutely incredible to me, how the entire record had opened up, expanding the mind and soul with each reading. A teacher of literature and would-be writer, one who specialized in communication, I had become convinced that, except perhaps for the Bible itself, there was no other record anywhere like the Book of Mormon—nothing more human, nothing more complex or profound, nothing more intricate in its plot structure. The thought, "even as we write," of producing a work of such magnitude by my own feeble instrumentality was totally ludicrous.

For some time I lay there considering some of the so-called "little things" in that record that were actually very big. Who, for example—especially a twenty-three-year-old rustic living in the backwoods a hundred and sixty years ago—would have thought to write a "record in the language of my father, which consists of the learning of the Jews and the language of the Egyptians"?

Who would have thought to write a book containing scores of different authors all the way from giants of the Lord like Nephi, Alma, and Mormon, to the man called Chemish who, during his custodianship of the sacred records, wrote only one terse verse, who decided to "make an end" as swiftly as he had started? Why, indeed had he written at all? At the insistence of a nagging wife? Or Abinadom, his son, who managed the equivalent of *two* verses! Who personally knew of "no revelation save that which has been written, neither prophecy . . ." What unlikely inclusions for someone writing a mere work of fiction, as some people claim the book to be. And yet, how real, how human! How like life itself!

"Dad?" Dare's voice was muffled yet full of inquiry.

"Yeah?"

"I've been lyin' here thinkin'." A pause. "About the Book of Mormon."

I smiled into the darkness. "Hmmmm . . . interesting coincidence." The capillaries in my skin fizzed pleasantly.

"About what Alma said to Korihor when they were having that big argument over the existence of God. Remember?"

"Verily!" At one time I had been quite a skeptic myself—hardly an atheist like Korihor and not consciously inclined to lead people astray, but something of a sign-seeker nonetheless.

"Remember where Alma talks to him about all the evidence?"

"Yes," I replied. "The scriptures, the testimony of 'these thy brethren,' the planets 'which do move in their regular order,' and so on. The entire universe, in fact."

"Yeah," he said, "that great big plan at work out there." There followed a minute or so of silence. A breeze sifted through the trees outside our open window. Crickets chanted faintly. From somewhere came the sound of footsteps along one of the cement walkways, and a little flirt of laughter. "But ya know one thing I keep wondering about?"

I was still smiling. Sheer joy—lying there, with my own boy, an arm's length away, on his *mission!* Talking about religion, about God. How many times in the fairly recent past had I broached the subject with him without success, sometimes provoking only impatience and irritation. "What's that?" I said. "Lay it on me."

"Well, Alma tells old Korihor that '*all* things testify to thee that there is a creator.' He says it a couple of times, in fact."

65

"Yes, that's true."

"So, do you interpret that literally? *All* things? *Everything*?"

"Yes," I said after a moment, "I think I do." I stretched and yawned, though not from boredom. "I don't know how to explain it right now, but . . . well, yes—I'm positive Alma was correct." Suddenly I could feel the rightness of it, the tingling confirmation. The full logic would perhaps come later. "It's just a matter of knowing how to look at things. Perspective, imagination . . . being in tune."

"Right on," Dare said. There was another pungent silence. I could smell a faint odor of scented soap and maybe aftershave wafting from the bathroom, barely hear the slow, measured drip of the shower. "I'm really glad you're here, Pop. You're a pretty cool dude."

"Thanks, pal," I said. "Same to you."

12

As we drove away from our meeting with the Williams family, my son, Elder Darren G. Connors, glanced at me and smiled. It was probably the broadest, most winning smile he had ever displayed. "How about *that* one?" He was at the wheel, shifting gears and zigzagging through the traffic with his usual, rather jerky abandon and, fortunately, good reflexes. But for some reason we almost seemed to be riding on air a foot or so above the ground. "Would you believe it?"

I shook my head, incredulous and highly euphoric. "I've never encountered anything quite like it." We had just completed our first meeting with the family Dare and Mac had met a few days earlier while I was tracting with Elder Huddleston. I have always had mixed feelings about the word *golden* as it applied to investigators. For some reason it seemed a bit pat, maybe goody-goody. I grope for words. A little like our use, in that same general connection, of the word *choice.* Nevertheless, the people we had just met qualified for the golden classification if anyone did. The wife, Allie, was a pretty, slender woman in her early thirties, with auburn hair and dark, rather oriental eyes. Her husband, Dan, was rugged-looking, about the same age, with a solid, deeply cleft chin, and blue eyes with a keen glint. He looked like a college wrestling champ or star quarterback.

They had welcomed us into their home almost as though we were their favorite neighbors, watched the *Together Forever* video with rapt attention, then asked questions for the next half hour. Their children, a boy and girl, ages ten and twelve, had greeted Dare and me as though we were an uncle and grandpa respectively.

"Well," Dare said, "this old area hasn't been too productive so far, not like a lot of the mission. In a way . . ." He looked reflective. "I wish you could have come a while back when we were baptizing like crazy over in Peoria. But maybe now things are going to start cookin' around these parts."

I nodded. "Maybe that meeting today will sort of open the doors." Dare stopped at a red light. "But even if it doesn't, I've got a feeling that this little Williams family will make the whole effort worthwhile."

Dare gave a single, enthusiastic nod. "You notice what the wife said when we were going out the door?"

"About our next appointment?"

"Right—if by any chance we couldn't make it Thursday could we *please* be sure to come Saturday!"

I laughed. "And what about Dan? 'You don't have to limit it to an hour—take a *couple* if you want to!'" I shook my head, still a bit disbelieving. "And those wonderful little kids! Coming up to give us hugs when we left. Such beautiful spirits—like angels!"

"Yeah, really!" Dare said.

Thus far, the Williams family was every missionary's dream of the way it ought to be but rarely is. "It was worth taking out some time from your P-Day, anyway. Right?"

"Absolutely," Dare said. "It was *that*." P-Day (Preparation Day) came every Monday in the Phoenix mission—a time for shopping, laundry, letters home, and for a bit of fun and recreation. Hence, no proselyting in most cases till afternoon or evening. But Dan Williams was a truck driver, often away from home for several days at a time, and this had been our first and best opportunity for a meeting. "Now, though," Dare continued, "just to celebrate our good fortune, why don't we head home, latch on to our buddies–"

"And go for a little basketball over at the stake center," I interjected, knowing how much Dare relished the sport. I still indulged a bit myself, and it was a great way to unwind.

"Good thought," Dare said, "but I had in mind something sort of different–maybe showing you around this part of the mission a little; seeing some of my old turf over Phoenix and Scottsdale way."

"Sounds great," I replied, "if it's okay with the president. I promised him I wasn't coming out here on a vacation or to interfere with the work."

"No sweat, my man," Dare said. "Pres Linford doesn't mind a little of that, long as we don't roam too far or do something stupid."

I chuckled. "Surely a Mormon missionary would never do anything stupid!"

"Never!" he said, and faked a look of great piety.

That afternoon, in the company of our friends Mac and Hud, we visited two of Dare's former companions who were now working together in nearby Sun City. Then we looked up some members, one of whom he had baptized a year earlier in Phoenix. Later, we stopped by the Scottsdale Ward, a few minutes drive to the north. The building was locked, but it was a large, handsome place from the outside with a slightly South American quality and constructed of white brick. It was surrounded by about two acres of lawn, quite a rarity for those arid climes, and the grounds were ringed by grapefruit trees, a hundred or so, all bearing abundant fruit in various stages of ripening.

"Very impressive," I said. "Who takes care of all these trees, and what do they do with this endless supply of fruit?" My three young friends seemed unsure. "Welfare project, maybe?" Maybe, they allowed, but none of them was certain. What they did know, they assured me, was that this particular ward was the richest in the Church, containing among its members some fifty millionaires! They joked about the number of Mercedes, Porsches, Cadillacs, and other costly vehicles in the parking lot on Sundays.

"The priests quorum is on permanent assignment as parking lot attendants," Elder Mac said. "Members drive up to the door in their big, shiny limousines, and the young priests hop to."

"You're putting me on," I said, but for the moment wasn't absolutely sure. My three companions laughed heartily.

"You about had Pop snaked there for a minute," Dare said.

"It's the highest tithe-paying ward in the Church," Elder Hud drawled after a moment, "and that's a faay-uct."

"Hmmm . . ." I stroked my chin and gazed at the building, squinting slightly because of the sunlight cascading off its white facade. "Sounds as though they have their priorities straight, anyway, a lot of them at least." I paused, waxing somewhat philosophical, perhaps even a bit wistful, since it now appeared fairly certain that I would never have to withstand the test of riches. "And . . . there's nothing wrong with money, per se, just the love of money. Some people do grand things with it, in addition to paying their tithes and offerings."

Shortly afterward we drove away, having collected some of the opulent fruit that had just fallen from the trees. "Remember those grapefruit bowling contests we used to have back there at the ward?" Dare asked. "During our district meetings?" Mac chortled. "First one to wing a grapefruit all the way across the parking lot and into the street was champ," Dare explained, "but old Huddleston here could do it every time."

"Darned near, anyhow," Mac said. "What a wing that mahn's got on him. Big old arms like a windmill."

Hud merely grinned. "Used to pitch a lot of fastball."

"Characters!" I chided, but couldn't avoid the amusement. "You're lucky somebody didn't come down on you—President Linford, or even the cops."

"No sweat, Pop," Dare said. "We always picked it up after and tossed it in the dumpster."

"*Almost* always," Elder Mac corrected. "Except for the ones that made the street and got squashed in the traffic."

"Characters!" I repeated. "So where next, back to the pad?" Dare was at the wheel as usual, since he knew the area.

"Nay, nay—we're heading for Camelback," he said, "to see how the rich folks live." He gestured ahead a short distance. "See that there mountain?"

"It looks more like a foothill," I said, "or sort of a mesa maybe, but it's obvious they've got some fancy dwellings up there."

"You'd better believe it," Hud said. "That's puttin' it mildly."

"Hey, Pop," Dare said. "Don't you remember, I was living up there with the Pedersons when I started out? Remember me saying what neat people they were and how they gave us the run of their whole spread?"

I frowned. "I remember the place and the people, all right, but I thought that was in Mesa."

"Nay, nay! That was where we lived in that rennovated bomb shelter."

Mac hooted. "Livin' in a *bomb* shelter!"

"Serious," Dare said. "Actually wasn't too bad the way they'd fixed it up, but the Pedersons' up there on the mountain, that's Shangri-la, man. Handball and tennis court, swimming pool—the whole bit."

"Too bad you couldn't go in swimmin'," Hud said.

"Aw . . ." Dare tilted his head to one side for a moment, then to the other. "It wasn't all that tough. I used to sit out there by the pool, sometimes in the mornings while I studied my lessons, or sometimes under the lights for a while at night. Maybe go wild once in a while and dangle my toes in the water. Besides, we got to use the courts and stuff on P-Day. Sometimes they'd have the

71

entire zone over for a steak fry." We were only a short distance away from the so-called Camelback now. "But anyway, I figured we could go up and show Pop the mountain, then maybe stop by Pedersons' for a visit."

"Good plan," Hud said. "Like to meet 'em myself. And why not show him the castle, too, long as we're at it?"

"Castle?" I waggled my eyebrows.

"For real," Mac assured me. "In fact, it was up for sale the last I heard."

"Good," I laughed. "Maybe I'll buy it."

The mountain, as I had observed earlier, was not exactly spectacular, but it did resemble a camel's back, even to the tan coloration. Many of the homes themselves appeared rather drab from the outside, blending with the landscape, and the so-called castle was something of a disappointment, walled like a small fortress from the side we were on, and somewhat forbidding. I could understand why it might be up for sale. "Have you ever tried to tract any of these places?"

"On occasion," Dare said, "but most of them are walled or fenced, with locked gates. Big, bad Dobermans inside, and German shepherds."

"That could be a little discouraging," I admitted.

"The Pedersons, though," Dare continued, "they're worth the whole place put together. I mean, they're your ideal members—faithful, dedicated—love everybody, no matter *who* they are."

"That's a fact!" Elder Mac said.

"And they're your classic example of rich people with their priorities straight, like you were talking about, Dad. Pay their tithing, give away tons to charity, and they're Grandpa and Grandma to all the missionaries around. They've been on three different missions themselves, I think it is—"

"Four!" Mac asserted. "Brother Pederson told me."

"Yeah, well, *four* then. How *about* that! And they're really terrif with the referrals. I don't know how many people they've helped bring in over the years, but it's a bunch, I promise you."

The Pederson residence, unlike many of the others, had no gate, nor was it guarded by any ferocious watchdogs. It was, as well, highly attractive from the outside. The foundations and lower portion of the walls were constructed of large copper-tinted rock slabs; the upper half of redwood, and it rambled over three different levels. A walkway flanked by orange and lemon trees formed a long gentle curve from the drive to the front door, passing a pond filled with large goldfish.

Three immense plate-glass windows along the front were outlined with colored lights, another reminder that Christmas was nigh. The doorbell even gave a Christmassy chiming when we pressed it. Moments later the door opened, and we were greeted by a woman who appeared to be about sixty-five, though Dare assured me later that she was several years older. Her face was round, pleasantly glowing, and almost wrinkle-free. It might well have belonged, in fact, to someone half her age except for the little cloud of pure white hair surrounding it.

"Hello, there," Dare said jovially, "is this the headquarters for the Mafia?"

"Oh, my goodness gracious!" she exclaimed, and put her hand over her mouth, smothering a gasp of excitement. "Elder Connors!" Reaching out, she gave him an ample maternal hug. Her large, brown eyes were suddenly glistening at the corners. "We were afraid your mission was over and that you'd gone home without seeing us."

"Naw—you don't get off that easy," Dare grinned. "I'm still kickin' around for another couple months."

"And Elder MacDougall!" Then he was receiving the same treatment. "Big as life," he replied, "and twice as ugly. I'll be around for a whole year yet." More burbles. "Can't kill the weeds!" Sister Genevieve Pederson joined in with some delightfully girlish titters, said something about what characters they both were, how thrilled she was to see

73

them again. Then Elder Hud and I were being introduced as she ushered us all into a spacious living room furnished with couches and loveseats of rose and cream. A grand piano resided in the corner of the room, gleaming darkly. A small Christmas tree, white-flocked with large red baubles, stood on top.

"Let me call Alonzo," Genevieve said. "He's just finished showering—been working around in the back yard."

"He keeps up this great big, gahgeous yahd all by himself?" Elder Huddleston asked, eyes widening.

"Well, no, not entirely," she replied. "He's retired now, though, and works around the yard for exercise, mostly for recreation because he loves growing things so much. But we do have a gardener."

"Yeah, Watanabe," Dare said. "He's a bad old dude."

A short while later Alonzo Pederson appeared, dressed in gray cotton slacks and a short-sleeved shirt with pink candy stripes. He was a man of about seventy-five with pale blue eyes, a long, sloping jaw, and lengthy lines deepening into folds on each side of his mouth. It was a face that somehow appeared mournful and amused at the same time, an honest, unpretentious face that left you feeling comfortable.

As our visit progressed, I learned that he had been a contractor and realtor, made quite a fortune and, though he was anything but boastful, devoted much of his life to philanthropy. He had been a naval commander in World War II, and active in the Church all his days—most notably as missionary, bishop, and stake president. For the past several years, he had, among other things, volunteered to act as chief furniture procurer for missionaries throughout the Phoenix area. Many of the items were obtained through direct donation from Church members and were stored within a small warehouse he had built for that very purpose in a secluded corner of the yard.

"Well sir . . ." he said at last and gave us a friendly wink. "We've sure missed having the Elders around these past few months."

Dare and Mac looked surprised. "No missionaries staying here now?"

The Pedersons shook their heads. "Nope," Alonzo said, "I guess this whole neighborhood's just too slow lately. We've pretty well run dry on prospects ourselves, in fact."

"So the guest house where you elders stayed is empty now," Genevieve said and looked quite sad. "Our kids all grown up and married off a long time ago—so we're just a couple of oldsters knocking around in this big place all on our lonesome."

"Well, it certainly was generous of you to let the missionaries stay here over the years the way you have," I said, "and to pretty much let them have the run of the place from what Dare's been telling us."

"Man, I'll say!" Dare laughed. "Only one problem; you stay with Alonzo and Gen, and you're completely ruined for anywhere else."

"I hear you're also helping to keep a lot of the mission in furniture," I continued.

"Cookin' stuff, too," Mac said, "lamps, washers, dryers—the works. You name it, Brother P's the man."

The smile wrinkles at the corners of Alonzo's eyes deepened for a moment. "Oh, just a little hobby to keep myself out of mischief. Of course, a lot of the apartments come furnished, so things are gradually settling out a little."

"Are you still selling any real estate?" Dare inquired.

"Oh . . ." Alonzo massaged his jaw. "Once in a blue moon—when I see something that catches my fancy."

"He sold the castle," Genevieve said, looking rather mysterious and proud. "Only a few weeks ago."

"No kidding!" Dare exclaimed.

"Well . . ." Alonzo said deprecatingly. "I was sort of a front man. It was really a group operation."

"The one right here on Camelback?" I asked.

He nodded. "It's been up for sale over two years and become kind of a white elephant. Finally the owners got desperate. They'd moved out of state, hit some bad times, and wanted to unload fast."

"Wanted to so much it went for only a little over half the original asking price," Gen added.

"Really!" I said. "Most interesting."

"Not much to look at from the outside," Alonzo mused, "but the interior's pretty nice."

"So who finally bought the place?" Elder Hud asked.

The Pedersons exchanged smiles. "A *mystery* lady . . ." Gen's eyebrows lilted. "Her name's Melana Gardner, and she's a member of the Church."

"Aah, you're puttin' us on now," Elder Mac said.

"No, Elder," Genevieve insisted. "At least, that's the rumor—although she's not active, apparently." She paused, reflecting. "I've never seen her out to church, anyway."

"Well, it's only been a month or so since she moved in," Alonzo reminded her. "Takes some doin'."

"I know," Gen replied, "but . . ."

Alonzo grinned, canting his head her way. "Her woman's intuition's taking hold."

I laughed. "Never want to fight that."

"Pretty lady," he mused, "real nice and friendly. How old?" He glanced at his wife. "Fifty, maybe?"

"How should I know?" she laughed. "I still haven't met her."

"Thought you'd been there on one of your Relief Society visits."

"Oh, we've been there, all right," she said. "Three different times. Maybe she's away, but I get a funny feeling she's there and just won't answer the door."

"I don't think her health's any too good," Alonzo said, "might be the reason. She looks sort of peaked, on the skinny side. Does lots of painting, incidentally. That's partly why she bought the place. Wants to turn the main floor into an art gallery of sorts eventually."

"Hmmmm, most interesting," I said. "and what about her family?"

"I understand she's going through a divorce," Gen volunteered, "and the children—her younger ones anyway—are over in Mesa for the present with their father. I guess there's quite a custody battle."

Alonzo shifted, crossing his lanky legs and gesturing toward his wife with a thumb. "She's never met the lady, but you can be sure Gen's in on all the latest scuttlebutt, sometimes before it even happens."

"Well, it helps to be Relief Society president," Gen laughed. "People sort of keep you apprised of what's going on." Her eyes narrowed speculatively. "You know . . ." The word "know" was attenuated with a kind of lilt in the middle as if something important were coming. "I have a *feeling*"—nodding a little and looking more confident—"that you elders ought to go pay her a brief visit and take Brother Connors with you."

Dare nodded. "Sounds like a winner. I'd sure love to have a look inside that place, anyway."

"Course, if she's not answering the doorbell . . ." Elder Hud began.

"She might not," Gen persisted, "but why not give it a try as long as you're here? It's only two or three minutes away."

He shrugged and gave her a boyish smile. "Yeah, why not?"

Later we had lunch on the Pedersons' back lawn and afterward bid them a fond, appreciative farewell. Then we drove on up the mountain to try our luck at the castle. The house stood atop a steep and winding drive. As with our friends' residence down the hill, however, there was no gate barring the way, and on the side was a basement triple garage. The castle itself looked more attractive from our present vantage point. It was constructed of red sandstone, and a glance at the recessed windows one high story above revealed that the walls were about two feet thick.

For an instant, in fact, during that same glance, I seemed to sense a presence, a motion within, perhaps just the faintest stirring of a curtain. On the other hand, it may merely have been my imagination or possibly a slight mote that sometimes drifted amoeba-like across my bad right eye.

Ringing the side doorbell at an entranceway beside the garage a moment later, we received no response. None after several tries and a lengthy wait. "Well?" I glanced at my companions and felt slightly amused. "It looks as if our mystery lady may remain that way." Moments later we were driving back to Glendale.

13

At five o'clock we returned to our apartments, Dare and I finding our mailbox full. "Hey, hey, hey!" Dare rejoiced. "Looks like we've been *livin'* good!" There was a letter from a missionary buddy in Japan addressed to "Big Dare Short-Timer Connors," one from his oldest brother, Matt, a captain with the USAF in Germany, another from an old high school pal, and, to his ill-concealed delight, one in a pale yellow, light-weight, crinkly envelope from his girlfriend, Cindy Stewart. Last of all was a letter addressed to both of us from Sally.

The letter from Matt contained a typically humorous, satirical account of his latest assignment as defense counsel at Sembok Air Base and a lively description of a trip down the Rhine with wife, Darla, and their five children. "The kids, as usual," he concluded, "started whining and pestering each other, generally acting like a bunch of chumps before it was halfway over." I could almost hear his voice, tinged with vexation but mostly wry, philosophical amusement. Few things ever ruffled the lad. "Adam kept insisting he wanted to be home playing with his motley bunch of pals instead of 'being on this stupid old river and having to see any more dumb castles.' You plan all these neat things for your kids, thinking they'll be the adventures of a lifetime, and they end up acting like brats. It was definitely not a scene from *The Sound of Music*."

I laughed aloud. One of the many gratifying aspects of becoming a grandparent is to see your own children begin to enter the same three-ring circus they once put you through. Sometimes my amusement in that regard almost verged on the sadistic.

Of course, all such things—and even they had their endearing elements worth treasuring—were outweighed by the truly great ones, the "heaven in the home" times that ultimately combined to render all the hassle rather trivial. Wife Sally's letter gave us that, focused upon decorating the Christmas tree—"the tallest, most bracingly fragrant ever"—with our three youngest daughters, a deepening snow that blanketed our yard and the adjoining hollow there at the end of Polk Street, overlooking Ogden Canyon. "Hollow's Edge," we called it, and sometimes "Polk's End," often feeling that we were somehow part of a Tolkein setting. "Just before dark," she wrote, "Nan looked out the window there off our side deck and called to us. Seven deer were drifting like ghosts through our yard, passing the pfitzers and peach trees on the fringe of the hollow. For a moment they seemed to be looking right at us, and their necks and backs caught a final gleam of sunlight that turned them a faint gold. For quite a while we just stood there with our arms around each other, until they wandered off into the night and the first stars appeared over the Great Salt Lake."

I had been away from my family for only a week and a half and already I was homesick. A senior citizen, almost, pushing sixty, and I still got homesick, even going away for a single night! But there was that little extra note enclosed with the main letter, especially for old Nate. (That's me.) Brief but full of endearments in her familiar, spidery handwriting. "Darling, it's so *terrific* that you can be there with Dare—there in the mission field with your own flesh and blood son! It's one of those things (I can tell from your letters, yet know regardless) that you will literally never forget worlds without end. But darn it, we MISS you! I don't *like* sleeping in that big old bed alone! In fact, it's not really a bed at all when you're not there too. It's just a *place*. The final words read: "XOX–ME!" These in turn, framed by a lipstick imprint of the mouth I knew so well.

At that moment I saw the lips themselves, the ones Sally herself considered too large and full, but not I. "Nay, nay!" in the words of my son. For one thing, they were exceptionally expressive lips, the only ones I had ever seen that could fully register a smile that was fond, wistful, and mischievous. I saw her eyes, bright sea-green, laugh crinkles at the corners which she had inherited from her dad— "fun lovin' " eyes as was the entire face framed in abundant hair the color of ripe June grass. Some of the strands were now turning white.

My fond reflections were decimated at this point by two different interruptions: the arrival of Elders MacDougall and Huddleston, and a weird, staticky voice emanating from the answering machine. "Get a load of this!" Dare regarded us with sly amusement. "Another message from Herr Erlichmann. Another of his hellfire and damnation sermons."

I found myself listening, much bemused, as the recording commenced with a bizarre salutation that continued in the same vein. It was a mishmash of weird threats and exhortations mingled with scripture regarding their alleged derelictions as missionaries in the cause—some of it verging on the sacrilegious but some quite hilarious. The lad had a flare for comedy, and indeed for mimicry, most of it a weird combination of King James and Book of Mormon wording. The accent however, often sounded more like Count Dracula than one of the prophets.

We were all chuckling and shaking our heads when it was over. "The laddie's *diff*-initely out of his tree," Elder Mac asserted, his own accent adding to the sense of hilarity. "Titched!"

I shook my head. "So what does the good mission president think of this character?" I wondered.

"Oh . . ." Dare squinched up his face. "He's pretty well got Erlichmann's number. Luckily, Pres has a great sense of humor himself."

"I hope to tell ya," Elder Hud laughed. "The pres learned ta expect about anything."

"Yeah, but he doesn't take any guff either. And his sense of humor—it's not weird or anything. I mean, it's mellow. Kind that makes you feel good and want to try harder."

They were all three seated on the couch, fairly consuming it—the big red-haired Huddleston, with his freckle-blasted face; MacDougall, short and stocky with broad shoulders, jutting lower jaw and teeth creating a slightly bulldoggish underbite. And Dare—kicked back, hands locked behind his head, purple tie loosened to make room for his Adam's apple. Back there for a while, for a year or two preceding his mission, it had seemed—as with many teenagers—that he was growing in odd proportions, hands and feet too big for his body, nose suddenly dominating his face, becoming rather large and pointed, creating the illusion that his chin was shrinking. Now the nose had gained its former stature, yet with a certain adult permanence, the jaw and cheekbones becoming more dominant. It was almost as though he had been under the hands of a talented plastic surgeon.

"But old Erlichmann," he mused, "he's quite the comedian."

"Speaking of comedians," I mused, "what about Elder Darren G. Connors? What about that poor fellow you met by the golf course a while back, for example?" Elders Mac and Hud guffawed. Obviously, they'd heard the story. I myself had learned of it a month or so before when a returned missionary—one of his former companions dropped by our home for a visit. Seems he and Dare had been parked on the edge of a golf course, having the standard missionary lunch away from home: burgers, shakes, and fries. A young course attendant had approached to ask what they were doing there and advise them that they were in a restricted parking zone. Without the slightest hesitation, Dare had beckoned the lad, cupped a hand to his mouth, and muttered: "FBI. Move out fast; act like you haven't noticed us." Utterly bamboozled, the attendant had actually backed off and gone his way.

"The old FBI ploy," I said. We were all laughing. Elder Mac himself fairly warbled. "Too cool—gotta *louve* it. Poor blighter didn't know which way was up after that, I'll bet."

"Where'd you hear about that one, Pop?" Dare's expression was sly, amused, slightly sheepish all in one. "That was supposed to be a secret."

"Oh, I have my sources," I replied, "my little spy network. Your former companion, actually. Dan Atkinson, the one from Tremonton, that time he dropped by for a visit."

"Oh, yeah—good old Elder Atkinson. He was a bad dude—outstanding missionary."

"What you should have done," I suggested, "was follow through on the guy—the golf course boy, I mean. Should have come back later and asked him if he'd like to know who you *really* are."

"Yeah." He began to look more serious. "Maybe I should have. It's pretty fantastic what can happen when you just go out and say hi to people on the street." He shrugged. "In the park, anywhere." He pursed his lips, squinting one eye. "Hey, maybe we should introduce Pop to it. That's one experience he hasn't had yet."

"You mean, just come up and buttonhole people on the street?" I asked. "Anybody that happens along?"

"Basically, yeah," Hud said. "However the Spirit directs. Just open your mouth and say what comes."

"Right now, though, I'd best call a few of the boys—see what's happenin'," Dare said. I took that to mean that he was going to confer a bit with some of the other missionaries within his zone. "See how Roberts and Cameron are comin' along." Plucking up the phone next to me on the table, he began punching numbers in a bouncy series of little chirps. Then he paused, waiting. Suddenly his face creased in a wide grin. "Hey, hey, Cameron my man! This is your old buddy The Con Man—yeah, Con Man Connors." A low chuckle. "Right! So what's happenin'?"

There was another pause while he nodded, still grinning. "Sis Edgar? Big feed comin' up, huh? Hey, good deal. Yeah, she's great that way, isn't she? Yeah, a real cool lady." Then, in an aside to the rest of us: "Sister Edgar's havin' Cameron and Roberts over for turkey dinner since nobody invited them for Thanksgiving."

"Hey, all right!" Hud said. "Tell her we'll be there too."

"Just in case they can't handle it," Mac added.

"By the way," Dare continued, "I understand you guys got one of those crazy Christmas cards . . . right, the weird Harold photo. 'Death and Destruction to all Mormon Missionaries.' Yeah, exactly. Looks sort of like a face—a bunch of faces, actually, sort of all melted into one." He waited, listening. "By the way, you fine, young Elders wouldn't have an idea who's behind it all, would you? Promise? Swear on the Bible?" Little chuckles and slight bobbing of the head. "Yeah, we thought it might be Erlichmann, but he says no real hard. Yeah, I sort of figured you two characters might be the next best bet."

There was more listening punctuated only by an occasional "Yeah," "right," or "uh-huh." Finally he said, "That's a fact. We just got another of Erlichmann's inspirational sermons on our answering machine, by the way. One of his real masterpieces—kookier than ever." Pause. "Well, anyway, the main reason I called was to tell you about my new companion. Already heard, huh? News gets around. Yeah, my pop. How's about if we drop by tomorrow and see how things are goin'—go out on some splits. Right, okay, we'll bless you boys with our presence around nine."

Then, on the verge of hanging up: "Okay, dude—you know what happens if you ain't telling the truth, the whole truth, and nothing but the truth. Right, it's down the chute with Old Scratch and the bad guys, shovelin' lots of coal. Yea, verily. Okay, peace, bruthah. Save us about half that turkey."

"So what's going on?" Elder Hud asked.

"Our highly esteemed colleague, Elder Charles H. Cameron, claims he doesn't know beans about who's doin' it. They just got one of the stupid things themselves."

14

That night, following several fruitless call-backs, Dare and I encountered Elders Mac and Hud entering their apartment complex via bicycle. They had just taught the first lesson to a family of six. All had gone well, with an invitation to return three days later.

Both elders were quite elated, and by way of celebration we all went to a drive-in for milkshakes. Heading home afterward, we journeyed momentarily in silence, watching the traffic flow by, the lights changing yellow, red, then green as though consciously timing themselves for our passage.

"You know . . ." I said eventually, then hesitated, cogitating.

"Know what?" my son prodded.

"Oh . . ." I squinted against the oncoming headlights. "I was just thinking of what you Elders were saying earlier about going out on the streets and talking to people, not being afraid to open your mouth. Guess I was kidding a little about Dare going back to check with that guy at the golf course. On the other hand, maybe he really should have."

"Could be," Dare allowed. "Maybe we can go look around

the place one of these days. It's only about fifteen minutes from here."

"Anyway," I continued, "that started me thinking about the fellow I met in the furniture store when I first hit Glendale—the one I told you about who finally got me headed straight." I hesitated. "Well, I have this little feeling, maybe just a hunch, that we should go pay the man a visit."

"Okay, let's do it," Mac said. "What's to lose? The place open this late?"

"It was the night I went there," I replied, "and it's not too far away—in that big mall down off Fifty-seventh Avenue—if I've finally got my directions right."

"Hey, let's go for it!" Mac said, and gave one of those little, missionary yelps. The "go-for-it," morale-builder special.

That was how I came to make my second visit to the establishment in question, this time accompanied by three companions. Initially, in fact, I wondered if I wasn't engaging in a little overkill. The store, however, was indeed open, people funneling out minutes shy of the advertised nine o'clock closing time. Several employees were completing their work behind a counter, and I could see one of the men I had encountered earlier seated behind a large desk in the rear. It was the rather swarthy, Latin-type I had met before, the man with the bristling moustache. An instant later we spotted his compatriot moving slowly in our direction through a grove of floor lamps, pausing here and there to examine price tags.

He glanced up inquiringly as I approached. "Yes, sir! Can I help you?"

"You probably won't remember me," I said, my entourage lingering a short distance in the background. For an instant, his face remained neutral, but he was unquestionably the gentleman I had encountered that first night. The same gray widow's peak, close-set eyes, and the dominating nose, a bit like the kind you sometimes see on Indian totem poles. "I came in here about two weeks ago," I explained. "You told me how to find West Eugie."

Suddenly his face broke into a crooked grin. "Ah yes! The man who was lost."

I nodded emphatically, laughing a little. "Right, and when I told you so, do you remember your reply?"

He frowned, pursed his lips, closed one eye as if sighting in on something within his head. "Hmmmm . . . guess you've got me. Something awfully clever, no doubt."

"Definitely," I told him. "You said . . . 'Aren't we all?' "

"Oh, yea-ahhh!" He gave a grand and knowing nod. "That *was* clever, wasn't it?" This followed by an infectious, asthmatic laugh.

"*I* thought so," I replied. "Anyway, you got me to West Eugie. I was looking for my son's place." I gestured toward Dare who was standing, hands on hips, beside our two companions. All were taking in the exchange with interest. "Well, for some reason I've been thinking about that statement ever since, wondering if by any chance it was also . . . oh, sort of a philosophical observation, say, on the state of mankind." He was watching me intently, wreathing a faintly quizzical smile. "If so," I concluded, "then, I've got news for you."

He continued to eye me for a moment, a good-natured glint in his yellow-gray eyes. "You one of those Mormons I keep hearing about?" He fired a glance at my friends. "Those characters with you have got to be."

"That's correct," I laughed, "and we'd like a chance to tell you a little about it one of these times." I guess that was an example of "opening my mouth"; I only hoped then it wasn't my *big* mouth.

"Hmmm . . ." He glanced down at his shoes, frowning. "An interesting proposition." Then he looked up, tossing his hands out in acquiescence. His gnome-like countenance was suddenly youthful and buoyant. "Well . . . why not? I've heard about everything else."

"Good," I said. "When's the best time?"

"Hmmm . . ." He arched one brow. "Well, it's past closing time. They're locking up, in fact. So, why don't we have at it right here for a little while?" I tossed the Elders a look and realized that they were mirroring my own surprise. "Fifteen minutes, a thousand well-chosen words. Then I've got to head home for my beauty rest." Another asthmatic chuckle. "By the way, name's George Steiner; call me Stein." Reaching for his extended hand, I introduced myself, then each of the Elders. He nodded. "Pleased to meet you fellows. And, by the way, *that* character . . ." He gestured toward his partner at the desk. "Is Robert Riverra, but I prefer to call him Geraldo." His friend glanced up smiling and tossed us a friendly little salute. "As you can see," Steiner added, "he not only has the requisite last name, he even *looks* like him, right down to the moustache." That prompted another smile from Riverra and a kind of "aw, come-off-it" gesture as though he were shooing away a fly.

Moments later we were seated in Steiner's glass-partitioned office, "Geraldo" having declined an invitation to join us on grounds that he had to complete the day's bookkeeping. "So!" Steiner exclaimed, then paused. "I gather you think we're lost after all, philosophically speaking. 'God's in his heaven, all's right with the world.' Is that it?" It was a quote from Browning that I, as professor of English literature, had known for years; but it surprised me somewhat coming from a furniture store manager.

I shrugged. "That line's a bit rosy, I'm afraid, for any of us these days. All is definitely not right with the world." I hesitated, wondering what to say next, and decided to make it simple. "Even so, we're convinced that God is in his heaven."

"Really?" He flicked me a look of mock surprise. "So what makes you think so?" His tone and expression were good-natured, but it was definitely a challenge. Possibly the oldest and most difficult we ever encounter, and suddenly there I was, on the firing line.

I gazed at my three young Elders, not wishing to usurp

their authority, but it was apparently my show. "Because for one thing," I replied cautiously, "despite all our woes and sorrows, the only alternative to God is no God, and I find that totally unacceptable."

He tossed out one hand, palm up, somewhat indifferently. "Why so?"

I reflected a moment, sensing that we were involved, all very unexpectedly, with someone who had probably heard all the standard answers more than once. "Because . . ." I squinted, looking about me. Geraldo was bending over the paperwork at his desk just outside the open door. "Despite all the chaos, the suffering, the unanswered questions"–I was choosing my words carefully, not wishing to over-generalize or appear fatuous–"I see his hand at work everywhere. Everywhere I look–things that simply could never have occurred by blind chance. Not in an eternity of coincidences."

I paused, knowing how easy it would be for good old Prof. Connors to launch one of his classroom-type lectures, resisting the inclination, reminding myself of our host's courtesy and the suggested fifteen-minute time limit.

"Like what?" he prodded slyly, "the birds and the bees?" We all laughed as though it were a great joke.

"Well, yes, as a matter of fact," I replied. "That's as good as any for openers. Birds and bees literally, and all that the phrase stands for." I had always been interested in biology, and from day one experienced a growing love affair with nature, even considered becoming a naturalist at one time. "Take the honey bee alone," I said. "The social order, the sophistication and consistency of their honey-gathering, of the entire operation. Billions upon billions of those remarkable little creatures, all exactly the same, and each one a complete miracle. Think of the color and design alone, or the wings, say, or the eye!"

"Or the brain!" Mac supplied.

"Yes, that above all."

"What about the stinger?" Stein winked at my companions.

90

I laughed, knowing what he was up to. "The old Blake dilemma about the tiger and the lamb," I said. "'Did he who made the lamb make thee?'" I was searching his face. "Did he who made the wing make the stinger?"

Steiner nodded, apparently conceding a *yes* answer on my part. Then he turned to Dare. "You think your dad here really believes what he's saying?"

My son smiled wryly and blinked as though a bit scandalized. "I most certainly hope so. Otherwise, I'm in for one big shock."

Our host chuckled, drew a pack of Viceroi's from his shirt pocket, casually extracting a cigarette. "Mind if I smoke?"

"No," I lied. "Go right ahead." I didn't relish the sidestream effect of tobacco by any means, but what could you say? It was his place, his time.

"By the way, talking about bees . . ." Dare said. "The beehive is our state emblem back home in Utah."

Steiner squirreled up one vestigial eyebrow, squinting through the smoke cloud he had just generated. "Yeah, right; I seem to recall now. Symbolical of industry, right? Industry in the positive human sense."

"Exactly," Dare assured him. The man continued to surprise me.

"It's part of our religious history, too," Elder Huddleston said. "Maybe we'll get a chance to tell you about that some time."

George Steiner shrugged, though not indifferently. "Why not?" He took another drag on his cigarette, coughing a little. "But for right now, let's pursue what Nathan here has to say about the existence of God. Okay to call you Nathan?"

"Why, sure," I replied, "or Nate—whatever." I reflected for a moment upon his continuing challenge. "Maybe in one sense the honeybee says it all. The rest is just a case of multiplying examples. But let's not forget the birds! If anything, they're even more remarkable examples of creation. Certainly more advanced."

91

"We get a lot of hummingbirds around our place in the summer," Dare said. "Put out feeders with red sugar water in them, and they really come in by the numbers. I mean, those little guys are just about the most fantastic things imaginable. About fifty wing vibrations per second in normal flight—about five times that when they go into their power dives."

"Hmmmm . . . fascinating." Steiner's words sounded genuine.

"So naturally, they burn up a terrific amount of energy," I said. "I read an article on the subject once that said a full-grown man who expended an equivalent amount of energy would have to consume twice his weight in food every day just to keep fueled, and he'd have to sweat more than a gallon of water an hour to prevent his blood from boiling."

"Incredible."

"Yes—fantastic little creatures. Very territorial also."

"I probably read the same article," Dare said. "That one in the *Smithsonian*?" I nodded. "Says they'll actually take on birds like crows and hawks, even eagles sometimes. Even snakes, if they have to protect their nests."

"Yes," I said. "On the other hand, they seem to have quite an affinity for people. They're a bit like dolphins in that respect. Occasionally they'll even let you hold them in your hand."

"Hmmm . . . most interesting." Our friend nodded, squinting through the smoke as if it hurt his eyes; it definitely hurt mine. "So those kinds of things—honeybees and hummingbirds—they tell of a divine power."

"Those things, yes," I said. "All life, for that matter, whether we're talking the birds and the bees or the flowers and the trees. Even a single living cell. That alone is an absolutely fantastic work of *creation*, not chance."

"Talking about miracles," Dare said, "what about the brain? One of my psych teachers back at Weber State was telling us that if you could string out all the neural tissue in the brain to the max . . . *Some* way," he laughed. "I don't

92

know how you'd do it, but if you could, it would stretch all the way to the moon and back. That's about half a million miles!"

"Ah yes," our friend observed. "The human brain—the ultimate miracle. So complex it may never fully comprehend itself!"

"I couldn't agree more," I told him. "Absolutely true. The greatest miracle and ultimate paradox." A handsome, darkly gleaming grandfather clock just outside the glass partition chimed ten. We had already consumed our allotted fifteen minutes. "And the great god Chance could never have brought it off, not by the remotest stretch of the imagination. Not any more than it could have brought off that fine clock. Agreed?"

Steiner dragged deeply on his cigarette, firing a jet of blue-gray smoke through his nostrils. "Maybe," he mused, then repeated the word a little more emphatically.

For a few seconds we sat in silence. I had first encountered the same basic argument at the old Missionary Training Center in Salt Lake City. In those days we had a mere week or so of preparation before funneling off into the great, wide world. But it was a sound and edifying concept, one that had grown within my mind and heart since then, steadily becoming more powerful. "And where within the entire realm of human experience do we ever have purpose without plan, and plan without personality? Let the intellectuals label it 'argument of design' and foolishly assume that in so doing they have disposed of its logic." I laughed and threw out my hands. "But not for me and my house."

Our interlocutor smiled cryptically. His gnome-like features, even to the all-consuming schnoz, were somehow quite appealing. "Saul, Saul," he said and stubbed out his cigarette in an ashtray. "Almost thou persuadest me."

15

The phone rang that night only moments after we had returned to our apartment. I answered, to be greeted by the pleasant voice of Genevieve Pederson. "I just wanted to call and let you know that my two counselors and I had a nice visit with Melana Gardner today."

"Melana Gardner?"

"The lady in the castle."

"Oh, yes! I'd forgotten her name. So what happened? What's she like?"

"Well . . . she's a very charming and gracious lady, and she spent quite a lot of time showing us around and telling us about her plans for the place. It's quite palatial, but also rather barren. Her former husband seems to have retained most of the furniture at their home in Mesa."

"Most interesting," I mused. "You said she was a member of the Church—right?"

"Yes, but in name only. She's never been active or learned much on the subject. She doesn't even know what's become of her records, but I guess that's something we can check into." Brief pause. "The important thing, though—and this is the main reason I called—she's definitely interested in learning more about it, about the gospel."

"Well, how nice!" I said.

"Yes, really. She doesn't feel like coming out to meetings at the moment but says she'd like to have someone come talk to her."

"Great! So who's going to meet with her, the ward missionaries? I suppose they're the ones who should."

"Well . . ." She dragged the word out thoughtfully. "Alonzo and I have been talking about that quite a bit. The fact is, two of our ward missionaries have just been released, and the other two happen to be an older couple who have gone back to Utah for the Christmas season to be with their children."

"Hmmm . . ." I stroked the bristles on my jaw, last shave fifteen hours or so earlier. Dare was watching me, his face full of inquiry, and I cupped my hand over the receiver. "Sister Pederson," I told him. "She's been in touch with the castle lady."

"So . . ." Genevieve continued, "well, Alonzo and I have sort of been thinking it might be nice if you and your son could pay her a visit before you head back to Utah."

"Maybe we *could*," I said, feeling both interested and uncertain. "She's not a part of Darren's zone, actually, but I suppose there wouldn't be anything wrong with an informal—"

"I really think it would be nice," Gen interjected. "Melana Gardner's . . . oh, a rather sophisticated, intellectual type, so I seriously doubt that the standard missionary approach is what she'd want at the moment. And besides that, she seems quite vulnerable emotionally. She's obviously going through some hard times with her divorce and all."

"That's too bad," I said. "One of the toughest things people undergo in this life, isn't it?"

"That's true," Gen replied. "Oh, by the way, she also showed us a few of her paintings. I'm no expert, but I think she's extremely talented."

Our conversation ended shortly afterward, and Dare was clearly pleased to learn what had happened. "Gen seems bound and determined that we visit this lady," I said and laughed a little. "But it might just be a good thing."

"Yeah," he replied. "I'll call Pres Linford and clue him in on things, but I'm sure he'll give us an okay, long as we're keeping up on stuff here. If she gets to the point where she's ready for the regular lessons, we'll let Gen work it out with her bishop in ward correlation—or whatever looks best." He hesitated, frowning. "Maybe we can take the full-time Sister missionaries from that ward area along with us."

Later as we lay in our beds almost ready for the sandman, Dare spoke quietly. "Well, Pop, you've been out here over two weeks now. How's it feel being a missionary again?"

"Great!" I said, though somewhat groggily. I had been hovering between wakefulness and dreams, hearing disconnected voices and snatches of conversation from my subconscious. "And the best part about the whole thing," I continued, reviving a little, "is that I have this terrific young compañero."

"Right on—so true!"

"Of course, now, he's kind of a whippersnapper at times. Occasionally I have to work him over a little, but he's shaping up." Momentarily I began to slide dreamward again, then thought of something. "So how are things these days with young Cindy?"

"Good . . . real good." For some reason I couldn't quite fathom, the words lacked full conviction. Something in the tone.

"Still waiting faithfully, I assume."

"Yeah, still waiting." A brief lull. "Goin' to school at Weber, lots of classes."

"Respiratory therapy—correct?"

"Right. It's what she's wanted for a long time, ever since high school." I had always been a little uncomfortable over the waiting part of their relationship, though certainly not because of any negative feelings toward Cindy Stewart. A bright and vivacious little blonde with electric blue eyes, she had a strong sense of direction, and was both sweet-natured and spiritual without being pious. About all one might hope for in a prospective daughter-in-law. It was simply that I didn't favor waiting in most cases. If the union was meant for eternity it should withstand the test of continued dating. If not . . .

"She still running marathons?"

"Not so much these days what with work and school. Seems like she hardly has time to write lately. That letter the other day was the first one in a couple of weeks."

"Well, I'm sure from what you just said she must be very busy."

"One sweet little woman." He sounded strangely wistful.

"She is indeed," I said. Silence . . . the returning of dreamscapes and voices.

"Pop?"

"Hmmnn?"

"Did you really *know* the first time you went with Mom? That she was the one, I mean."

"The first time I went with your mom, she was a darling young thing of only seventeen."

"Really? You never told me that."

"No? Always thought I had. Anyway, she was seventeen, and I was an old man of twenty-three, a couple of years after my mission." I was back there now, through the decades with the speed of light. "The first time I went with her? No, I didn't really know she was the one, but I did tell myself she would make somebody a terrific wife someday when she grew up. Of course, I was enough older that I felt a little guilty dating her—the old cradle-robber syndrome. Then I went waltzing off into the army for a couple of years, off to Japan—the Land of the Rising Sun. I returned home on a Saturday night in early June, 1956, and the next morning when I went to Church, this beautiful, glowing girl in a yellow dress came walking up to me in the foyer, stuck out her hand, and said, 'Welcome home, Nathan Connors.'"

"That was Mom?"

"You'd better believe it—that was our Sally Girl."

"And *then* you knew for sure, right?"

"Not exactly, but something pretty remarkable started going to work on me. I remember going home from sunday school that day, walking toward our place on upper Lake Street up there by the mountains. The sun was shining very brightly, and this voice in my mind was saying over and over again—'You're going to marry that girl.' Then my alter ego would start arguing that it was all a purely emotional reaction to the first pretty girl I'd met back home." I paused, feeling it all again, more strongly than ever. "But I'll tell you something, the absolute truth . . . that other voice in my mind knew exactly what it was talking about. Absolutely would not be denied."

"I'm sure glad, Pop." He gave a sleepy laugh. "Otherwise, we wouldn't be here talkin' it all over like we are right now. Man, I might not even be around!"

"That *would* be sad," I said. "I suppose, in actuality, you'd be around in somebody's family, but maybe not mine." I heard footsteps coming down the walk outside our window, muffled voices, a trailing rill of feminine laughter. A car started up in a parking lot and rolled away down the street.

"Pop?"

"Roger—still here."

"How do you really know in stuff like that—I mean like knowing you were going to marry Mom. That it's the Spirit and not just imagination or wishful thinking?"

I hesitated; it was a good question. "Maybe you can't always, not every time you want to. At least, I can't. But sometimes the Spirit is so powerful, downright pungent, you can't deny it. Sometimes it's so strong it feels as if all your cells are sort of fizzing, carbonated maybe. And the tear ducts usually go into action, even though you aren't necessarily crying. In some cases, in fact, it seems as if your whole body is filled with light. Sometimes it actually feels as if you might start floating." I waited. "Know what I'm saying?"

"Yeah," he said, "I do. Sometimes it just helps to get a little different perspective."

"And it really *was* that way in the case of your mother, as soon as I stopped offering dumb, so-called logical counter-arguments and really started listening."

"I know what you mean," he said. "Things along that line happen pretty often out here in the field, but still . . . sometimes you're not certain. Maybe just not operating on a spiritual enough level."

"Right," I replied, "and there are definitely different levels of awareness. The past day or two, in particular, I've had a growing feeling that I've come here for some special reason. First, naturally, to be with you—that's reason enough in and of itself."

"Absolutely," he chuckled. "That's a *glorious* reason!"

"True . . . and secondly to do some research. But . . ." I hesitated, speaking cautiously. "There's something else along with it. Something pretty important and specific, even though I don't have any idea what it is at the moment." Even as I spoke, however, a pleasant fizzing began within my cells and veins. My tear ducts started to activate very slightly. Mere power of suggestion? No, it definitely went beyond that.

Dare gave a sleep-filled laugh. "Well, you'd better find out pretty quick, Pop, if you plan to make it home for Christmas."

16

Two days later we had our first meeting with Melana Gardner in the castle, one arranged by our ever-attentive friend Gen Pederson. We were accompanied by two full-time Sister missionaries from that area, whom Dare had phoned following a discussion of the matter with President Linford.

The entire place, as Gen had explained during our phone conversation, was almost bare. Within the living room—more accurately, perhaps, a small banquet hall—there was little but patio furniture. Expensive furniture, however, including a plush, flowered lounge couch in peach and soft-orange tones, also white, wrought-iron chairs containing the same flowered padding. A large, oval table with a heavy glass top sat next to us, framed with wrought iron. In the center was a big vase of pink and cream-colored roses.

Dare and I sat on the lounge, our Sister missionaries and Melana Gardner on chairs surrounding the table and facing us. "As you can see," Melana was saying, "I'm terribly shy on furniture. I've pretty well spent my inheritance, and right now I'm hoping to live off my paintings."

"Fascinating," I said, and meant it. "An enterprise like

that requires a lot of resourcefulness. A lot of vision and courage."

Melana, however, laughed self-deprecatingly. "Maybe it's sheer insanity, but as you may know, this place has been empty for over two years. The former owners had left the area and were pretty desperate. And their realtors, thanks to Alonzo Pederson, simply made me an offer I could not refuse."

If some day you might happen to be writing about this woman, the thought came, how would you describe her? Beautiful? Well, maybe not, but certainly very charming and attractive. Her face was a slender oval with a delicate, finely chiseled nose and slightly flaring nostrils that somehow seemed familiar. Wide, rather thin lips that constantly changed their expression, often curling up at the corners in a smile that appeared both knowing and rueful. Short, ash-colored hair, a wing of which angled becomingly across her brow.

"My big dream at present," she was saying, "is to convert this downstairs area into a gallery and hold exhibitions for local artists. I'll live and do my painting upstairs."

"Great idea," Dare said. "I mean, there's a lot of bad artists all over this state."

I smiled. "By *bad* he means *good*, in case you're wondering."

"Yes," Melana laughed. It was a sound that tinkled faintly, like wind chimes. "I'm on to the argot, thanks to my own teenagers."

"Yeah, some pretty darned good artists. I've even run into a couple," Dare continued, "mainly up on the res."

"The 'res'?" Her brows winged up as though on the verge of flight. They were surprisingly dark, as were her lashes, in contrast to the pale ash of her hair.

"Navajo Reservation, up north near Window Rock," he explained.

"Ahhh, Window Rock!" She rolled her eyes half swooningly, tossing her head slightly to one side, and I must confess that the expression was remarkably appealing. It was the eyes, most of all, that really entranced. They were large and silver-gray—the kind that had probably generated much comment throughout her life. Comments like: "Did you see those *eyes?*" Especially, of course, by appreciative males. "You kidding? How could you *miss* them?"

"It really is a terrific place," Dare was saying. "I spent about four months up that way a while back. That whole area . . . well, some of it's sort of bleak, but lots of it's really beautiful. Kind of gets into your bloodstream."

"Yes, it truly does," Melana said. "I've done quite a bit of painting in that locale myself, in fact—not recently, but a few year ago I spent about two weeks there with my son and daughter . . . driving around, painting, taking hundreds of slides, and . . ." She gestured gracefully with a slender hand. "Just soaking it up." Her body was also slender, perhaps even a bit anorexic, and as she turned her head, glancing at the young Sisters, her face caught the light, revealing a mosaic of fine lines I hadn't noticed before. The magnificent eyes, in fact, were discolored around parts of the sockets, almost bruised-looking. Increasingly, though, it seemed as if I had met her before.

She was talking now about Indian art, its unique properties, its appeal, how she hoped to feature a lot of it in her future gallery. How old was she? Hard to tell. Forty-five, possibly fifty.

"Well!" Melana exclaimed at last. "I'm sure you're very busy people, and I suppose Genevieve explained why I asked you to come."

"She said you might like to discuss some things regarding the Church," Dare said.

"Well—ah, yes!" It was a combined exclamation and sigh. Then she gazed at the ceiling for a moment. "Yes, I really do, but perhaps I should give you a little of my background first." For a time, she hesitated, glancing about reflectively. "Where to begin? Hmmm . . ." We were sipping pink lemonade from pink-tinted goblets with clinking ice cubes and bright red maraschino cherries. In the brief lull, I gazed at our two lady missionaries. Sister Bronson was short, curvaceous, rather muscular, with cheeks that reminded me of apples. Sister Keller was tall and somewhat gaunt, with red hair and freckles much like those of our friend Huddleston. Both countenances were very pleasant, smiling politely with a kind of sweet inquiry.

"Wherever you like," I said finally. "We're here to listen."

"Well, I'll just go back partway," Melana concluded. "Otherwise, I might have you here the rest of the day. "Where to begin?" she repeated, still hesitant. "My marriage I suppose, I was married pretty early in life, age eighteen—practically a child bride. And to a man who was about twelve years older than I. We were living in Nova Scotia at the time, and he was into ship-building very heavily, and very successfully." She sipped her lemonade, eyelids lowered. Dare was sampling some of the macaroons she had provided, slyly attempting to acquire three or four by secreting most of them in his palm. He glanced up a bit sheepishly, suddenly aware that he had been caught in the act. The young Sisters were trying to avoid the giggles, Sister Bronson's eyes blue as periwinkles. Melana herself was trying to hide a smile.

"He's become very adroit at that sort of thing, thanks to the example set by several older brothers," I noted.

"Well, heavens!" Melana laughed. "That's what they're for, to eat. Besides, they're awfully small." Dare's face was actually turning red. "Anyway . . ." our hostess continued. "It was not exactly a marriage made on high—or one my parents were especially thrilled with, for reasons you might imagine. Not merely because of the age difference, but because despite his financial talents, they thought he was unstable, and because . . . Well, there I was, an innocent little Mormon girl who actually didn't know what she believed or why, and there he was, the sophisticated playboy and adventurer—an agnostic on top of that."

I shook my head. "Quite a combination."

"Oh, indeed!" She rolled her remarkable eyes. "I'm

still not quite sure what he saw in me." *He saw the eyes*, I thought. "But I suppose that in *some* ways I was pretty mature and rather independent, something of a free spirit." Her shoulders rose and fell in a mild shrug. "I guess maybe he liked that." She was wearing white slacks, sandals, and a lilac-colored blouse that accentuated her graceful arms. "Well, anyway, I was quite enamored of the man." Her brow arched eloquently, with a touch of seduction. "Dazzled."

Sister Keller laughed. "Oh, I'd be too—who wouldn't be! Even an orthodox little Mormon girl like myself." She was wearing rather large glasses with red frames that somehow seemed rather unorthodox even though they complemented her hair and freckles.

"Oh, it was quite a life to begin with," Melana continued. "We spent the first few years in Nova Scotia, then moved to Barbados. That's where our first two children were born—Lance and Lorelie."

"Cool names," Dare said.

"Yes, a nice combination," I added.

"They made a nice combination as siblings, too," she said. "I've never known a brother and sister who related so harmoniously, who had so much downright fun together or shared more love and respect. Eventually they both married, drifted apart geographically, and started their own little families. But the love and rapport never faded." She said no more for several seconds, but I could tell from her expression that something unhappy would follow. "Then, about two years ago, we lost Lance in a plane crash. He had acquired his own private plane, a Cessna, and went down with it in a storm near Lake Tahoe."

"Oh, I'm *sorry!*" I exclaimed, while the Sisters and Dare offered their own condolences.

Melana's eyes misted, and her voice thickened, but it was apparent that she had trained herself to keep it under control. "One of those seemingly ridiculous, utterly senseless things that springs out of nowhere." Her tone was almost sing-songy for an instant, lightly indifferent, though that was clearly an ironic disguise. "But getting back to the main story. My husband and I—his name's Court, by the way—had some pretty exciting times during our first several years. Travelled the world—Europe, the Orient, Africa, Australia, much of South America—and he was, still is, a genius at making money, virtually anything he turns his hand to."

"An enviable talent," I said.

"Well, yes, in some respects. I can remember that sometimes he used to look at me with this slightly unfocused stare as if he couldn't quite believe it himself. Despite all his sophistication and worldliness, he had a kind of child-like innocence that often surfaced quite unexpectedly." She hesitated, her own expression rather innocent too, perhaps somewhat fond as well. "Sometimes he'd look at me and say, 'You know, Lanie, it's actually as if I don't know how *not* to make money. It's as if I'm fated to or something!'"

We all laughed a little, exchanging glances. "That's an affliction I've never suffered," I said.

Her own laughter was more subdued. "It's almost a metabolic thing, an inborn gift or talent like mechanical or athletic ability. Unfortunately, though, he's not much good at retaining it. Literally here today and gone tomorrow much of the time."

"Intriguing," I said.

She nodded, her slender smile flowing and curling upward at the corners. "And being an alcoholic doesn't always enhance sound judgment."

"I hear you," Dare said. "I've run into a lot of people with problems along that line the past couple of years."

"Yes, I suspect." She shook her head. "At first it wasn't much of a problem. For quite a while it actually seemed as if he had unlimited tolerance for the stuff—the macho man who could always hold his liquor even when practically swimming in it. But eventually he pushed it too far and went over the brink." She frowned; then her features smoothed out. "Oh, we lived the high and lavish life and, as you can see, I managed to cling on to a bit." She glanced across the ceiling, letting her gaze sweep the room. "Enough to acquire this poor little hovel." Her laughter was lyrical with an ironic note. A woman who knew how to poke fun at herself. For an instant her face seemed quite girlish, some twenty years younger. "Enough, at least, to make my escape."

"So you're now in the process of . . ." I began, but she anticipated my question.

"A divorce?" I nodded and she continued. "We've been separated for a year now, and I want all the way out desperately, but Court's really making it tough. I won't bore you with the grisly details, but among other things he's making it very hard for me to gain custody of our two youngest children—Aaron and Amber."

"How old are they?" Sister Bronson asked.

"Aaron's fifteen and Amber's twelve," she said. "I'm hoping and praying to have them by the first of the year, and I know I will eventually. He's definitely an unfit father, and I have the evidence to prove it."

"So where's your husband now?" Dare inquired.

"Oh, not that far away, unfortunately. He's building a ship in Mesa for treasure hunting off the Florida Keys."

"You're kidding!" Sis. Keller shrilled. Her eyes magnified with surprise behind the red-framed glasses. "That's out of sight!"

Melana smiled. "That's only one of many little enterprises, but it's his entertainment for the moment."

"But building a ship in *Mesa*?" I stared at her. "Isn't that a bit inland?"

She laughed. "You might think so, yes. But that's where he's putting it all together businesswise and otherwise. They'll transport it in sections by semi to the Gulf when the time arrives." Melana then related at length many of the technical aspects involved, how countless millions in gold, silver, and jewelry still lay on the ocean floor, much of it dating back to the time of the Spanish galleons. It was a fascinating story that held our interest throughout.

"But that's all prologue," she sighed. Once more her gaze ascended to the ceiling and flowed about the room. "And again, I don't know quite where to begin." She sipped her lemonade. "Except to tell you that for a long, long time there's been a terrific void in my life—not only maritally but also theologically."

Already, I felt the vibes. Fascinating though our previous dialogue had been, her latest observation portended greater excitement. That single word *theologically* resonated with potential.

"For a long time I refused to admit it," she continued. "Ever since those girlhood days in Nova Scotia when I first met Court, I've prided myself on being an independent thinker and highly self-sufficient when it came to religion." She shrugged and made a wry face. "Like 'who needs it?' All very foolishly and egotistically, of course; I'm beginning to realize that more now, especially the past two years." Her voice became dry and fractured. Her eyes glistened. Women's tears, incidentally, have always rendered me vulnerable, perhaps too much in some cases.

"But you actually were," I inquired gently, "baptized a member of the Church?"

She nodded. "Except for my early childhood, though, I've never been active. It's only recently, as I say, that I've begun to consider it at all seriously . . . not only because of Lance's death, but also because my life is in such turmoil. But I won't keep going over that. Here's what I've been working around to for all this time. The other night I was at the home of a woman I know, a long-time friend, over in Sun City. We were taking in some TV, trying to find something worth watching, and not succeeding. So finally, she asked if I'd like to see a short video she had, put out by the LDS Church. *Families Forever?*"

"*Together Forever*," Sister Bronson said.

"Yes, that's it," she replied. "Well, I agreed, but frankly, just to be polite. Before long, though, I became quite engrossed in it—especially the final part involving the young couple who had . . ." She sucked in her cheeks and took a deep breath. "Lost their little girl in an accident. It was all so sensitive and real that . . ." Again she struggled for composure and her eyes filled with tears. "I'm sorry," she managed after a few moments, dabbing at the corners of her eyes with a paper napkin.

"Don't be," I said. "You aren't the only one who has reacted this way, believe me."

For a while, no one spoke. "I truly do want to be with my children forever," Melana said, "and eventually—who knows—find the right man who can somehow become a part of it all. Yet right now . . ." Her hands were tremulous, and she was biting her lips, eyes still glistening. "I'm still not sure whether there is a forever—whether there's anything out there at all."

Sitting there next to her, I wanted greatly to reach out. It seemed unkind not to, but I resisted.

17

Nearly three-fourths of my mini-mission to Arizona had fled—magically, incredibly. The days were still warm and summery, temperatures reaching the low eighties each afternoon, but the nights were turning somewhat cooler, enough to make our suit coats more pleasure than burden. It was December 18, and the Christmas lights were proliferating. As we travelled about among our slowly growing pool of investigators, and members willing to aid in the finding, those lights seemed increasingly appropriate.

Our favorite display, one we passed regularly coming and going, involved a team of plywood reindeer towing a life-sized Snoopy in an old-time aviator helmet and goggles, ensconced in a fancy speed boat. A *real* one! The whole thing was outlined in a skein of blinking red and blue lights and extended across the owner's entire front yard.

Unfailingly it caused us amusement, making the entire night a bit brighter, and somehow, despite its craziness, it seemed to make Christmas a growing reality. The day after our visit with Melana Gardner, however, we journeyed with some of the local ward missionaries and our "golden" Williams family to see the Mesa Temple and a very different kind of display. Lights in all colors festooned the white temple and visitors' center, and outlined the decorative pools, illumined also from beneath their surface in a vivid, morning-glory blue. Lights drifted in skeins from every tree, abounded in the shrubbery, and blinked in constellations among the fronds of tall palm trees.

"This almost rivals the Snoopy display," Elder Mac said. "Wouldn't you say?"

I laughed. "Almost!"

Elder Hud shook his head, marveling. "How many lights they supposed to have here? Something like two-hundred and forty thousand? That's what I heard."

I shrugged. "Maybe so, wouldn't surprise me. It looks like the next best thing to the one at Temple Square in Salt Lake City." Nightly, a different religious organization from the area sang carols on a cement veranda near the pools. At the moment, a group of about forty were harmonizing well: "Angels we have heard on high sweetly singing o'er the plains, And the mountains in reply echoing their joyous strains." Visitors, nearly all of them smiling, thronged the grounds, emanating a special Christmas-time glow, and the Williams family was no exception.

The light of our surroundings, of the entire evening, reflected in their faces, reaching its greatest intensity as we stood together in the visitors' center before the Christus. There it was: a great, white statue of the Savior, hands graciously extended as if to welcome and bless all of mankind.

For perhaps two or three minutes the Williams family stood there with us, no one speaking. "A lot of people," Dare said finally, "think Mormons aren't Christians." Visitors were drifting all about us, but for the moment it seemed as if we were alone together. "But that's as far from the truth as anything could be." Leaning down, he placed his arms around the shoulders of Lisa and Ronny. "You know who that is, right? That big white statue?" They nodded promptly, smiling shyly. "Yeah, it's Jesus," Ronny said.

"That's right, and do you know why he's here in the very *center* of this place?" Their expressions were uncertain, though still highly receptive. "It's because Jesus Christ is the center of our lives," Dare said quietly. He paused, watching. "Nobody else anywhere is that important except for our Heavenly Father himself." Again the quick little nods, in perfect unison, faces aglow, and suddenly I felt awash with the Spirit, a pronounced enrichment of the blood. Glancing at Dare and the others, I realized that they felt the same thing, a little, perhaps, the way we might all be feeling in the resurrection with the fluid of immortality flowing in our veins.

Gradually the intensity decreased, but it remained to some degree throughout the following tour, was still there as we concluded the evening in one of the center's little auditoriums watching the movie *Mr. Kreuger's Christmas*. It was an old favorite starring James Stewart and the Mormon Tabernacle Choir. The mood persisted, in fact, during our hour-long return home in the van owned and driven by the ward mission leader, Clayton Foley.

The Williams family was riding with us, and they were now enthusiastically talking over their first experience in attending LDS church services the previous Sunday—of the welcome they had received, including three different dinner invitations, of the invitation to Ronny from the ward Cub scoutmaster to come join the ranks, of an offer from the Primary president to give Lisa free piano lessons.

"Now *that* . . ." Elder Mac was speaking quietly into Dare's ear. His accent at the moment was almost too thick for comprehension, but I got the interpretation thereof even so: "That is what I call *friendshipping!*"

"Ain't it the truth," Dare replied. I was seated with our full-time elders in the rear, trying to tune in on all the conversation over the road rumble and the hum of the motor. At the moment Allie was saying, "Maybe it's just coincidence, or maybe we just started to keep our eyes open, but I really think there's more to it than that."

"Like maybe it was planned upstairs?" Clayton asked. Allie and Dan were seated beside him, and he tossed them a friendly glance before returning his attention to the road. He was a chubby young man with an affable round face and thick-lensed glasses, invariably cheerful and energetic.

"Well, yes," Allie continued. "This past year while we've begun wondering about where to find answers to our religious questions, and suddenly these elders have started cropping up all over the place!"

"Really!" Dan said. "Before we even knew who they were. At first we thought they were Amway salesmen or something!" Clayton chuckled heartily.

"Or FBI!" Ronny piped. The laughter mounted. Then, of course, we had to recount Dare's experience with the golf course attendant earlier in his mission.

"Back on my own mission," I related, "we all had to wear those felt fedoras, the kind with a brim like you see in the old-time movies. Then we *really* got mistaken for the FBI, because most of their agents not only went in pairs but they also wore suits and the same fedoras—even the youngest."

"You had to wear those crazy old gizmos all the time?" Dare asked. He sounded skeptical, incredulous. "Like the ones Grampa Wallace has in the top of the hall closet?"

"Absolutely! Haven't you ever seen that old photo album of mine—from my days in Canada? Failure to wear your fedora was almost enough to get you a dishonorable discharge."

"Well, ever since the elders came," Dan continued, "ever since they walked in the door, there was this fantastic *feeling*. I mean, our kids have always been friendly but never anything like this—coming up and hugging them right off like they were long-lost relatives. I mean, they act like Elder Connors and his dad here are their uncle and grandfather or something."

"That's the honest truth," Allie laughed. "Even our Siamese cat, who doesn't like strangers a bit. He jumps up and settles right down next to them on the couch every time they come."

"Yeah, and he starts purring real loud," Lisa said, "then goes to sleep."

"We sometimes put people to sleep too," I laughed. And yet, what they were saying was entirely true and quite remarkable. It was something Dare and I had commented on several times without taking any personal credit for it. We had simply experienced the great good fortune of finding people who were receptive to the nth degree, and the Spirit had been with us.

We had just passed one of the turn-offs to Phoenix and were rolling onward toward Glendale along a highway brightened by amber lights. The traffic on all sides was still heavy. "And the past while," Dan went on, "we've just had this terrific feeling that . . ." He glanced at his wife. "Well, how do *you* explain it, hon?"

"I don't know," she said, "but it's really powerful . . . a feeling of absolute rightness about what we're doing."

"Yeah," Dan said, "and a feeling about this little family of ours, that it's lots more important than we ever dreamed, like it's the center of something really big that can just keep expanding forever."

18

It was almost ten o'clock by the time we arrived at our apartment. I had completed some of my exercises, showered, and donned my shimmering, light-green pj's. We were lounging back on the couch celebrating our happy evening with large bowls of mint-chocolate-chip ice cream. Yes, my low cholesterol diet had been somewhat compromised the past while, but I promised myself I'd repent when it was convenient.

"Terrific evening," I observed.

"Was it ever!" My young companion was spooning it down voraciously, clad now in his robe of dark-red satin with a black collar and cuffs. It had been rescued from our attic, that great, dark maw from which few things ever return at our big and rather battered home on Hollow's Edge. It was inherited actually from his late Grandfather Connors, and Dare had considered it "pretty cool"—cool enough to take along on his mission. It combined rather strangely, though, with his bright yellow pajamas and the old brown mucklucks he was wearing in place of house slippers. "Yep," he said contentedly. "Great evening—the lights, the music . . . the Christus. And what about those Williamses? Aren't they something else?" Then he began to look amused, mischievously reminiscing. "I keep thinking about you guys and those crazy hats," he said.

"The old fedoras?"

He nodded, wolfing a couple of cookies for added ballast.

"It was part of the standard attire then. I remember, my dad bought me a nice, expensive, gray one with a wide, black band. Pretty dignified for a nineteen-year-old kid." I sat there remembering, hearing somewhere faintly in the smog-veiled sky the sound of a jet. "Unfortunately, the hat was a little too large, and one night when we were heading home from a 'cottage meeting'—that's what we called them then—a storm moved in and whipped my hat off into the Welland Canal. Right into the path of a gigantic coal barge about a block long."

"Crazy!"

"I didn't know whether to laugh or cry, because I definitely didn't enjoy wearing the thing, but still . . . it was a gift from my dad and it reminded me of him." For a time I was right back there in the rain on the edge of that big canal, gazing into the dark and sullen waters after my hapless hat. "Well, it really cracked my companion up. He nearly fell apart, and pretty soon we were both laughing so hard, right there in the middle of that downpour, that our sides hurt. It was literally painful."

"I know what you mean," Dare said. "I've run into deals sort of like that when there's nothing to do but laugh. I mean that's all you've got. If you can't see the funny side, you'll go down. Especially be able to laugh at yourself."

"So true. Gung ho but mellow at the same time—right?"

"Exactly."

For a time we simply enjoyed our dessert.

"Did you ever get another hat?"

"Oh, yes—it was obligatory. A missionary without his hat was like a minister without his collar. But this time I got one that fit better. A brown one with a little red feather in the band. I flattened the top until it was only about three inches high, making it into what they called a pork pie. And I wore it at a slight angle with the brim snapped down over my right eye. That was lots cooler, sort of racy, in fact." There in the midst of my special, three-week mission, the memories of the old two-year mission were steadily growing stronger. Sometimes they came in fragments, sometimes entire episodes, but many of them were things that might otherwise have been lost forever.

"Really something, isn't it?" Dare said after a while.

"What's that?"

"The whole thing, this whole big old mission."

"Nothing quite like it," I said. "I can remember . . ." I shifted, massaging the back of my neck. "Who was it? One of the General Authorities, I think, saying that a mission is a kind of mini earth life in and of itself. Then he thought about it a second and said, 'And not so *mini*, in fact.'"

"Yeah, for sure." Dare yawned and stretched his long, wiry frame.

"Well," I said, and arose to rinse my bowl in the sink. "Time to hit the hay." But he wasn't quite ready yet.

"Ya know what, Pop?" he mused. He leaned back, hands laced behind his head, looking his most thoughtful.

"What?" I said.

"I'm really glad you and Mom never tried to force this down our throats."

I grinned inwardly, knowing that nothing had ever been forced on Darren Connors, even when he was a little kid and we called him Darry. "Nobody ever did that very well with any of you guys, beginning Day One when you weren't much bigger than gophers. And we certainly didn't try it when it came to your missions." I paused. "Oh, sure, there's always a lot of social pressure. After all, mission-arying is the thing to *do*! And RMs, even though we don't exactly advertise it, are the fair-haired boys."

"Yeah, I guess so."

I was standing there, arms folded, head bowed in

116

thought, half sitting on the sink for support. "And a mission, in Mormon culture, is a rite of passage in a way, an initiation into manhood." I hadn't thought of it in those exact terms before, but now the truthfulness of it struck home. "And, of course, that's only part of it. The Church of Jesus Christ has always been a missionary operation, always will be. That's one of its hallmarks. But still— you've got to go because *you* want to, not because somebody's arm-twisting you into it or putting you on a big guilt trip if you don't."

"You and Mom never did that," he said. "I knew you'd still love me just as much, no matter what."

I laughed and tousled his hair. It was so blond it reflected the yellow of his pajamas. "Now, where did you ever get the crazy idea that we loved you?"

"Aw, I dunno," he said. "Maybe 'cause you didn't whop on me too often."

"But you need to know in advance how tough it's going to be in a lot of ways," I continued, "one of the biggest challenges, from a positive standpoint, most young people ever face. And consequently, their greatest growing experience."

"Right. I think that's been one of Hud's biggest problems. He had this idea that he'd go out there on the 'mish' and that people would actually be lining up to get in the water. That everybody he ever met would throw their arms around him and start singin' 'Praise the Lord.'"

I nodded. "Hmmmm, maybe so. But I have a feeling he's going to win."

"Yeah, he's taking hold better every day. Great potential."

"Well, keep your arm around him." I laughed a little. "*Part* of him, anyhow. That's a lot of missionary."

We sat for a while in silence. Three teenage girls from the ward had come by that afternoon to set up a little Christmas tree for us and decorated it with a skein of pink lights shaped like miniature candles. The tree occupied most of our study table, but it was much appreciated, especially in view of the fact that one of the girls was a paraplegic confined to a wheelchair. The tiny lights blinked sweetly on the tree's frosted branches and, unexpectedly, were making me feel very happy and tender. Beneath it lay the presents I had brought from home, and two, elaborately wrapped with silver paper and gold ribbon, from his beloved Cindy S. Gradually the whole scene was beginning to melt into a warm and soporific pool.

Suddenly I bestirred myself, stretched and yawned mightily. "We'd best hit it," Dare said. "Toddle away to our little trundle beds." Seconds later, that's exactly where we were, drifting off in our little trundle beds. "But Dad?"

"Hmmm?"

"It's worth all the sacrifice, right?"

"Verily." The good and great things outweighed the bad so prodigiously that there was no comparison in the end, but I'd save the sermon for another time. "Experiences like the one with the Williamses tonight alone, even—aren't they worth it all?"

"Yeah," Dare said. His voice was muffled. "It's so great, in fact, I'm running scared. Practically holding my breath wondering when old Lucifer's going to make his move."

19

We were sitting together, Dare and I and the two Sister missionaries, on the fringe of Melana Gardner's swimming pool. The pool was about twenty yards long, shaped like a curving teardrop, a beckoning pastel blue. Our hostess had entered the castle to obtain a few refreshments, and meanwhile Dare and the Sisters were joking rather longingly about all the magnificent, forbidden water. The sun reflected brightly off the pool, dazzled from the chrome ladder near the diving board, suddenly reminding me of my missionary days in North Bay, Ontario, on the shores of Lake Nippissing long ago. I recalled, also, how readily and mischievously my companion and I had succumbed to the lure of the water.

"We'd wake up on the morning of P-Day, which happened to be on Saturday back then, and look out the window of our third-story bedroom at the lake only a few hundred yards away. Then Elder Bradley would give me a grin and say, 'That's really not a *dangerous* body of water, is it?' And, of course, I'd always go along with it. 'No, Elder,' I'd tell him, 'that's not a *dangerous* body of water–that's just good old Lake Nippissing.' Back in those days the *Missionary Handbook* didn't specifically forbid swimming and boating, but it did warn against being on 'dangerous bodies of water,' and I'm afraid we wrested the scriptures, so to speak, pretty badly in that regard."

"So you'd go out on the lake on P-Day?" Sister Keller asked. Her expression combined amusement and slight disbelief.

"Yes, I'm afraid so," I replied, "and one day, in fact, we learned quite a lesson in that connection. We were about half a mile out, in a rowboat, fishing for pike and pickerel, when a terrific storm moved in with waves about six feet high. Several times we were nearly swamped. We barely made it to shore after a really tough, hour-long struggle."

"Wow!" Sister Bronson exclaimed.

"Wow is right," I laughed. "Two extremely lucky young fools."

Just then the lady of the castle appeared bearing a tray of fancy little sandwiches, a bowl of veggies and dip, and a pitcher of orange juice. She was wearing a dress of pale gold, and her gray hair was fluffed, lying in that becoming silvery wing across her brow. Somehow her entire features, body itself, seemed healthier, less emaciated. "And who are the lucky young fools?" her voice lilted. She didn't merely walk, she flowed entrancingly—enough so, in fact, to leave us momentarily speechless. For a second or two my mind swam with lines from one of Herrick's "Julia" poems: "When as in silks my Julia goes—then, then me thinks how sweetly flows the liquefaction of her clothes." The Melana Gardner of that moment was a very different person from the sweet but wistful lady of our previous meeting, one who had looked as though she might need a doctor's care.

"Oh, I was just carrying on about some of my own missionary experiences back in prehistoric times," I told her. "How my companion and I perverted the rules and nearly managed to drown ourselves in a lake in eastern Canada."

"Well!" she exclaimed as she set her tray upon the umbrella table next to us. "I'm surely glad you didn't. It would have been an immense loss." I laughed, said I wasn't so sure about that, but Melana was insistent. "Oh, it definitely *would* have been!" she continued, and I wondered a little whether she talked to most men that way. "Besides," she added, "if that had happened, maybe none of you would be here with me today." The silver-gray eyes scintillated with mischief yet also seemed watchful and serious underneath. Herrick had written about Julia's clothes, also her voice. Eyes too? Certainly he must have if they were anything like Melana Gardner's.

"And to talk with me about what?" She posed the question for us, one brow lofting coquettishly, then became more serious. "About the reality of an afterlife, most of all, I guess. That's where we left off last time, wasn't it? And . . ." She hesitated as if uncertain whether to say more at the moment or not. "And this is what I *dreamed* about last night, believe it or not—all four of you right here like this beside the pool, dressed exactly as you are . . . all of you with the same polite, quizzical smiles."

For a moment it seemed a bit much; for an instant I wondered, albeit somewhat guiltily, if we were dealing with a phony, or perhaps an actress who enjoyed creating roles for herself. Then I decided against it. In one respect, of course, her dream might simply have been a logical process of association, since she was already expecting us.

I glanced at Dare and the Sisters, reluctant to take over the show, to follow my natural inclinations as professor of the classroom. Dare shrugged, waggled his brows, blinked a few times, pursed his lips. "Whatever's fair," he said, and waited as though leaving it in my hands for now.

Smiling, I barely shrugged back, but realizing I was on deck I started to search my mind rather nervously. For a few moments, I found nothing. Then, very unexpectedly, I began to recollect something from my early childhood; visualize, actually, another kind of dream. "Back when I was a little boy," I said, "only four or five years old, I had a recurring dream. I'm not really sure whether it was a night dream or a daydream—maybe both—but it involved a little kid who looked a lot like me, who each time even seemed to become me. For some reason I was always alone, walking down a long, empty road in the hot sunshine, and eventually—always without fail—the road ended at a high wall. The wall contained two words painted in large block letters: THE END."

"How interesting," Melana said quietly, looking highly attentive.

Everyone was watching me, wondering no doubt what I expected to prove. At the time, in fact, I wasn't entirely sure. "Well, interesting to me," I replied, "because for one thing, those were the only words I could read. I remember seeing them on the last page of a book one time and asking my mother what they meant. But the words on the wall were also highly frustrating because that wall was about ten feet high, and there was no way to climb it." I waited, searching my mind. "One thing I knew, though, with absolute certainty." I paused, reflecting.

"What was that, Dad?" Dare inquired.

"I knew, absolutely *knew*, that if I ever *could* climb that wall . . . well, maybe there wouldn't be any more road, but there would have to be something. I mean, you don't ever climb a wall then look over into nothing."

Melana smiled, nodding.

"I didn't realize what that signified way back then," I continued. "In fact, it wasn't until I was midway into my mission, with a strong testimony of the gospel, that I realized what the experience meant." Again I waited. "It was symbolical of eternal life, of feelings that as a child I had experienced strongly but hadn't comprehended."

"That life itself doesn't end?" Melana asked. "Maybe even can't end. Is that it?"

"Precisely. Obviously, it can undergo some radical change—when the spirit leaves the body, for instance, or when it unites with it at birth or in the resurrection. So, yes, it can be altered, but never annihilated. And, if you can conceive of it in that light, maybe you can also see that life itself can't have a beginning either—not the primal life element, force, whatever you want to call it that makes us who we are, that makes us individuals."

Melana Gardner laughed. "That's getting pretty deep for my mind. In a way I can see the logic in it, though, at least sense it a bit." She made a helpless little gesture like someone trying to capture scattered raindrops. "But it's still incomprehensible."

I nodded. "True, and yet the human mind can accept the idea of non-beginning and non-ending quite readily regarding other things, even if it is not fully comprehensible. I'm thinking, for example, of something we call time. Can you imagine time itself having a beginning or ending?"

Her eyes narrowed in contemplation. "No . . ." she said cautiously. "I suppose I can't. It's like your dream wall, isn't it? Something had to come before and something has to come after."

"Correct—exactly," I said and eyed her with growing respect. No airhead there, to say the least.

"And I imagine," she mused, "that the same goes for space. At least, that's what the astronomers keep telling us, isn't it?"

"Definitely."

"Same with matter and energy," Dare said. "They can be transformed but not created or destroyed."

"Right again," I said.

He chuckled self-deprecatingly. "Just a little something I learned back at Weber in a physics class."

"I remember reading an account somewhere . . ." Sister Keller began and frowned. "Where was it? I can't recall now, but it was about one of our Church leaders back in the early days. At one time he was having trouble with the same question and, well, couldn't quite come to terms with the concept of no beginning or ending. Then he had this dream—speaking of dreams—in which he saw a stream. The stream flowed out of some hills in the distance, then wandered through a beautiful, sunlit meadow and vanished into a forest. Somehow that little dream seemed to make it all lots clearer. The hills that the stream came from represented our pre-earth life, and the sunlit meadow was mortality, the part we can see right now. The forest beyond was the life to come . . . but all three areas were equally real and very important."

"How fascinating!" Melana said. "I really like that."

High overhead, a jet had materialized, seemingly from nowhere. Soon it had vanished to the north, reflecting sunlight, leaving a white vapor trail and a faint, delayed-action rumbling sound. Perhaps, I reflected, it was heading for Salt Lake City.

"So that's a little of the general philosophy, the logic behind it, but you'd probably also like something more specific, I suspect." I was watching her face. "Real evidence that we continue as actual individuals, as *spirits* in the next realm. Right?"

Her smile was very sweet. It mingled uncertainty and hope. "That would indeed be comforting . . . although I don't imagine that's something we'll ever prove scientifically, at least by our current scientific procedures."

"Perhaps not," I replied. "Science by very definition involves itself with earthly, material things—things that are empirically, consistently verifiable to anybody who performs the tests correctly."

"But aren't those books by people like Moody pretty scientific?" Dare asked.

"Well . . ." I squinted. "About as scientific as you can get in such matters, I guess." I glanced at Melana. "Are you familiar with the works of Dr. Raymond Moody regarding life-after-death experiences?"

"No," she replied, but sounded uncertain. "I seem to have heard the name, but . . ."

"Raymond Moody is a psychiatrist who also holds a doctorate in philosophy," I explained, "and he has written three books based upon his studies of people who have died, withdrawn from their bodies in the spirit, then returned to mortal life and reported what they experienced."

Melana sipped her juice, then set the glass down and stared at me, waiting. "Well, don't stop there," she laughed. "Tell me all about it."

I smiled. "Well, I hardly pretend to know *everything* about it, and it's a long story, but maybe I can give you the overall picture. These books are based to a large extent upon actual interviews Moody has conducted with such people—over a thousand in the case of his latest work, *The Light Beyond.*"

"Come to think of it . . ." Melana's eyes grew distant for a moment. "Yes, maybe I *did* read the first one. What was it called? *Life After Life?*"

Dare nodded. "Right. That was the one that really created a big interest in the subject."

"Yes, I remember now. But, unfortunately, that was a long time ago—fifteen years or so as I recall—and I didn't get into it that much. Just too many distractions at the time, or maybe simply lack of interest and motivation."

"Now, though, you really feel quite different," Sister Bronson said. It was half statement, half question.

"Oh, yes—absolutely. Ever since Lance died, I've . . ." She said nothing for several seconds. "Well, my attitude's changed a great deal."

I nodded. "Yes, that's surely understandable." After a moment I continued. "Of course, these books by Moody aren't the only ones on the subject, but they've probably exerted more impact than any of the others. I'm especially impressed with the last one because it's not only based on a thousand interviews but it also includes some fascinating responses from a number of other authorities."

There was a brief wait while Melana replenished our glasses.

"Anyway," I continued, "Moody tries to analyze such experiences as objectively as possible, and even though each one is somewhat, occasionally quite dramatically, different there are some strong threads of commonality running throughout most of them. Withdrawing in the spirit, for example, and looking back on one's own body from a

125

short distance away, observing the reactions of others—medical people, family, whatever—who are on hand. And almost immediately, wondering why all the frantic efforts at resuscitation if, say, the death occurred in a hospital . . . why all the lamentation and sorrow in cases of family members. After all, there's that immediate awareness that what has just occurred is *really not the end*, just a transition. That sort of thing."

"Ah yes, I seem to recall now," Melana said. "And after that, don't a lot of them seem to go down a long, dark tunnel with a light at the end?"

"Right," Dare said. "And at the end there're people, friends and family, waiting there to welcome them to the other side."

I nodded. "Frequently, also, a heavenly being is on hand. A lot of people refer to him as a being of light and even believe he's Jesus Christ."

"And doesn't the being of light usually ask them questions about their lives on the earth?" Sister Keller asked.

"Right," Dare said, "like, 'What have you learned?' "

"Now *that's* downright scary," Melana laughed. "I'm afraid I'd be utterly speechless."

"I know what you mean," I said, "but there's an even tougher follow-up question in some cases. 'What have you *done?*' "

"Hmmmm, yes, even more traumatic."

"And quite a few people also experience a kind of instant playback," I went on, "in which somehow they relive the key events of their lives in a matter of moments."

Melana glanced at me from the corners of her eyes, more fearful, perhaps, than amused. "You'd better stop, Nathan. You're frightening me more with every sentence."

"But at least we now have the advantage of knowing what to expect in advance," Sister Keller said. "And according to what I've read, the being of light is never harsh or threatening—just wonderfully kind and understanding."

"Wasn't there some kind of poll that showed about

eight million Americans claim to have died and come back again?" Dare asked.

"Yes," I replied, "eight million American *adults*, in fact, based on a Gallup poll. Moody refers to it, in fact, in *The Light Beyond*. And there are books now dealing exclusively with children who have undergone the same kind of experiences. Anyway, I've read a lot of these accounts and actually heard quite a few from people I know in the Church, and I guess the one thing that impresses me most is how genuine they all seem. It's not as if these people are trying to win attention, and they never try to argue the matter. It's just something that *happened* as far as they're concerned, just as real as a trip to some other state or country."

"A lot of people are even reluctant to talk about it for fear of ridicule," Sister Bronson said.

Melana was watching us almost dreamily. "Absolutely fascinating," she said. "But what brings them back once they've died? Can you simply decide, 'Hey, I'd like to return,' and presto, you're there?"

"Well, not quite," I laughed. "Sometimes it's a result of direct, divine intervention—Christ and Lazarus, going back a while—but there are quite a number in the Church today. Most of those recorded by people like Moody, however, are the result of medical resuscitation, especially electric shock to stimulate the heart. Somehow, it's as if the spirit is still linked to the body for a brief while afterward. In such cases, though, it seems the person who has died can actually make a conscious decision either to remain on the other side or to return to earth life. Initially most of them actually want to stay, because it's so peaceful and happy there. Nevertheless, many of them do come back mainly from a sense of obligation to those left behind, important unfinished business, whatever."

A flashy-looking sports car, fire-engine red, was winding up the side of Camelback mountain above us, occasionally vanishing along a tree-lined curve then reappearing, its windshield exploding sunlight.

127

"So how do these people feel about what happened, once they're back to stay for a while?" Melana wondered.

"Really great in most cases," Sister Bronson replied. "Most of them are very happy, and they see life in an entirely different light."

"Yes," I said. "There's an initial period of adjustment in some cases; sometimes the transition is rather difficult, in fact, but they do come back changed for the better almost invariably. Almost all of them return convinced that two things are of utmost importance—above all else." I paused, searching their faces. "First, and most vital of all, love. Second, knowledge—the conviction that learning is eternal and that it needn't end, by any means, with death. In effect, that we can and should progress eternally, and that we should make the best use of our time wherever possible."

"On *both* sides of the veil," Melana said.

"Right on," Dare replied. He leaned back in his chair, looking reflective. "When you think about it, though, what could be more logical?" For a moment I wondered what he meant. "Love and learning," he explained. "After all, isn't that pretty much what we've been told all along? What's more basic to the whole gospel?"

Two bright-green hummingbirds streaked across the pool, wings trilling, throats scintillating, ruby-colored and blaze pink. Rippled by a warm breeze, the waters dappled in the sunlight, a few tiny waves exploding into sparklers. "It all sounds so right and so beautiful," Melana said quietly. "I truly *want* to believe it."

20

It was ten o'clock, and I was updating my combination letter-journal while Dare talked to our friend Elder MacDougall on the phone. "Incidentally," I heard him say, "we had another meeting with Mrs. Gardner, the castle lady, yesterday. Right, took the Sisters along again. Yeah, we talked with Pres Linford; he says it's okay to handle it that way for now. Once the ward missionaries get back maybe they'll give her the discussions, I'm not sure. If not, possibly the Sisters." A pause. "Uh-huh . . . well, I kind of hope they get to. They're pretty sharp, and they've already got an in there."

For a time I tuned him out, attending to my writing, typing away on an ancient little portable that had actually belonged to my mother. "Yeah, Pop's been a real help, and this Gardner lady thinks he's all right. Told the Sisters he's 'an *adorable* man with a brilliant mind.'"

Naturally my ears perked up at that point. I could tell from the way he emphasized those final words that they were supposed to be a direct quote. My brows lifted high enough that I could feel the ripples in my receding hairline. My chin tucked in, crowding my larynx, and my mouth compressed, hooking down at the corners. Dare was regarding me with sly amusement, and I was feigning, yet also feeling, no small surprise. I had always considered myself reasonably intelligent, maybe even attractive also, to certain attractive women. But surely not brilliant, and far from adorable! "Yeah," he continued. "We've got another appointment for Saturday morning."

The conversation continued for some time. Then Dare hung up and headed for the fridge. "Guess what?" he said.

"What?"

"Mac got a call from Erlichmann today. Says he's got this new greenie companion who won't talk—so shy he can't pry two words out of him. Erlichmann's about ready to flip out and go a-boogyin' off into the sunset again."

"I hope not," I said. "If he cuts out early it will dog him the rest of his days."

"True. I'll have to give the dude a call and tell him to hang in. One way or another, he's almost made it over the hump. The Great Divide. Gotta tell him it's all downhill from now on. Once you hit the year mark, it starts slipping by so fast you get nervous. Right now it seems like every week only lasts about two days."

I nodded. "I know what you mean." There are two parts to almost every missionary: one that often misses the joys and comforts of home, longs—sometimes very painfully—for the great day of reunion, another that becomes increasingly engrossed in the work, tries ever more earnestly to seize each fleeting moment.

Dare had pulled off his shoes, and one of his socks had a hole in the big toe. "Looks like you're having a coming-out party," I said.

"Yeah—practically all my socks are worn right down to the threads, if not worse."

"Well . . ." I reflected, and stretched. "Maybe old Santa can help out in that connection if you try to be a good boy." Several new pairs lay wrapped there under the little tree, in fact, a humble part of his forthcoming Christmas.

"That would be *veerrry* nice, very nice indeed." Then his thoughts returned to the notorious Elder E. "Such a character! That dude, I promise you, has the weirdest sense of humor in the world, bar none. And yet . . . he's got a fantastic lot of talent. Might still end up one terrific old missionary if he'll just quit clowning around and do the job." He had acquired a large cluster of grapes from a supply purchased during our grocery shopping earlier and was popping them into his mouth with considerable alacrity. "Want some?"

"No thanks, not for the moment." Then, recalling his conversation with Elder Mac minutes before: "By the way, what was that stuff you were telling Mac about Melana Gardner?" It was another vainer moment, I suppose, and my male ego could not resist hearing a bit more.

Dare returned to the couch with another cluster of grapes and treated me to one of his special looks—sly and knowing. "It's true, Pop—the lady thinks you're a very bright guy—also 'an adorable man.'" This was followed by a few low-volume "heh-heh's" and a "yuk-yuk" or two for good measure. The latter was something he had begun to pick up from his pal Mac. Obviously, he considered the whole thing quite enjoyable, if not humorous.

"You're putting your old dad on," I said.

But Dare shook his head vigorously. "It's the gospel truth," he insisted. "She told the Sisters that, when they called up about our next meeting." Removing his socks, he placed one size-twelve foot on the side of the study table, hooking on with a big toe that looked almost prehensile. "Wait till I tell Mom!"

Periodically during the night I thought about Melana Gardner. Once, unable to sleep, I got up for a drink of water. For years I had suffered from sinus trouble and a deviated septum. In consequence, I often ended up breathing through my mouth at night, snoring and acquiring a parched throat. Often I had to arise two or three times for a drink of water to alleviate the problem. While up this time, I wandered into the front room and (always having been a great snoop) glanced over a terse entry in Dare's missionary journal dated a few days earlier. "It's eleven o'clock and Pop is snoring away, snorting like a porpus." I had put a large "Sp" through the final word, unable to resist.

Stopping by the bathroom on my way back to bed, I regarded myself in the mirror to see if by some wild stretch of the imagination I looked adorable. My hair, what there was of it, was disheveled, suddenly more gray than brindle, and there were slight bags under my eyes, especially the left one. "Adorable?" I gave a dry little laugh and shook my head. And yet . . . well, I was a wee bit flattered by the idea, especially coming from one as charming as Melana Gardner. But maybe, I decided, it was at least a masculine face, fairly wise, perhaps even empathic. Sally Girl had always told me so, but then she was a biased witness. Prominent chin, jaw muscles that swelled when I clamped my teeth together, something of an unconscious affectation at times when I want to appear impressive.

The following day I decided to remain at the apartment while Darren and our elders down the street attended a district conference. I had already sat in on one of them and wanted to continue my letter-journal. It was then, at about 10 a.m., that the call came.

"Hello, LDS missionaries," I said.

"Hello," the voice replied hesitantly, "is this Nathan Connors?"

"Yes, speaking," I replied, and instantly had a feeling of expectation.

"This is Melana Gardner." The voice was gentle, cultured without being at all pretentious. I realized that, now more than ever, isolated as it was from her direct person. Highly feminine, with a kind of silvery quality that reminded me of her eyes. For an instant I felt a faint stirring of the heart, a twinge of surprise. And yet, it was *not* surprise—as if, as with so many things lately, I had somehow anticipated it.

"Yes, Melana," I said, and heard my own voice fill with respect and cordiality. "How *are* you?"

"Oh . . . " There was a long pause. "Not so well, I'm afraid. I'm feeling a bit depressed, frankly."

"Well," I replied, "I'm sorry to hear that. Has something . . . " I hesitated, reluctant to appear nosy. "Has something happened to upset you?"

"Oh, nothing I haven't encountered before. It's just that Court keeps trying to give me a bad time. Constant phone calls and letters that might seem rather innocuous on the surface, but in reality they're quite demoralizing."

"Aw, that's too bad," I said. "Is there anything we can do to help?" At the moment, I had no idea what might be done, but I had to ask.

"Well . . . I was wondering," she said, sounding very uncertain. "I wouldn't want to impose and, of course, I don't know whether your schedule might possibly permit it. But I was wondering if, by any chance, you might be able to come by for a little while. Before our regular meeting on Saturday, I mean."

"I'm sure we could," I replied. "I don't know what Darren has scheduled, but he should be back from a meeting within a couple of hours or so."

"I actually need to talk with someone in private if possible," Melana said. Her voice suddenly sounded very forlorn. "I really apologize for asking you, and I'm afraid it's awfully presumptuous."

"Not at all," I said, sensing simultaneously a potential dilemma.

"It's just that the things you explained during our last visit were so comforting and enlightening. And . . . I honestly feel that you have so much *understanding*." I began to demur, but Melana persisted, sounding as if she were on the verge of tears. "That perhaps . . . oh, I don't really know how to say this without being misunderstood. That possibly we're, well, on the same wavelength."

"That's a very nice compliment," I said, "I'm truly honored that you would feel that way." My emotions at that point were very contradictory. I was moved by the imminence of her tears, flattered (or perhaps "honored" is more apt) over what she had just disclosed, but definitely dubious about visiting her by myself, for obvious reasons.

"I'm sure your time is well occupied," she continued, "and believe me, I wouldn't impose upon you this way if I didn't feel so down. It's really strange in a way because I was so excited after your last visit—but for some reason this past day or two . . . " I waited while she fought to collect herself. "I've felt as if I'm in an immense black cloud. As if I'd just like to forget the whole thing and end it all."

"Oh, I'm truly sorry," I said, and felt myself frowning with dismay. I hesitated, struggling with a painful moment of indecision. On the one hand, it seemed inhumane to put her off, even for an hour or two. Threats about "ending it all" must always be taken seriously. On the other hand, despite a strong temptation to respond immediately, the conviction that such response might even be crucial, I had to demur. Simultaneously, I felt I was appearing to be very callous.

"Look," I said quietly, "I really appreciate what you're saying, Melana, and I want you to know I'm deeply concerned. But as a missionary . . . Well, we have to observe some pretty strict requirements, and one of them is to work together—as companions." In reality I was *not* a missionary in the sense that I had been set apart for it, and in point of fact, I was companionless at the very moment. Nevertheless, it was the best I could do under the circumstances.

There was a moment of painful silence. "Of course," her voice came, and it was very subdued. "I apologize for . . . I mean, I'm sure I've been terribly presumptuous."

"No, not at all," I insisted. "And I assure you, Melana, that I do want to visit you as soon as possible—if you don't mind my bringing Darren along. I'm certain he'll be back within an hour or so."

"Of course," she repeated, and this time her tone was a bit more positive. "But I'm still afraid I'm imposing."

"Definitely not," I insisted. "I'll call you the minute he returns."

"Thank you—you're very kind," she said.

That was how our conversation ended, and I hung up the phone with very mixed feelings. The lady was alone without any close friends in the area and clearly needed someone in whom to confide. Now, however, she might be reluctant. It was one of those dilemmas that springs from the shadows, when somehow you have no choice but to select "the lesser of the evils."

21

$D$are and I arrived at Melana Gardner's residence an hour and a half later, and she was a dramatic contrast to the woman we had visited only two days earlier. Her face was drawn and ashen, and her body appeared more fragile than ever, even somewhat hunched. "Please come in," she murmured; and as we entered: "Thank you both ever so much. I do hope this isn't too inconvenient."

"Not a bit," Dare replied. "Nothing on the agenda but some afternoon tracting, and that can definitely wait."

"Well, I'm glad," she said. "As you can see, this place is still as barren as a mausoleum, but I *will* be getting a few things ere long. Meanwhile, perhaps you won't mind visiting out by the pool again."

"Sounds fine," I replied. There seemed, in fact, to be a somberness about the castle I hadn't noticed before. The pool would definitely be cheerier—a better place in general in this situation.

"I hardly know where to begin," Melana said once we were seated. "First maybe the good news—then the bad."

"All right, anything you feel like sharing," I replied. "I still have at least *one* good ear, and Dare has two." Dare grinned and nodded.

Her smile was faint and wan. The dark rings that I had

noticed beneath her eyes on our first meeting were now even darker. "Well . . . " she sighed. "The good is that the things you were all talking about last time have really offered me a ray of hope. After our last discussion, I felt so uplifted! For a while . . . " She shook her head as though words were inadequate. "I almost felt transformed. And that night—maybe because we'd been talking about dreams—I had a very vivid one. I dreamed my son Lance had come to my bedside. That . . . " She bowed her head, a hand to her brow, the fingertips tremulous. "That he was dressed in white and that his face and eyes were absolutely luminous."

She waited some time before continuing. "I'm sure, as I say, that it could all be explained very logically as mere association based upon our discussion. And yet, there seemed to be more to it than that. A dream, yes, but it felt so real, and even though he didn't speak, he seemed to radiate this powerful kind of approval. It was as if he was saying, 'You're following the right path with these new friends of yours, Mom. Stay in contact with them and listen with your heart to their message.' "

I smiled. "Very moving, and needless to say, in my opinion, you were getting the right impression. Maybe it truly was something more than a dream."

Dare looked thoughtful. "Yeah—could be."

Melana was shaking her head a bit in amazement. "It was so *beautiful*, so *right*, and I felt so *happy*!" Even as she spoke her face began to change, emanating a little of the light she had just described. I had, in fact, never encountered anyone more chameleon-like in terms of how her outer self reflected the feelings of the moment.

Across the swimming pool was a high fence of redwood stakes festooned with orange-flowered trumpet vine. Half a dozen of the usual hummingbirds flitted among them, stealing their nectar.

"So that's the good part," Melana murmured. She too was watching the hummingbirds. Her gaze lifted as one of them arched upward, ringing off into the morning, followed shortly by the rest as though in urgent summons. I waited now for the bad news, uneasy, even mildly superstitious, but also curious. "The bad is that—well, for one thing, I've had quite a few health problems the past year or more. Been on so many medications I'm beginning to feel like a hypochondriac."

"Oh, really?" I said. "I'm sorry to hear that."

"Sometimes my heart rate becomes rather erratic and even misses a few strokes."

"That's disturbing indeed," I said.

"Yeah," Dare added.

"Have you seen a doctor recently?"

"Oh yes," she answered wearily. "Just a few days ago, in fact, but nobody seems to have any explanation. Nothing but a lot of double-talk disguised in medical jargon, as far as I'm concerned. I'm pretty sure, in fact, that they all think it's merely psychological." She gave another wan smile. "And who knows, maybe they're right. But that doesn't necessarily make the problem any less *real*, does it?"

"Absolutely not," I said.

"And the worst part of it is that almost every time my heart acts up, I get these hideous migraines and end up looking as if I'd taken a beating and had both eyes blackened." I remonstrated for the sake of chivalry alone, because her description really was quite accurate. "But finally, on top of all that—I get these awful feelings of depression, this kind of dark despair that doesn't have any logic or reason."

"Despair often doesn't," I said. "I'm wondering, though, from what you said earlier, how much it may relate in part to your marital problems."

"Oh yes, that's unquestionably a factor—especially since I've escaped his clutches and moved here to Scottsdale." She waited, seeming to ponder the matter. "My husband is a very strange man. *Former* husband—the divorce is now all but final, and in consequence Court has been

138

harassing me almost night and day. He still loves me, I suppose, in his own warped manner. But he's always been terribly possessive, and he can't stand the thought that I'm no longer in his control."

"So what exactly is the man doing?" Dare inquired.

"Nothing really threatening, just constant psychological warfare. Constant phone calls and letters feigning great concern, at the same time implying that I've betrayed him, betrayed the children by 'breaking up our happy home!' " She threw out her hands, and her smile was bitter. "That is the ultimate irony, believe me. And lots of brainwashing to the effect that I can't survive without him. Much of it's so subtle that anyone who doesn't know him as well as I do would never detect it. You have to learn the code, so to speak."

"Hmmmm . . . " I nodded a little. "I've known a few people of his kind, though none, I'm sure, that extreme."

"Oh, he's extreme, all right, to the point of being diabolical. And whenever anyone calls him on it, he'll either deny any malice aforethought whatever or pretend it's all a big joke and ridicule you for being so 'thin-skinned,' so 'childish and defensive.' Lately, though, it's become a lot more blatant. Last night, for example, he called me and said, in a tone of great solicitude, 'Well, liebchen, I really and truly hope you can make it on your own and that you can handle the big D (meaning my depression) when it comes, because it's really going to clobber you pretty hard now that you're all alone.' "

"Diabolical is right," Dare said. "Ought to have his tongue tied."

Melana nodded and sighed. "Then this morning he called again and said he was really concerned that I might 'flip out and start getting suicidal again'! Those were his exact words." She closed her eyes, looking rather faint. "But you'll never really know, unless you can actually tune in on it direct, how the man can play cat and mouse with your mind. Sometimes it's downright hypnotic, except that everything's irony and innuendo. It's . . . " Melana seemed to be struggling with herself. "Almost as if he's in league with some evil power. Something extra-terrestrial."

"Is there also any chance the guy might really hurt you?" Dare asked. "Physically, I mean."

"Oh . . . " Melana's eyes narrowed, and she seemed to weigh the idea. "Not much. Occasionally, he's become rather heavy-handed, you might say. Knocked me down some stairs once, broke three of my ribs and dislocated my jaw in the process." Melana's smile was wry and wan, as if it had been a good little joke on her.

"No, not really!" I exclaimed. I was genuinely distressed and also angered. "Sounds as if you may be in *great* physical danger."

Melana looked down at her hands. They were folded in her lap and the delicate fingers trembled slightly. "No," she sighed, "not really. Those things are rather rare and only when he's thoroughly intoxicated."

"Yes, but still—"

"No, the big danger is the constant psychological warfare and what it does to my morale. Court Gardner is the ultimate master of the mind game, of power through intimidation. And he does it with practically everybody." She paused, gazing at the pool. "And he's constantly playing these bizarre jokes on people. Once, for example, he got into some kind of disagreement with a business acquaintance and apparently came out on the losing end. So later, when the man's wife and children were away in Europe on a vacation, Court called him up posing as a member of the State Department or something—he's a fantastic actor and mimic, by the way—and told the poor man that they had been kidnapped by terrorists!"

"Wild!" Dare said.

"Really. Another time, some firm outbid him on a big contract involving water recreational equipment. Anyway, Court was practically frothing at the mouth, and he wrote letters to every single person in the organization under the name of the company president, telling them they'd been fired for disloyalty and inferior performance."

I could not refrain from laughing. "The man's insane!"

Dare was laughing even harder. "Really something else!"

"Yes," she said. "He ought to be in a mental institution—or maybe a penal institution—it's a toss-up. But he's crazy like a fox and slippery as an eel. He's a real computer wizard, incidentally, and he got the names of the employees by tapping into their computer system some way."

"What a fellow!" I mused.

Melana nodded. "Whenever he pulls these things off, he can't resist telling people how clever he is. He thinks tricks of that kind are utterly hilarious and prove what a brilliant mind he has. But one of these days . . . " Her expression was suddenly rather grim. "He's going to get nailed."

I nodded. "Sounds like it."

"In a way, though," she continued, "it's all rather pathetic. Underneath that sinister facade, he's a very insecure person. Now, with me gone, and—I hope and pray—the children leaving soon, he's a terribly lonely man. Despite all his talent and charisma, he doesn't have any real friends because people soon realize he's the world's champion manipulator. The Great Exploiter."

"That's sad," I said, "but much sadder for his victims. A classic case of self-alienation if there ever was one. And it's abundantly apparent that you're on the right track. The only answer is to sever relations with the man completely as soon as possible."

"That's true," Melana said. "There's absolutely no way in the world that I can survive any longer under that kind of domination, and I simply can't permit it to continue with Aaron and Amber. I'd literally rather die first."

I nodded, pondering the situation. "For the time being, though, why don't you just hang up on him whenever he calls and chuck all his letters, if he sends any, in the trash can?"

"Yes," Melana said, "that makes sense, and I've actually done it from time to time, but he's so fiendishly cunning, he'll imitate other people, friends of mine, and sometimes I'm taken in until it's too late. Then he'll start cackling like a hyena and say 'Well, well, well, now—how *about* that! Fooled you again, didn't I, sweetheart?'"

"Out of sight!" Dare exclaimed. "Has he always been that way?"

"Well, not to that kind of awful extreme. In the early days it was more playful, less malicious. People quite enjoyed him. He was a man with fantastic charm, but now it has all turned sour—rancid."

"The minute you recognize who it is, though," I said, "on the phone, why not just hang up?"

"What you ought to do," Dare told her, "is get a police whistle. Then every time he calls give him the full blast. Ream his ears out!"

Her laughter was almost delighted. "That would *really* do the trick, wouldn't it." Then she became solemn again. "But I'd never get away with it. Court would always find some way of getting back at me. He's a terribly poor loser."

"Do you have an answering machine?" I asked.

"No," she replied, "but I'll be getting one soon. That way, hopefully, I can pretty well screen him out. But I do need to be in touch with my children. I rarely call them, for fear Court will answer and try to interfere. They call me instead, collect, when he's not around."

"So what does this husband dude of yours look like?" Dare wondered.

"Look like," she mused, frowning. "Look like . . . hmmm. Well, fairly handsome, I suppose. Rather hawk-like profile, full head of white hair. But his moustache and beard—well, a goatee, actually—are a dark red, almost black." She shrugged faintly and squinted, angling her glance to the side then upward. "Tall, lean, quite agile and athletic."

"Cool," Dare said. He seemed impressed despite himself.

"Athletic when he's *sober*," Melana qualified. "When he's drunk, even slightly, he sprawls all over himself and whoever's unfortunate enough to be in the way."

"Ha!" Dare grinned and shook his head. "What a character!"

Somewhere a dog began to bark but soon fell silent. Dragonflies added entrancement to the swimming pool, and one—large and blue-green—fenced briefly with a tassel on the patio umbrella overhead.

"But what about the depression per se?" I asked. "Have you found any of the medications helpful?"

"To some extent, yes," she replied. "I was on Tofranil and Lithium for quite a while." She shrugged. "Although sometimes the side effects outweigh the benefits. My doctor in Mesa started me on Prozac this past year, and that seems to help, but I need to renew my prescription."

"I hope you will," I said, "if it's truly helping." I paused, watching her face, hoping what followed would not seem presumptuous. "Soon, okay?"

"Okay," she said, and gave me a gentle smile. "Thanks." The dragonflies increased in number, cavorting, some with bodies of pale red and gold, slender as darning needles. "I do have a problem in that general regard, though," she said. "I think that gradually I've become *over*-medicated. Pills for my heart, my spastic stomach, for depression . . . insulin." She made an offhand gesture as if assigning it all to the ridiculous.

"Insulin? You're diabetic also?"

"Oh, yes." She repeated the gesture. "A little of everything." I saw the wistful smile that curled mysteriously at the corners of her mouth. "Poor, pathetic Melana Gardner—right?"

"Brave, intelligent Melana Gardner," I replied. "A lady who is facing great trials. But I predict she's going to win."

"Thank you," she said and gazed down again at her hands. "Sometimes, though, I don't face them very wisely, I'm afraid. I do things occasionally, or sometimes fail to, almost to spite myself. I really think I'm somewhat masochistic. Otherwise, why would I have put up with all that I have for so long?" She laughed, tossing her head. "What a splendid symbiotic relationship!"

I smiled. "What about counseling? There are a lot of knowledgeable people in the ward and stake here, I'm sure, who could place you in touch with someone who might be of real help."

Again the knowing, enigmatic smile, the disconcerting gaze. "Oh, they already have. I'm sure I've found him, in fact, but unfortunately for me, he'll be returning to his wife and family in Utah before long."

22

At least, I have a lot to keep me occupied," Melana continued. "Trying to make this place habitable, and I want to get back to my painting. It should be good therapy."

"I hope you will," I said. "A talent like yours should flourish to the full, and I'm sure it *will* be very therapeutic."

Melana laughed with the tinkling, glass-chimes quality I had so enjoyed before. "Aw, you haven't even *seen* my paintings!"

"No," I said, "but the Pedersons have, and they've told me how great they are."

"Really have," Dare said.

"And besides," I continued, "I can tell—strictly from the way you talk about art, the love you project in that connection—that you have to be very good, to say the least."

"You're very kind."

"No, just truthful."

"By the way," Melana said. "You said earlier that you were here to research material for a book."

I nodded. "Yes. I'm not sure what direction it will take. Just in the raw material stage right now, but it will probably be a novel."

"How fascinating!" It sounded as if she meant it. "I've

wanted to talk to you about your writing, but I've been so wrapped up in my own little problems, I'm afraid I must seem awfully narcissistic."

"Not in the least," I insisted. "Melana Gardner is why we're here."

"What a nice thing to say," she said. Unexpectedly, her eyes appeared a bit moist. Then, brightening she said: "But *tell* me about it—your writing . . . your philosophy in that regard . . . whatever." Tossing out her hands as if, indeed, the sky itself were not the limit.

I laughed a bit nervously. Where could I possibly begin? "I'll either have to make this extremely short or go on for hours."

Dare chuckled. "He really will if you give him a chance."

"Oh, do go on for hours," she replied. "I'd love it."

"Bless you," I said, "but I'd better stick with the former. Maybe I should just say the whole thing's a nervous habit, a unique brand of insanity, and let it go at that." I paused. "I'm not sure what to tell you, really. It's something I got into long ago, on my mission, in fact. Clear back then, I began combining my journal writing and my letters to the family. On P-Day I'd start typing away on my little Remington portable, recounting the events of the week as descriptively as possible. One copy went into my journal looseleaf; the carbon went home in the mail. That's when I got hooked on writing, and I've been at it in most of my spare time ever since. Took all the classes I could in college—finally even got a doctorate in creative writing and modern lit. The practice ties in perfectly with my *teaching* of writing and literature at Weber State. Each one reinforces the other—what you might call a benign circle."

Dare's eyebrows rose. "Opposite of a vicious circle, right?" I nodded.

"I like that," Melana exclaimed. "We all need more benign circles in our lives, don't we? The vicious ones we can do without entirely." Her glance was exceptionally sweet and inquiring. "And you obviously blended your

146

writing and teaching to find your work, correct? Work, as opposed to a mere job; something that affords constant fulfillment, much of your *raison d'etre.*"

"Absolutely," I said. I was steadily becoming fonder of the woman, feeling an ever-greater affinity and respect. "And yet . . . " I mused, "writing is probably the hardest work I ever do. That blank page—or computer screen for most of us these days—can be incredibly intimidating."

"Oh, yes!" Melana said, "I'm sure. It's the same way with a canvas. That blank canvas can be so formidable! Sometimes, utterly repelling."

I nodded, smiling. "And getting that first word on paper, or daub of paint on the canvas, is often a tremendous act of faith—merely imagining that something of value may materialize. Sometimes you may have a pretty good idea where you're headed, and sometimes, none at all. The whole thing's *terra incognita*, and it requires a special kind of courage to take that first step."

"Yes," she said, "that's absolutely true. Yet, on the other hand, that page or canvas can be a kind of magical carte blanche, can't it? Sometimes, if you really care enough, and you're creating from the heart, miracles truly can happen."

I nodded. "In my own case, I'm afraid they're rather minor ones, but yes, you're one hundred percent correct, Melana. Whenever I think about the challenge of writing, incidentally, I'm reminded of a cartoon one of my students gave me. Charles Dickens is sitting in a chair beside a desk, looking rather bemused. Seated on the other side is an editor who appears a bit disgruntled, and he's saying, 'Come, come now, Mr. Dickens—was it the *best* of times or the *worst* of times? After all, it can hardly have been both!'"

Melana Gardner's laughter not only tinkled, it also was delightfully girlish. The face that had looked so haunted and careworn only a short time earlier was—speaking of magic and miracles—almost radiant. "Oh, that's fabulous!"

"But that's, literally, the way it is, with writing and,

I'm sure, painting. Probably all the arts, wouldn't you say? It can range in a given day, even hour, from the best of times to the worst of times and vice versa."

"Definitely. I maintain, in fact, that truly creative art is not merely a reflection of life but that it actually is life. Ultimately, the life we live and the art we create become inseparable. Do you understand what I'm saying?" Her gaze was transfixing.

"Yes, I do," I replied, "but I've never been able to explain it fully, to articulate it very well. Maybe for me the concept is so profound it is also elusive."

Melana nodded, but I could tell from her expression that she was well ahead of me. "I'd love to read something you've written, in any case."

I laughed. "Now that is faith! I'm afraid you may be in for a letdown."

"Oh, no, I'm sure I won't," she said. The cryptic, flowing smile welled and lingered. The gray eyes sparkled with fragments of quicksilver, emanating a glint of mischief. She glanced at Darren "And, who knows? Maybe one of these days your father will write that novel about his season here in Arizona and include—at least as one of your minor, less consequential characters—the strange and neurotic Melana Gardner. Cleverly disguised, of course!"

"Right on!" Dare laughed.

"Without question, but she can't possibly be a minor figure," I insisted, "either in life or its reflection. Furthermore, I would find it very difficult, psychologically speaking, to disguise the lady very much." Almost inadvertently, I looked at my watch.

"Oh," she said apologetically, "I've been keeping you both far longer than I expected, monopolizing your time."

"No, no, no!" I protested. "Nothing could be further from the truth. The pleasure has been ours, believe me. And I assure you, we'd immensely enjoy seeing some of your work before I return home."

"Definitely," Dare said.

"Well . . . " Melana's glance rose toward the second story

of her castle. "Most of my work hasn't arrived from Mesa yet, and some of it's on display at the University of Phoenix."

"Really!" I began to say something about how well that must reflect her talent but was interrupted.

"But I am starting to hang a few things in my upstairs hallway," Melana said, "and I'm working on another—quite a different approach, in fact." She was watching us closely. "If you could spare another five minutes or so, maybe . . . "

"Why, sure," Dare replied. "I'd really like to see some of it. Wouldn't you, Pop?"

"Absolutely," I said.

"Just a glance," she insisted, and moments later we entered the castle. "I'm setting up a photo lab in the basement," she added as we mounted the stairs. "I'm starting to take up photography a bit now, too."

"Good," I said. We were ascending the stairs. "I do a little myself, mostly family stuff."

"That's one thing I can say in Court's favor," she continued. "He's a brilliant photographer, does all his own processing and developing. He's the one who got me started. But . . . well, for now I'll just show you a few of my more recent paintings."

Moments later we were looking at them with great admiration and astonishment. Several involved Arizona and New Mexico desert scenes, somewhat in the Navajo Indian style, with starkly contrasting light and shadow, shimmering dunes resounding with sunshine, giant saguaro cacti. Night scenes with the silhouette of a lone coyote on a ridge, drifting ravens, distant mountains and mercury-colored stars that actually seemed to pulsate. One painting contained an immense owl, lofting against a full moon of almost celestial whiteness.

"Melana," I exclaimed, "these are wonderful, utterly entrancing!" Her reply was light and self-effacing, but I remained insistent. "Don't sell yourself short. These are remarkable!"

"They're terrific," Dare agreed. "You are one talented lady."

149

And there were others of widely varying subject material, mood, and style—wild and rugged seascapes, somewhat in the Rockwell Kent vein; portraits of beautiful Jamaican women, and of Melana's children. One, about eighteen inches wide and two feet long, of her son Lance was especially captivating and powerful. In some respects he resembled Dare, the same general facial features, same full, blond hair with a kind of coppery, almost russet glow, but his eyes somehow seemed quite Christ-like and were an intense, emery-spark blue.

"Marvelous," I said, "all of them. But especially this one of your son. It absolutely exudes life and personality. Were his eyes really this blue?"

"Yes, even more," she replied, and for an instant I had the strange-yet-pleasant feeling that they were actually looking at each other. She gave a little laugh. "People who didn't know him sometimes thought he had on colored contacts."

"I can understand why," I said. Her paintings lined a long hallway floored with dull red tile, and at the far end was a stack of canvasses leaning against the wall. The outer one faced inward so that only the frame was visible. "And what might those be?" I inquired. My interest was steadily growing.

"Oh . . . " Melana sounded rather indifferent. Or perhaps it was reluctant—dubious. "I don't think I'll ever display those again. They were all created during what I call my Goya periods, at the low, black end of my mood swings." A cold little laugh. "The very nadir."

"I know what you're saying," I told her. "I haven't experienced it very much, but I've done a little writing on the subject." I hesitated, musing. "I guess the thing I remember best about it all is a quote I came across from F. Scott Fitzgerald: 'In a dark night of the soul it's always three o'clock in the morning.'"

"That's marvelous," she said. "Nothing could be more true. And I suppose poor Scott knew whereof he spoke."

"That he did," I replied.

150

"Anyway," Melana continued. "One of these fine days, I'm going to light a gigantic bonfire—maybe have a bonfire *party*—and consign them to the flames." I was about to suggest that it would be a shame to destroy any of her work, no matter what it reflected, but my hostess continued. "For the moment, though, I'd like to show you one more thing—something fairly upbeat—out on the verandah."

Beckoning, she led us back down the hallway toward the stairs and on into a spacious room with Persian rugs. Overhead were three large skylights, and a long, felt couch of mallard-head green bisected the room, flanked by matching easy chairs. "This," she announced with a graceful wafting of the hand, "is in the very gradual process of becoming my studio. At present, though, I'm spending most of my time out here beneath the sky." Again, she beckoned, leading the way, and we followed through open glass doors at the room's far end onto the waiting verandah.

"Man, what a layout!" Dare marveled.

"Right, you could practically see the whole of Arizona if it weren't for the smog."

I smiled. "No doubt."

"Hopefully some rainstorms will come along and clear things off occasionally," she said. "But here's what I wanted to show you." On one corner of the verandah, overlooking the back yard and pool, was a huge drafting table approximately six feet long and half that wide. It contained large castors for easy transportation indoors or out, apparently, and upon its surface was a canvas of almost the same dimensions. The painting itself was incomplete, but even so it was remarkable—a strange and compelling semi-abstraction unlike anything I had ever seen or imagined. It fairly flowed with vaporous, rainbow-tinted swirls that looked like fire and water combined, enough to make one slightly dizzy. Beginning in its center and dominating much of the canvas, in fact, was a great bird only half materialized, still awaiting its realization. A fantastic hybridization—flamingo, peacock, and perhaps pheasant—starting into flight from what might have been ashes. Ashes of a funeral pyre? Dare and I were both staring in near amazement. "Part of it . . . " He squinted, tilting his head to one side. "Part of it looks like an Indian thunderbird."

Melana smiled. "Yes, that was some of what I wanted to convey."

"Melana!" I said at last. "This is incredible, a work of genius." It seemed as though for the past while, I had been speaking in ever greater superlatives, yet they were inescapable. "How do you *do* it—I mean, *seriously!*"

"With mirrors," she laughed. Her smile was quite bewitching, and her face steadily grew brighter as though reflecting candle flames.

"All right," I laughed, "I asked."

"Hey, I'm not joking," she insisted. "Mirrors and prisms, actually. Here, let me show you." Reaching beneath the table, she produced an ingenious contraption constructed of a stand and frame perhaps two feet square. The frame was affixed to the stand at the center of two uprights with bolts and wing nuts so that it could be tilted at various angles. It was also spanned every few inches by rotatable rods, each containing either rows of tiny mirrors or prisms. It looked like some science fiction creation from another planet or perhaps even an exotic musical instrument. An eccentric yet ingenious work of art in and of itself. As I soon discovered, however, it was merely a means to an end.

"This is something I sort of dreamed up one time," Melana explained, "literally saw in a dream. It's designed to capture the sunlight and diffuse it onto the canvas in some rather different patterns and color combinations. Then I attempt to recreate the general effect with an airbrush and at times even a perfume atomizer."

"Hey, that's *bad!*"

"He means great," I reminded her, "and so do I." I paused, observing more closely. "And that's how you achieve that . . . well, what? That sense of constant motion."

She nodded. "That, and a special paint I've finally

come up with. Very refined stuff, actually—a banana oil base along with old-time model airplane dope, neither of which is very easy to obtain these days. Remember the flying models made of balsa wood sticks and tissue paper?"

"Do I ever!" I said. "With the elastic-powered propeller that you wound by hand. I used to make a lot of them back in my early teens. The dope went on the tissue paper to make it more resilient."

Melana nodded, smiling nostalgically. "I was the only girl I've ever known who made and flew model airplanes. My whole family kidded me about it, but I really didn't care. There was something so gratifying—exhilarating, in fact—about the whole experience, especially when the planes took wing."

"So true," I said, and for an instant I saw myself at age twelve or thirteen, running with two friends through a long, green field, in pursuit of a newly created yellow flying model—a "Pacific Ace"—that danced along the summer morning as though its time might never end. Then I looked again at Melana's current "flying model," the one ever rising on an expanse of canvas. Unfortunately the sun was now veiled by a growing overcast. Yet even so I could detect a subtle interplay of color, something mysteriously captured and interpolated by all those little mirrors and prisms. An exotic, mind-spinning swirl, culminating, yet ever evolving, in her winged creation.

"Clearly," I said, "this is not your standard little songbird; it's the ultimate bird of birds, or will be when you're finished. But what else does it represent?" I cast her a quick glance. "Or is that a dumb question?"

"No, no, not dumb at all," she said, and gently touched my arm in that open yet intimate way some women have. "I think perhaps I'll call it *Phoenix Rising*!"

"Aha! Excellent—bravo!" I actually found myself applauding.

"Yeah, first-rate," Dare said.

The whole idea transfixed and enchanted me. "And no doubt, with all due respect to this noble state, it symbolizes

153

more things than Phoenix, Arizona. First, of course, it epitomizes magnificently the old myth, right? The phoenix bird that every few hundred years burns itself up in an excess of foolishness, but then somehow eventually springs forth from the ashes, renewed and resurrected. Correct?"

She nodded. "One hundred percent correct."

"But what does it represent, specifically, for Melana Gardner, I wonder?"

She shook her head, eyes dreamy, shrugged eloquently with her slender shoulders. "That I have yet to discover. But definitely *something*, something very fundamental, or it never would have laid hold upon me so irresistibly." For an instant our gazes fused empathically, unsettlingly so. "Perhaps the kind Professor Connors can help me discover it."

"Perhaps he can," I said quietly. "Rest assured, he'll be thinking about it."

Minutes later we were downstairs again, saying goodbye at the front door. "Just one thing," I said, "something I was wondering when we were discussing some of your problems." I hesitated, not wishing to overstep my bounds. "I'm sure the Pedersons would be delighted to have you come stay with them for a while until . . . well, things level off. They have a nice guest house that's empty, and—"

But Melana promptly demurred. "No, no." She shook her head gently but firmly. "I wouldn't want to impose, and I'm sure things will start looking up. Our visit has done wonders already, believe me."

"Maybe you could just stay there nights," Dare suggested. "Or just any time you start feeling down."

"No, bless you," Melana said, as she clasped his hand warmly in both her own. "I'll be *fine!*" The final words came brightly, perhaps too brightly. For an instant she glanced at me. Her eyes glistened. "Your visit has done wonders."

23

Shortly after returning to our apartment we were visited by Elders Mac and Hud. Both were quite jubilant over having just completed a highly successful discussion with an elderly couple in their apartment complex. "Sounds like a celebration's in order," I observed. "You Elders go for some pizza?" They would, without question. "Great!" I said. "I'll run down to the supermarket and pick some up—maybe a few other items to go with them too."

When I returned a short while later, however, the mood was dramatically different. "Looks like we've got some bad news, Pop," Dare informed me. His brow was furrowed, and they all looked pretty glum.

"It must be pretty serious," I said. "What's the story?"

"Well, it's happened . . . with the Williamses. Their darling little 'saved today' neighbors just dumped on them—a whole ton of anti-Mormon garbage."

"No!" I said. I was momentarily stunned. "You're kidding!" It was almost like hearing about the death of a close friend.

"It's a fact," he said. Elders Mac and Hud merely looked doleful and muttered a bit.

"So, when did you receive this delightful news?" I asked.

155

"About twenty minutes ago. I just called up to confirm our appointment tomorrow, and Dan said they needed some time to sort things out, that they'd call us later."

"And you know what that means," Elder Mac said.

"Yep," I said. "'Don't call us, we'll call you.'" I began pacing about the little room, crunched the knuckles of one hand in the opposite palm, felt an urge to swear but resisted it. "What a revolting development!"

"Those stupid 'saved todayers,'" Dare said. "Why don't they just keep their long noses where they belong?"

Momentarily, right in the midst of it all, I wanted to laugh. My son could be a most impatient and scornful young man when he wanted to—at times, even when he didn't.

"Well, I guess they're doing what they think is right," I said.

"The 'saved todayers'? Yeah, because they're all out of wack. Wouldn't surprise me one little bit if they're the ones circulating those weird photos."

For a second his reference failed to register. "Photos of what?"

"The *Study in Tar* or whatever you call it."

"Oh . . . yeah, of course."

"All those crazy faces," Elder Hud said.

"Yes, The Morass. That's what I'm beginning to call it. Well, maybe it's the 'saved todayers,' but it could be anybody. But what about the Williamses? There *has* to be *something* we can do besides just sit on our hands and wait for the call that never comes. Maybe we ought to phone them and say we'd just like to drop by for a little while and try to answer their questions."

"We already tried that, Pop," Dare said. He sounded a bit vexed with me for assuming anything to the contrary. "But it was no go. Somebody's really gotten to them, and they don't know which way's up."

I was pacing the room, in what scant space it offered, hands locked behind my back like a drill instructor, almost tripping over the feet of my young companions as they

156

sprawled disconsolately on the couch. But I didn't feel like a drill instructor; I felt very despondent and uncertain. "Well . . . " I mused and glanced out the front window. The curtains were barely parted. For some reason all the residents of Glendale and environs kept their curtains closed day and night, and the missionaries had adopted the custom. "Maybe it might help if we double-teamed them. Possibly I could call and tell them I'd just like to see them before I return home."

Darren shrugged. "Go for it." Through the slit in the curtains I saw a maple tree stirring in the breeze. A few of its winged seeds came spinning down to land on a small, dry island of lawn. "Just don't feel too bad if they give you the negative."

"I couldn't feel much worse than I already do," I replied. "Let's live with it for a while and see if we get any promptings."

Several times during the day I was on the verge of calling the Williamses but always, almost at the last second, felt restrained. Possibly it was merely cold feet from fear of rejection, yet I also felt that there was something beyond that. Some other approach I wasn't yet on to.

That night we conversed at length again about our respective missions, reiterating our concerns about the Williams family, wondering also what might become of our remarkable friend Melana Gardner.

Then, on the brink of dreamland, I heard Dare's voice. "Pop?"

"Roger," I said groggily.

"Whatever happens with the Williams family, Melana, or anybody else, it's sure neat having you here. Things like this don't come along very often."

"That's true, old buddy," I replied. "Wouldn't have missed this for the world. It's something I'll never forget."

A moment later I heard him stir, felt more than saw his long, wiry arm reach out there in the darkness. Then his hand was giving my balding dome a little massage.

24

Despite that happy concluding note, however, my dreams were restless and tangled. Only a few days remained until my return to Ogden, and at times it seemed I was journeying through the desert, lost in mists of darkness, fearful I wouldn't arrive for Christmas. All this interwoven with dreams of Melana Gardner and the Williams family. Eventually, about 3:00 A.M., the dreams became so tangled and obsessive that I arose. That way I could at least have control over my mind.

Entering the cramped little kitchen, I poured myself a glass of milk from the carton in the fridge. Then I strolled into the adjoining room and sat down at the study table. Before me was the little white Christmas tree and, scarcely thinking, I flipped on the lights; that automatically made me feel a bit cheerier. Moments later, almost as unthinkingly, I inserted two sheets of paper, along with a faded carbon, into the roller of my little portable and began to type as follows:

My Dear Williams Family:

I have been thinking about all of you with deep and prayerful concern over the past few days—especially upon learning that you have been exposed to some anti-Mormon literature. Several times I have been tempted to call you but now feel that it would be best to set forth some of my reflections in writing.

Well, so much for a beginning, of one sort or another. Now for the more important consideration: what *were* my reflections? My mind at that point was as blank as the remaining page. Although I intended nothing in terms of a real literary effort, the problem I had discussed with Melana applied—blank wall or carte blanche. For now I could only rely upon the old saying, "How can I know what I think until I see what I say?"

Thus, after some small hesitation, a bit of yawning, stretching, sighing, and sipping more milk . . . I could discover no additional delaying tactics and gradually began to get words on paper. At the onset I told the Williamses that I could empathize with their feelings of doubt and confusion having, back in my young and skeptical days, read a good deal of anti-Mormon literature myself. Indeed, that for a time I had been quite disturbed by it. I also spoke at length of discussions with ministers of other faiths, on my mission and occasionally afterward, explaining that I had been able to refute to my own satisfaction most of their accusations and arguments. Included as follows were my comments in that regard:

Some of those arguments, I still can't answer fully, at least not as specifically as I might desire. But here is my basic position . . . *Many* of the alleged discrepancies and contradictions in LDS teachings and practices cited by our opponents are the result of statements wrenched and often combined out of context. Many others occur when people contrast opinions of our Church leaders either with other opinions, or with declared, canonized *revelation*. All the prophets throughout time have readily admitted that they were not uttering revelation twenty-four hours a day and that some of their private views, no matter how well educated or intended, *might* be at variance with what God himself has revealed or may decide to reveal. By contrasting opinion with opinion, opinion with revelation, or even revelation with revelation (when such things are not viewed in a broad and enlightened perspective), one can create almost any impression imaginable.

"So where from here?" I wondered. I pondered the matter for several minutes, prayed for the Spirit, and received only one answer: "Keep writing." It was an answer I had arrived at on more than one occasion, and it always left me with mixed feelings. Were such words coming from on high or merely the mind of one Nathan R. Connors? And even if they were in very deed the whisperings of the Spirit, I sometimes felt that perhaps the Lord was saying in effect, "My son, you're a man now; do what seems best, for it is not meet that I should command in all things."

I therefore continued:

Let me stress as well, that a person can also discover all kinds of *apparent* contradictions within the Bible itself. Consider what a mass of confusion and downright absurdity one can create, for example, if he wishes to play some of the statements and happenings in the Old Testament against the New. Consider also the writings of Paul or, for that matter, even parts of the four Gospels.

I proceeded in that vein a bit further, then concluded:

And yet, despite all these things, you and I are both quick to affirm our belief in the Bible and in Jesus Christ as our Savior. In the existence of God the Father. Because we prefer to accentuate the positive, and because we genuinely believe that it *overwhelmingly outweighs* the apparent negative. On the other hand, I also believe that it is entirely possible for all of us to lose our testimony of Christ's divinity if we abandon ourselves to the arguments of his numerous detractors. Imagine what might have happened, for instance, to those in the Savior's day who spent all their time listening to the Pharisees and the Saducees!

I went on now with less and less hesitation, discussing "the great outpourings of positive evidence which I am convinced beyond all doubt profoundly outweigh any negative I have ever encountered." I compared briefly the doctrines, ordinances, and organization of the restored Church with those of Christ's church in Jerusalem. I spoke of the great evidence for the Book of Mormon, exhorted the Williamses to pray earnestly for guidance from the Spirit as the only sure and ultimate answer, then ended with perhaps the most sincere testimony I have ever borne. At that point it truly seemed that the words were not mine alone.

"Hey, what's happenin', Pop?" a voice said. The frail light of dawn was permeating the curtains, streaking a vague blue through the slit in them.

I glanced up—half groggy, half startled—to see my son standing beside me in his red-satin bathrobe, the one inherited from his Grandfather Connors. "Testifying," I replied, but I also realized that I had fallen asleep praying some time earlier, my head cradled on my forearms over the little green typewriter.

25

It looks as if I have only a couple of days left," I said. "But I did want to drop by for a brief visit and thank you for letting me invade the Arizona Phoenix Mission."

President Linford bathed us in a cordial smile. "Delighted to have had you here, and I'm sure it's been a memorable experience for both of you."

"Exceptionally," I replied. "I tried to phone you a time or two. We even dropped by a while back, but you weren't in."

"True," he laughed. "I rarely am—out galavantin'. Been covering the mission end to end this past two or three weeks, in fact." President Linford was a handsome fellow of about fifty, rather short, but powerfully built, with a rugged, jutting chin that gave him an air of great determination. His dark hair contained islands of white, and, though very thick, was cropped so close that his skull gleamed through. His eyes were a metallic blue, his grin broad and white-toothed. Dare had told me earlier that President Linford was a retired Air Force colonel, and he certainly fit the idealized image.

"So, how's Elder Connors the Younger treating Elder Connors the Elder?" he asked heartily.

"He's giving me a rough time," I said, "working old Dad right down to the nub."

"Don't let him kid ya," Dare said. "Pop's a goer—can't hold him down."

The chit-chat continued for a little while then shifted to a more serious tone. "We've had a few disappointments along the way, though," I said, and I proceeded to relate the melancholy tale of our once-golden Williams family.

President Linford nodded solemnly, clucked his tongue. "It *happens*. Amazing how often, at almost the final moment, just when you think you're home free."

"Yeah," Dare sighed. "And this one's a real downer. We've been some unhappy campers the past couple days, I wanna tell ya. Dad and I been ready to call them back a bunch of times, but, well, it just didn't feel right for some reason."

Another nod from the president. "Well you're right to rely on your feelings." More clucking of the tongue. A quick, resigned twist of the head. "The Old Boy's one shrewd customer. His battle plans are laid and he just *revels* in catching the troops off guard."

"So true," I said. Maybe, despite our feelings that it had all been "a little too good to be true," we had somehow taken the situation too much for granted. We probably hadn't prayed hard enough, or specifically enough, for one thing. "Maybe we should have warned them in advance that the Church always has plenty of enemies," I sighed. "Maybe I should have emphasized the fact even more this morning."

President Linford's brow raised. "Oh, so you *did* get through to them?"

"Well, no, not directly," I replied. "But I started worrying about it last night and couldn't go back to sleep. About three o'clock I decided to write them a letter. It ended up running a lot longer than I expected, and—"

Dare laughed. "When I got up this morning to study, there Pop was, conked out dead to the world over the typewriter."

I laughed, feeling a bit sheepish for some reason. "I can't even remember what I said at the moment, not very clearly anyway."

"And you've mailed it?" the president asked.

"Yes, about nine this morning. I hope I did the right thing."

"Well . . . " President Linford leaned forward on his desk, lips pursed, massaging his granitic chin with one square hand. Large square hands with formidable knuckles but long, tapering fingers. "I suspect you did."

"I hope so," I said. "It seemed as if I was getting a little direction, maybe quite a lot, especially toward the end."

"Then, so be it." His gaze was frank, absorbing, utterly guileless. The kind of man I would like to have as an intimate friend, one I could always rely upon to hold the rope. "Sometimes the written word is even more persuasive than the spoken. Certainly it's a lot more permanent." Then, the white smile broadening: "What's that old Chinese proverb? 'Faintest ink stronger than most retentive memory'?"

I laughed again. "That's a new one on me. Maybe I'd better jot it down right now; otherwise, my memory may not be that retentive."

On the wall behind his desk was a large map of the mission sprinkled with the typed names and locations of each missionary, all of them affixed with red-headed pins. Beside the map was a fabric board containing photos of each missionary along with their names and current addresses. There, in fact, was Elder Darren Connors himself, looking rather camera shy, grinning like someone who had just committed a faux pas. He appeared surprisingly young and . . . what? Vulnerable. Suddenly, I realized that this was the boy of nearly two years ago—age nineteen and brand new in the field, instead of the present twenty-one. Time, time . . . how inexorably it flowed. How he had grown!

Then I was back to the moment. "But I can tell you one thing," I said.

"What's that?"

"Toward the end there, typing that letter, I was practically praying over every paragraph—every sentence!"

Our good mission president squinted, stroked his darkly gleaming chin again. "Well, that's surely got to count for something," he said. "After all, what did you have to lose? An honest, prayerful effort's almost always better than none."

Dare was less philosophical, however. "Those 'saved todayers,'" he said. "Haven't they ever got anything better to do than knock the Church?"

President Linford flashed another smile, one that also contained a trace of empathy. "Sometimes it almost seems they don't. But I suppose, looking at it from their own standpoint we're constantly putting *them* down too. The attack on our part is just more general." Dare frowned, looking dubious. "Well," the president shrugged, "merely by virtue of the fact that we claim what we claim. After all, we're *it*. We claim to be the only true church, the one that Christ himself established, restored. *Numero uno!* Right?"

I nodded, gazing at all those beaming young faces on the wall who were out proclaiming that very message, many of them probably at that precise moment. Part of a steadily growing army now numbering some forty thousand.

"Yeah," Dare said, "but we don't spend our time just *knocking* other religions and, well . . . always putting 'em down."

"True," came the reply, "although a lot of them know we believe in the Great Apostasy; that's what we teach in our discussions. And they realize that we consider all other Christian religions the ultimate consequence." He paused, searching my son's face with an intense blue eye. "Remember Joseph Smith's own account? The one involving his visitation by the Father and the Son? 'I was answered that I must join none of them.'" He held up an admonitory forefinger. "And *why*?" Actually shaking it a little.

Dare grinned, conceding the point. "'For they were all wrong.'"

"Precisely. '. ... and the Personage who addressed me said that all their creeds were an abomination in his sight;

165

that those professors were all corrupt; that: "they draw near to me with their lips, but their hearts are far from me, they teach for doctrines the commandments of men, having a form of godliness, but they deny the power thereof."'"

He waited, still eyeing my son with fatherly fondness and amusement. "Them's pretty strong words, Elder, and how many of those 'Joseph Smith Histories' do you imagine we've circulated throughout the world by now, along with all our other books and pamphlets and tracts on related subjects? Millions!"

"President," Dare laughed, "whose side are you *on?*"

"The Lord's," President Linford replied. "I'm just trying to put things in an objective perspective. Sometimes it's helpful, even healthy, to see ourselves as others see us."

"I agree," I said.

We sat there pondering the idea for a moment. Then Dare reached into the breast pocket of his suit and extracted something. It was our postcard-sized photo of the nefarious Study in Tar or The Morass. "So what do you make of this, president? This is the thing I called you about." President Linford nodded, acknowledging that he had already seen it, even had a duplicate given him by one of the other missionaries only the day before. "Pretty weird, right?"

The mission president shook his head, frowning. "It is that." He stretched and blinked. The whites of his eyes were red from what I suspected was lack of sleep during his many travels. "Don't know *what* to make of it, but I'm firing off a memo tomorrow to the whole mission on several different matters, and that's one of them. If any of our Elders are playing games and think this is some sort of a joke, they'd better shape up and repent." He paused, brow deeply knit. "I don't mind a little humor, but if that's what this is supposed to be, it's pretty sick: 'Death and Destruction to all Mormon Missionaries.'"

"Yes," I agreed. "Doesn't make it in the humor department at all. Some of them just have the initials MMs, but the message is clear."

He was scrutinizing the photo intently. "This *might* be more than a joke. If the problem continues, I want to be notified immediately."

"Whoever it is," Dare said, "it's got to be somebody who has access to our addresses."

I glanced at the president. "True, but that could be almost anybody," he noted. "Our missionaries give their phone numbers out to investigators, even their addresses in some cases, and a lot of the people in every ward know where the missionaries in that particular area live."

"Yeah," Dare said. "People all over the place know where *we* live. There's no way of hiding it even if we wanted to. See us going in and out all day long. But anyway, I'll lay you ten to one those 'saved todayers' are behind it."

"Maybe," President Linford mused, "but this doesn't quite seem their style to me. And after all, Elder, there are plenty of kooks out there in every religion." His laughter was wry. "Even a few in our own."

26

That night, despite having spent much of the previous one writing my epistle to the Williams family, I remained awake, unable to put my mind at rest. I reflected at length upon our various investigators, our meetings with member families in hopes that they would help us unearth additional prospects.

I thought of Melana Gardner, her brilliant artistry, her loneliness and depression, her perverted husband, her longing for spiritual sustenance, especially regarding the afterlife. Most of all, I thought about my wife and children. A letter had arrived from Sally that afternoon recounting her latest pre-Christmas activities, describing the tree, largest ever, fifteen feet tall or more, its tip brushing the high apex of our living room ceiling on one side of my loft. She told, as well, the "magnificent yuletide snowfall that left everything—our two acres here on Hollow's Edge, El Monte Golf Course across the highway below, the surrounding mountains—a glorious, pristine white."

Further on in her letter she described how the "sun exploded from the clouds for a few minutes, almost blindingly, and a cock pheasant came cackling and soaring across the back lawn as if it had actually been startled by all that light. Moments later the clouds moved in bringing more snow and more of our good old Robert Frost." I knew what she meant: "Stopping by Woods on a Snowy Evening." It was a poem we had both memorized long ago in our college days, even recited to each other betimes, there on the edge of our own little woods.

"Well," she concluded, "we won't be getting our missionary back until Valentine's Day, bless him, but maybe we can put up a Valentine Tree!" Knowing Sally, I suspected she might well do that very thing—a large branch from the scrub oak in the hollow, say . . . sprayed white, bedecked with a skein of tiny pink lights, strings of red beads, many valentines. Something like that, anyway, because she was delightfully inventive and reveled in doing things of that kind for those she loved most. "Dare, hon, we all miss you so! And we're so *proud* of you! Maybe we'd better not start counting the days, though—not for a *little* while. But we do hope that your itinerant father makes it home a bit sooner. A *few* hours before Christmas, anyway!" And there were short, crazy notes from our three youngest daughters, including a scribbled cartoon from Nan, our twelve-year-old "artist in residence," of Elder Connors and his balding "junior companion" attempting to tract a cactus. The cactus, a large saguaro, had a face, and appeared very startled indeed.

In some ways it seemed as though I had left home only a day or two before. In others, my three-week absence was beginning to feel like three months. And yet, I was relishing, literally relishing, every hour with my boy, trying to treasure up each moment. It was the kind of experience I would always remember in vivid detail. In addition, I'm sure we both sensed that, good as our relationship had been before, it would now and henceforth retain a certain touch of closeness and speciality. Mingling with it all, as well, was that persisting sense of unfinished business, along with my concern over Melana Gardner and the Williams family.

Lying there, hearing the gentle fuzzing of Darren's snores, I recalled our latest discussion with Steiner and "Geraldo." We had gone with them that very evening to a McDonald's, with little more in mind at the time than a brief visit. Steiner, we had discovered, was a widower whose children were all grown and living outside the area. Geraldo, having undergone a divorce months earlier, now pronounced himself an "incorrigible bachelor," insisting that he fully intended to remain that way henceforth and forever. Both seemed very self-sufficient on the one hand, lonely on the other, happy for a bit of company.

That night, over burgers and chocolate shakes, we had drifted into a friendly little exchange regarding organic evolution, Dare and I explaining that in the Church view it was indeed merely a theory even though so many alleged experts taught it as law—law supposedly as verifiable as those of gravity or thermodynamics. Even the great televised nature programs by such organizations as *National Geographic*, I pointed out, begin with that premise. Assume it as a foregone conclusion and go from there.

During our conversation I discovered that my shake was too thick for the straw and was trying to sip it from the cup without having a large glob suddenly descend and engulf my nose. Realizing that danger was imminent, I opted for a long plastic spoon instead. Dare, having inhaled his own supply of fries, was making forays into my own. "Oh, I was a disciple of Darwin at one time," I reflected, "but then I caught religion, and it began to shake my faith in the theory." Steiner exploded a dry, asthmatic laugh. Geraldo merely grinned enigmatically. "I remember my own classes," I continued, "Zoo 100 with its famous, ever-present chart covering much of the blackboard. The phylogenetic tree, depicting the ascent of man from an amoeba floating happily in its own private swamp. It was all very neat and authoritative and exact; at the time I considered it the final word. Anybody who ever *questioned* the proposition was regarded as a benighted nincompoop."

"Ah, yes, the phylogenetic tree," Steiner exclaimed,

170

lofting his proboscis eloquently. As usual, it was hard to tell whose side the man was on, or if, in fact, he ever belonged to any side. Homo sapiens in general seemed to furnish him great funds of interest and entertainment, whatever their persuasion–religious, political, or otherwise. "We don't see it around much anymore, do we?"

"No, we really don't," I acknowledged. "The good old phylogenetic tree seems to have become as extinct as the creatures it depicts. Even the most ardent evolutionists have come to realize that it needs a lot of qualification."

We went on to discuss some of the immense gaps in the so-called fossil record, still as wide as ever after a hundred and thirty years of searching, and some of the fantastic hoaxes that had been perpetrated when it came to the "missing links" in man's alleged biological history. Dare himself was surprisingly well informed in that regard, having written a research paper on the subject in one of his freshman English classes. "A lot of those 'missing links'– or whatever you want to call them," he said, "have turned out to be nothing but hogwash." I was slightly taken aback at his outspokenness, but he went on to make the point rather effectively.

"Some of them are complete hoaxes," he continued. "Guys having lots of fun making fools out of the experts."

"Piltdown Man!" Steiner said.

"Yeah, right on–exactly!" Dare finished his shake. "Turns out Piltdown Man was the head of an ape! Some joker had filed the teeth down, then stained them with potassium permanganate or something so they'd look real old. Then they buried it in this gravel pit where some of those guys were digging." The whole idea caused us considerable merriment.

"Then there was Java Man," Dare continued. "That one turned out to be a chimp." He frowned, grinning. "Or maybe it was a gibbon–one or the other."

"And wasn't there one based on nothing but a *tooth*?" Geraldo inquired.

"Nebraska Man," Dare said.

"Yeah, I guess that was it." Geraldo favored us with a wolfish grin. "Not only did they create an entire prehistoric man on the basis of a single tooth but also his wife and family as well."

"No!" Steiner guffawed.

"Seriously," I said. "It's the truth. I think, in fact, that it finally proved to be a pig's tooth—a prehistoric pig."

More laughter. "Now that's what I call a grand leap of faith," Steiner enthused. "*That* I admire! Forget all this wishy-washy temporizing stuff called verification."

We went on to discuss fairly recent "finds" which had little more to support them, and the fact that modern evolutionists had been compelled to reject the gradual change theory expounded by Darwin. "Man, they've *had* to!" Dare said, starting to work on another burger. "Now they're talking about these big genetic leaps instead of the old gradual transition theory. Nobody knows how these supposed leaps took place, but they've had to trump up something to fill in all those humongous gaps. So now everything's just started leaping."

"Right!" Steiner said. "That's how we got all those jackrabbits and kangaroos, in fact!" And that broke us up again.

After reflecting on this earlier conversation, I considered, for a time, the many things that for me personally, and for quite a few others, simply didn't support the evolutionary theory. For one thing, evolution would never explain the magnificent color patterning in a bird like a cock pheasant, a mallard drake, or a peacock; or, indeed, its astounding uniformity within a given species. Then I recalled again Steiner's final words on the subject and began to chortle.

"Hey, Pop," a sleepy voice drifted, "what's goin' on?"

"Oh, nothing," I said. "I just got to thinking about all those rabbits and kangaroos."

"Yeeaahhh," he sighed. It ended in a snort of amusement. I could feel the mirth surfacing through his mantle of sleep, but he was too groggy to give it full play. Besides, he already knew that I was a bit crazy, that I had a habit, in fact, of awakening from a dead sleep laughing about things that often seemed only mildly funny in the saner light of day.

27

I awakened the next morning (in the saner light of day) still convinced that the idea was pretty humorous, thinking also that I'd be leaving on the morrow.

"That will put me back the evening of the twenty-second," I said, "with only two days left till Christmas." Dare and I were breakfasting on canned pears and cracked-wheat toast with peanut butter and raspberry jelly. "Your mater has attended to most of the shopping as usual, but I'd better be on hand to help her in the final crunch." I glanced at him and took another bite of my toast. "Really hate to leave, old buddy. Truly has been great."

"Yeah, it has," Dare replied. "Really somethin' else. *But* . . . " he sounded reluctant. "It's about time, I guess. Elder Begay will probably be back in a few days, from what the pres was saying." He shrugged, chewed, squinted meditatively. "Till then, I can just hang out with Mac and Hud like before."

"Good," I said, "I'd hate to have you getting into mischief."

"We've already got invites out for dinner Christmas and New Year's, and the stake's throwin' a big New Year's Eve party."

"I'm glad," I said and felt happy that he wouldn't be

lonely, that also he had never suffered much homesickness. That would make the departure easier for a dad who would definitely be a bit "homesick" for him.

Half an hour later, we were out calling on members who had promised to provide us with some referrals, and at noon we returned to the apartment for lunch feeling rather pleased with the results. One good sister, wife of the first counselor in the ward bishopric, had provided us with three different names. We had also gleaned two more as a result of several other visits. "Not a bad morning," I said.

"Yeah, well worth the effort," Dare replied. He had just opened the mailbox to find it literally overflowing with letters and Christmas cards. "Hey-hey-hey! Feast your eyes, Pop—hit the jackpot again!"

"Sure looks like it," I said, thinking how much mail had meant on my own mission and later during my army days in Japan. Among the offerings was a letter to both of us addressed in Sally Girl's familiar spidery hand, cards from members and missionaries in the field and a pal or two in Ogden. There was also one from Cindy Stewart.

"Hey, hey!" Dare wafted it before my nose. "Passionate, perfumed purple!"

I chuckled. "You'd better let the old man review it first to see if it needs censoring. Can't allow anything too passionate while you're still on call."

"Naw, I can handle it," he said, "my strength is as the strength of ten. Know what I mean, Vern?" The final sentence was a perfect imitation of Jim Varney and his TV ads extolling the joys of various dairy products.

"Okay," I laughed, "if you're really positive. I'll just go ahead and read this one to both of us from my own special girlfriend while you're otherwise occupied. Know what I mean, Vern?"

Dare grinned knowingly, tossing his head. "Yea, verily, brothah!"

The letter from my wife was a long one, happily recounting a trip she had taken with our two youngest daughters and several grandchildren to Christmas Village in downtown Ogden, hot cider, donuts, and stories afterward beside the living room fireplace. A great lover of tradition, my wife, Sally–a girl of the hearth. And few things delighted her more than reading to her progeny. Always very animatedly and interpretively, having majored in drama in college and starred in several movies produced by the Church. Often she would go on and on, face glowing, sometimes continuing long after her most ardent listeners, including the dog, had succumbed to Morpheus.

"Well!" I stretched and yawned with pleasure at the conclusion. "Another of your mother's wonderful epistles." I truly meant it, but Dare failed to hear me. He was reading from the passionate purple stationery, but his face hardly mirrored my own satisfaction. His brow was deeply knit, his gaze frustrated and perplexed like someone with dyslexia.

"Something wrong?" I inquired.

Momentarily, there was no response. "Yeah . . . " he said at last. He was staring at the letter as though hypnotized, baffled, shocked, incredulous, oddly amused. "Pop, I've been Dear *Johnned!*"

"Naw," I said, dragging the word out with disbelief. "You've got to be kidding!"

He shook his head slowly, closed his eyes for an instant, inhaled through narrowed nostrils. "I kid you not. I've just been knifed in the neck, dumped like a bag of garbage."

"I'll be hornswoggled. What a revolting development!" I wasn't joking in the least.

"Revolting is right." Again he shook his head and closed his eyes. "Like getting zapped with a laser. Here, you wanna read the crummy thing?" He flipped the pages onto the table before me and they fluttered apart like dying butterflies.

I looked at him. "Why sure, if you really want me to. I don't want to be snooping into your private problems."

"No, that's fine, Pop. Go ahead and read it–tell me I'm just having some wild hallucination or something."

176

I nodded a little. "Okay." Then I began to read:

"Dear Darren: . . . " That in and of itself might have been a slight warning. To my knowledge, she had always called him "Dare" before, both in writing and in the flesh. "I really don't know how to begin this letter . . . " Even more suspicious. Sinister. I was empathizing strongly already, for even though I had never received a bona fide "Dear John" on my own mission, I had at one point been treated to a reasonable facsimile—the next best (worst) thing. In addition, I had suffered a few painful affairs of the heart back in my youth. So long ago, and yet so recent. "But I guess the only fair and honest thing to do is come right out and say it." Fair and honest? The little A-bomb from out of nowhere, without the faintest foreshadowing, right amid all the moonlight and roses. I was relating very strongly, feeling much of my son's own resentment and disillusionment. "I'm engaged." *Engaged!* Whammo!

Well, that was certainly laying it on the line—nice and direct, like a bludgeon. But, of course, I was and am a biased father. Maybe that really was the kindest way it could be handled, a bit like extracting a loose tooth via the old string-door-slam method instead of much protracted worrying and wiggling. It was simply that he hadn't ever been accorded the faintest notion that an extraction was necessary. Or had he? Reflecting back on our last conversation about Cindy Stewart, I wondered. Maybe the subtle clues had all been there before, merely rejected as a part of his natural protective mechanism. All these impressions flitted through my mind in seconds, like a swirl of bats.

"I'm sure you're wondering, Dare, why I haven't said anything before, and just tossed the whole thing at you out of the blue this way. Well, I don't know if I can ever give you a complete answer, and I'm positive (looking at it from your standpoint) that it can't be a good one. But, here's the thing. I really do think the world of you, Dare, and I still love you a whole lot. In fact, you're one of the neatest guys a girl could ever meet up with. I honestly mean that."

Very politic, a little kindly anesthesia before the big *coup de grace*. Simultaneously, another part of me was being won over a bit. Maybe the girl had somehow gotten herself into a tough dilemma without intending to and was now doing the best she knew how to explain. Her next words tended to confirm that thought, at least in some small measure.

"So, okay—here's what happened as straight and honest as I can tell it. About two months ago I wound up in a psych class at Weber with this guy I know named Jack Sorenson. We used to date a fair amount before I started going with you. Then he went on a mission to Australia. We didn't have any commitment or anything. Jack knew I'd be going out and even told me to, just said to write him once in a while.

"And that's the way it was. All the time you and I were together, I really thought Jack was history, even though I liked him a lot. I wasn't playing games, Dare, I promise. But that first day in class when he just walked in out of nowhere and sat down by me . . . I can't explain it. The only thing I can tell you is that for some reason, all the old feelings started coming back for both of us, but about five times as strong.

"That evening Jack asked me for a date, but I told him that I was waiting for you. He's not sure whether you know him, by the way, but he remembers you from Ogden High, what a great runner you were and everything, says you're a really fine guy." Cold comfort. Great runner, fine guy, big-time loser—the guy who gets dumped. "Well, Jack said okay, that he understood, and wouldn't interfere. That was the plan, Dare—the very best of intentions. Yet somehow it didn't work out that way. Maybe, to be as honest as possible, our big mistake was sitting next to each other in class, because every single day the feelings got stronger. Then . . . " I could almost hear a little feminine sigh of distress at having to relate the truth in all its harshness, at having to hurt him. "Well, then we started studying together over in the library and sometimes having lunch in the UB, never really admitting that things were getting more serious. Always telling ourselves we weren't really dating.

"And at the very same time, Dare, I was always reminding myself, 'Hey I've got this terrific missionary down in Arizona I've promised to wait for, somebody I love and respect in a real big way.' So that's why, when things kept getting more serious with Jack, when he started dropping by the house and everything, that I just didn't know what to do. I was in this great big dilemma, and I didn't say anything to you about it till now because I truly didn't know my own mind and heart. Besides that, I kept telling myself that I didn't want to worry you about something that might never happen. 'Dare's going to be home in a couple of months,' I kept telling myself, 'and the very least I can do for *both* of us is to hang in until he gets here so we can see each other face to face and talk things out.'

"I kept telling Jack that same thing, and he even agreed. In fact, he even said it was the only fair thing. He's really a terrific person, Dare, and I know you'd like him, just as much as he likes you, if you ever got acquainted." I found myself smiling, or maybe grimacing, inwardly at the innocent irony of it all. Telling my son how well he'd like the oh-so-wonderful fellow who has just aced him out in the romance department, taken the very girl Dare had wanted forever. Kindly, understandingly, accommodatingly taken him to the cleaners.

"But this past week, and again I don't know how to say it. (Can anybody ever say these things the *right* way???) It's just that we both suddenly realized that we can't stand being away from each other, and that we have just about everything in the world in common, including our religion." And that made me wonder whether the girl was implying that she and my son "only" had their religion in common.

"So finally, the other night, Jack just came right out and said he was madly in love with me, and that if I had any question about where the relationship was headed,

179

we'd better do a lot of fasting and praying about it. That's what we both did, Dare, and I think I have my answer."

And, I thought wryly, constantly relating to my son's immediate frame of reference, *it sure ain't you.* But perhaps I was being unkind, even irreverent. Maybe the two of them had indeed received an answer, and if so . . . Of course, that might be the big question in Dare's mind. Even my own. Was it really an answer, or just believing what they wanted to believe in the height of romantic emotion?

Well, who was I to judge? Very possibly they were making exactly the right move. It was fairly apparent, in any case, that what had happened was not the result of some cunning scheme to undermine my boy or from a desire to be unfair or unkind. Rather, it was simply a part of the time-honored pattern, a way of life, an inevitable element in the endlessly growing missionary experience.

The letter continued for another page or so full of regret that she had to hurt him, begging his understanding and forgiveness, insisting that she would always love and respect him, that she hoped they could remain friends (!). It concluded by stating that she knew there was "someone very special out there—the ideal girl for you" and that they'd both know it when the time came, just as she and Jack Sorenson had.

Yes, yes, probably he would. I felt the morose inner smile. Irony. Resignation. It was not only a part of the time-honored pattern—it was the connubial law of the jungle. Maybe, the thought fluttered, maybe some enterprising soul would one day assemble a whole book of such letters and simply entitle the entire collection *Dear John.* You think of things like that once you've succumbed to the writing virus—sometimes at moments otherwise inappropriate.

For a time Dare had been sitting beside me on the couch, leaning forward, elbows on knees, chin in hands, staring bleakly at the floor. Now he was up, pacing about the little apartment, back and forth from the front room to the kitchenette, and occasionally the bedroom. "Well," I said quietly, "That's a tough one, very tough indeed." I couldn't think of a single thing to add at the moment that wouldn't be trite or preachy.

His eyes were the slightest bit red, but I knew for certain that he wasn't going to compromise his manhood by being a boob about it or humiliate himself by bawling. Nor was he going to allow the "fickle female" who had betrayed him the "satisfaction" (even though she would never really know his reactions at that crucial moment) of learning how much he was hurting.

"It's not much comfort," I hazarded, "but at least you aren't alone. It almost seems to come with the territory."

"Yep," he muttered, tight-lipped, "that it does, my man, that it does."

Arising, I headed for the kitchen to get a drink and clapped his shoulder in passing, far closer suddenly to bawling myself than he seemed to be. "Anything we can do? Take a drive, a long walk?"

"A long *jog*," he replied. "Get on your sweats, Pop." For an instant, he seemed almost playful.

"Sounds good," I said. In fact, I could think of nothing better for the moment. "Just don't run the old man into the ground."

Minutes later we had donned our jogging attire, Dare in royal purple with white letters across the chest reading Weber State, and white stripes down the side of each leg. That, plus his white Nikes, made him look pretty cool and, of itself, had to be something of a morale booster. His dad, on the other hand, was sporting some ancient gray specimens that went back years beyond recollection. They were growing threadbare and bagged somewhat at the knees, but I kept them for sentimental reasons, my "security blanket" sweats.

Anyway, as the saying goes, he led me on a merry chase, or it would have been if we were feeling merrier. We jogged up the sidewalk along a nearby avenue until we reached the downtown campus mentioned earlier—trotting

181

our way along broad walkways bordered by parched sands decorated with tumbleweeds, cacti, puncture weed, and an occasional golden sunflower. Along a broad diagonal path toward the facades of immense buildings, passing between strips of green lawn and columns of palm trees topped by their distinctive headdress of fronds. We then entered a residential area beyond, eventually wending our way through the parking lot of a large shopping mall.

On and on for the better part of an hour. The young Elder Connors was running his heavy heart out and literally would have run my own out, had I not been in pretty good shape. Even at that, he was making his pater familias sweat heavily toward the end, perspiration so much on my balding, freckled dome that I had to slick the dampness off with the palm of my hand at times to keep it from bathing my eyes and half-blinding me. Large damp splotches were forming under my armpits and across my back, and I was trailing him by nearly half a block as we approached our apartment.

As we entered the living room I heaved a great "poooffff!" and mopped my brow with the back of one hand. Dare headed for the sink, bending over it and craning his neck to drink long and deep directly from the tap. He rarely bothered with glasses when he was thirsty. I pulled off my saturated sweatshirt with difficulty, thinking that I should have listened to the old bod more carefully, not permitted my pride to push it quite so long and hard in all that heat. "Well?" I said. "Any help?"

He was now sluicing his face and neck from the same tap. "The run or the drink?"

"The former," I replied.

Dare mopped his face with his hands, blinked, shrugged. "Yeah, I reckon. Anything's better than sitting around on your duff."

"Yes," I said. "That's very true." I hesitated. "Care to go for a drive somewhere? Just to get away from it all? I'm sure the president would understand."

"No, I don't think so, Pop. Thanks just the same, but let's just get out and do the work." A slight grin, and game little wink. "That's what we're here for, right?"

"Yea, verily," I said.

28

We prayed together before leaving the apartment, and I asked for blessings upon my son in his present trial, for both of us that we might accomplish something of special significance in our remaining time together, that his final weeks in the field might somehow become the highlight of his entire mission.

"Thanks, Pop," Dare said.

"You're welcome," I replied. Then after a momentary pause: "So what's on the agenda? Need to visit some of your missionaries?" We had been working pretty hard together, accomplishing quite a bit, but I had also begun to fear that I might be interfering with his work among the Elders in his zone.

"Naw, maybe a little tracting for now," he said, "but I do need to visit the boys right away. Tonight I've got to make a bunch of calls and start following through on some zone conference assignments for next month."

Two hours of tracting followed, all futile. After that, we decided to check back on more members who had promised to find us some investigators. Several, however, were not at home, and the two we visited, both good Sisters in the ward Relief Society, had nothing to suggest. Apologetically, they confessed that they had been engrossed in so many other activities that they had allowed the appointed date to slip by without realizing it. It was understandable, considering the myriad responsibilities they undoubtedly faced, and we could hardly afford to be critical. Nor did we wish to be coercive, though admittedly it is sometimes tricky business walking the fine line between exhortation and encouragement on the one side and arm-twisting on the other.

Our final visit, however, produced some gratifying results—an unexpected first discussion with a young couple by the name of Martin. The husband, a superbly built fellow named Al, was a member of the Church. A former gymnast, he now made part of his living as a movie stuntman, the rest in real estate. His wife, Shauna, was indeed "golden," the very personification of the word. She even looked golden from the glowing tones of her skin to the abundant flaxen hair that flowed almost to her waist. And her emerald-colored eyes, much like Sally Girl's, provided a beautiful contrast.

Shauna Martin was one of those people who, in effect, had been a Latter-day Saint for her entire life and simply had not realized it. Not aware that the gospel had indeed been restored. Now she had found her priceless pearl, religiously speaking, and a husband who admirably exemplified it simultaneously. The lesson went perfectly (another of those rare experiences that some missionaries only dream of) and concluded with plans for a baptism two weeks hence. The Martins hoped to be sealed in the Mesa Temple exactly one year later, the earliest date possible.

All during our discussion, however, I kept glancing at Dare. I was certain that he was feeling some very mixed emotions, especially in light of what we had learned about their relationship earlier. We had called on Al briefly one evening the week before, while Shauna was visiting her family in Colorado. A bit shyly, yet with obvious pride, he had shown us a page from her most recent letter. It was one of literal rejoicing over the fact that she had finally found what she'd been searching for during her entire life, and it included the most profound expressions of incredulity and gratitude because her husband loved her so much he wanted to "seal our relationship in the house of the Lord forever—for ETERNITY!" The conclusion read as follows: "Al, darling, it's been great being here with my family, and I'm trying to plant a few seeds, even though it's not exactly easy. But, I just miss you so much I can hardly stand it. Sometimes I still keep thinking—I mean literally—I'll wake up and find it's all a dream. But it's *not* a dream is it? It's the best of all worlds. I just hope and pray about twenty times a day, and every time I wake up in the night, that I'll be worthy of such blessings."

It is rather easy to remember something like that almost verbatim for me now as I write, and for Dare as well, no doubt, perhaps at any time. He was reflecting upon it, in fact, as we drove home after our lesson. "Some lady, isn't she?" he said.

"She is indeed," I replied. "Just a terrific young couple."

"Remember that letter of hers?"

"How could I forget?" I said.

"Pretty amazing how different two letters can be, isn't it?" he mused after a moment. "How they can change your whole life, up or down, in just a few words."

"Yes," I replied. He said no more on the subject. That was all he would allow himself by way of self-pity, at least openly, for the present.

"Well, as I said before," I continued, "even though it might sound like cold comfort, you're not alone. And sometimes that means more than we might realize when we're right there in the big storm." No reply. He simply pursed his lips, sort of flickered his eyebrows, a facial shrug. "I remember Brigham Young once saying that there never was a time when there were not worlds without people on them undergoing the same basic experiences that we are now." I paused, hoping I wasn't pushing it, getting too philosophical at the wrong time. "Believe that?"

He was driving fairly fast, a bit too fast, but watching the road with his twenty-twenty vision. This time, his

186

shoulders shrugged along with the eyebrows, but there was something positive about it. "Checks," he said.

"Brother Brigham was talking about people who had been through the wringer, a lot of them, and I remember that he also told them something like, 'You can't comprehend that now, but when you do it will be a great source of consolation to you.'" In my own view, it was an absolutely magnificent concept, something the world knew nothing about, but I refrained from elaborating at the moment. Dare nodded, looked knowing and even slightly amused—amused with himself, possibly. "Dear Johns and all?"

I could not restrain the laughter. "Undoubtedly, in my opinion; I suspect that Dear Johns are an integral part of the grand eternal scheme." A yellow taxi nosed in front of us, causing Dare to brake sharply and mutter a mild insult. Rough roads and hazardous driving also seemed to be a part of that scheme. "Who knows, old boy, you may go home and one fine day find a terrific young girl who will end up writing a letter to some poor missionary off in Timbuktu or some place. 'Dear Harold: I don't quite know how to tell you this, but I've just come across this wonderful guy named Darren Connors.'"

He snorted. "Not likely."

"Don't be too sure, my friend—in fact, I'll lay fifty-fifty odds right now." We were both smiling. Humor definitely was and is a saving grace. "And just think of your bro John over in Japan. Every single letter he *got* was a 'Dear John.'"

He snorted another laugh. "Aw, Pop—you're a blast."

"Back on my own mission," I continued, "I got *three* Dear Johns."

"Yeah?" He was waiting for the joke. "And I'm sure all of them had agreed to wait the duration, right?"

"Oh sure—most definitely."

"So what if they all had?"

"That's a good question—guess I was hoping for a return to plural marriage." I paused, watching traffic drift by like the passage of time. "No, I wasn't *quite* that fickle.

No real commitments with anybody, but I did have three or four young ladies I liked a lot, sort of viewed as prospects, you might say. But then—one by one!"

He gave a quiet laugh. "One by one!"

"Yep, that was the story. They *all* gave me the fond and fatal farewell." Once more I was back there forty years in Canada. "There was a popular song going around in those days that really applied to a lot of us: 'So long, it's been good to know ya . . .'" The stake center was coming up, red-brick, the traditional LDS architecture, simple yet graceful lines, the single spire, and (for Arizona) an abundance of green lawn.

"So, no," I admitted. "I don't *really* know what it's like, because there was never an actual commitment with anybody. I had agreed with myself before I ever left that they all might have gone by the way before I made it back to Zion." And then I saw her face—heart shaped, framed by short black hair, large eyes a dark brown yet light-filled, like syrup in the bottle. For a few seconds, I was way back there, the ardent youth of twenty in North Bay, Ontario. "Lovely little girl named Carol who looked a bit Hispanic. We had actually been 'going steady,' as they used to call it, for two or three months before my mission. Then, by mutual agreement, we broke it off. But, even so . . . "

"Yeah, even so." He tossed me an amused glance of comprehension.

We had turned down W. Eugie, heading for the apartment, so there wasn't much time to reminisce. "I kept thinking about her, anyway, even though we didn't write much . . . carried her picture in my wallet for old time's sake or something. Then, along toward the end of my mission, I got to thinking it might be a nice idea to resurrect things. So I wrote her a long, sort of romantic letter—a little on the mushy side, to tell the truth—recalling some of those old times, suggesting we at least ought to have a visit when I returned. I was just egotistical enough, in fact, to imagine that I was doing her a kind of favor since it had been my idea, initially, to break things off."

188

Dare tossed me another glance. "So what happened?"

A short burst of laughter on my part. "The very next week, the very next *week*, I got a letter from my sister Penny with a clipping from the *Standard Examiner* society section. One Carol Tolman, my former steady, had just gotten married!"

"You're kidding!" Precisely my own response upon reading his Dear John.

"Nope—not at all. And get this—to one of my old high school buddies."

"Ha! That's too much!"

I laughed. "That's what *I* thought, and I never should have told my companion, because he showed no mercy and wouldn't let me live it down for a couple of weeks." We had pulled into our parking stall by the dun-colored dumpster. Sparrows were twittering, and we could smell the fragrance of peach-colored roses against a cinder block wall. "But, I got back at him. About a month later, he was hit with a *real* Dear John from a girl he'd planned to marry right after his return. And that—that nearly put him under."

"I believe it," Dare said, with a little more passion than he perhaps realized.

"He'd kept a picture of her on the bureau in our bedroom. Swimsuit special, sitting on the pontoon of a catamaran on some lake shore. She really was a good-looking girl, but after a while when I saw how down he was, I tried to convince him that she had thick ankles, and I kept at it until he finally sort of believed me."

Dare chuckled and shook his head.

"Every time he'd start looking glum, I'd catch his eye and say, 'Old Thick Ankles.' And he'd start to laugh in spite of himself. Eventually, in fact, he started calling her Old Thick Ankles himself.

"It didn't exactly solve the problem," I said, "but it definitely helped a little."

"Yeah," Dare sighed, his smile slowly evaporating. "But you never could convince me of anything like that with Cindy. She was a perfect ten—looks, personality, and everything else." He opened the door. "At least, that's what I thought up until about four hours ago."

29

It was 8:30 P.M., following a late supper—still the fateful "DJ" Day, better known as "Dear John" Day—and we were preparing to leave for a meeting with an elderly couple to whom we had given a copy of the Book of Mormon a few days earlier. The phone rang just as we were going out of the door, and Dare answered. "LDS missionaries." Glancing at his face, I suddenly had a wild impression, a childish hope, whatever, as if I were inside my son's own mind: a call from Cindy Stewart in Ogden, saying that she had made a bad mistake and wanted to keep their love afloat after all. Even mature adults snatch at wisps of that kind occasionally, no matter how far-fetched they may appear in the light of objectivity. Men condemned to death even experience it in the final moments of life, suddenly convincing themselves that some fantastic form of deliverance is nigh. It is known to psychologists as "the delusion of reprieve."

"Oh, hi, Sister Keller," Dare said. The delusion of reprieve was over, and the initial look of expectation that he had barely disguised (or was it all just a bit of foolish fatherly imagination?) transformed to mere pleasantry. "Oh, really?" There was a long pause. The smile became a frown. "Melana Gardner, huh?" Another wait. "Hmmm . . .

really down again. That's too bad." I waited in the doorway, watching, as he squinched up his mouth, nodded periodically, looking increasingly somber. He was wearing a paisley, purple and red tie that seemed a bit incongruous.

"Yeah, that's why we went to visit her the other day." Long pause. "No kiddin'. Hmmm, that husband—former husband, whatever—has got to be one of the world's champion flakes. Yeah, a first-class weirdo." He waited, bobbing his head a little, shifting his stance, left hand on his hip, occasionally sitting back on the edge of the table, mashing one of his Christmas presents slightly. "Okay, sure enough. We'll be there." Then he hung up, glance tracing across the room to meet my own.

"More problems with Melana, I take it," I said.

"Yep. That sicko husband is still giving her a bad time, driving her out of her tree." I clucked my tongue and actually seemed to feel a sour taste in the mouth. "So now she's talking about ending it all again. Wants us to come give her a blessing in the morning."

"Ah, me," I sighed. "What a sad state of affairs. Maybe we should alert the Pedersons so they know what's going on."

"Sister K. already has."

"Okay, good. I wish Melana would go stay with them for a while, the way we suggested."

Dare and I had been home from our investigator meeting for more than two hours, had talked for some time about Cindy Stewart and love's labors lost, then a bit about life in general. So far, despite all the hurt, he was handling the situation admirably. After that, we had gone to bed, and he was sleeping more soundly than I had dared hope, so soundly that he never heard the phone ringing. Groping my way into the front room, I picked up the receiver. "Hello," I said a bit groggily, "LDS Missionaries."

"Nathan?" The voice sounded faint and muffled as though coming long distance with a bad connection.

For an instant I thought it was Sally and felt a slight

sense of alarm. "Hi," I said, resisting appending one of my favorite pet names—Sweetheart, Babe, Angel, Doll, and so forth—thanks to some faint sense of uncertainty. "Is everything all right?"

Nothing but the humming silence. "Hello?" More silence. "*Hehhh-lo!*" I dragged it out, stressing both syllables in a slight sing-song. No answer. Again the hello with the same, even stronger, intonation.

Eventually I heard the faintest sigh or gasp. Maybe even a sob. Somebody playing jokes? "Hello," I repeated, "who is this?"

"Nathan . . ." The voice had a strange languid quality, almost subliminal yet highly disconcerting. "Nathan . . . I think I'm dying."

Again, muted as though coming through a dense layer of cotton, but I knew who it was with a certainty, and my heart seemed to stumble. There was a long silence appended by a gasp, much like a death rattle. "Dying . . . "

"Dying from what?" I implored. "Is someone trying to *harm* you?"

Suddenly I realized that Dare was standing beside me in his oriole yellow pajamas, one hand coming to rest on my shoulder. "Melana Gardner?" His face was intense, eyes dark and searching. I nodded.

"I just . . . " the voice faltered. "Just wanted to thank you and your . . . wonderful son . . . for all your kindness. And everybody else . . . " It must have been a thirty-second wait but seemed much longer. Nevertheless, I restrained myself from asking more questions for fear of disrupting any further communication. "Thank you and everyone involved with all my . . . " Her voice trailed off into the frailest weeping. "Heart."

That was the last I heard despite more urgent requests, even demands, on my part for added information. And finally: "Hang on, Melana, we're coming." For an instant Dare and I merely stared at each other. "She says she's dying," I told him, "from what, I don't know, but I think maybe she's OD'd on something." I stood up, exploding a long "whew" to ease the pressure. "Let's grab our duds and head out."

Dare nodded. "But it takes half an hour to get there, Pop. Maybe we'd better call the Pedersons; they're only a few minutes away."

"Right," I said, "that's good thinking. Ask them to get there as fast as possible, and they may need to call the paramedics. We'll join them as quick as we can."

Minutes later we were on our way, having talked to Alonzo Pederson and received his full cooperation. The trip that normally took thirty minutes we managed in slightly over twenty, thanks to my son's race car tactics and the fact that there was little traffic at that hour. Exceeding the speed limit, yes, but we honestly felt there was no choice.

As it turned out, in fact, Alonzo's fine old Continental had, for the first time in its history, refused to start, and Genevieve's little Celica was in the body shop because someone had backed into its side door. It was almost as though fate or the forces of darkness had engineered the problem, but the elderly couple refused to be stymied. Setting out on foot under a full moon, they had hiked the winding road up Camelback Mountain for about five hundred yards to reach the castle.

And then another problem: the castle was locked, all entrances—a fact the Pedersons had just ascertained upon our arrival. "So what now?" Gen asked. They were both still breathing hard from their exertions. "Maybe we should have called the police." The thought had entered my mind during my limited phone conversation with Melana, and given the unknowns confronting us, that might have been the wisest course. There was no time to worry about it now, though.

"Tried them *all*?" Dare queried, "garage too?"

"That too," Alonzo said. His profile appeared exceptionally craggy in the contrasting light and shadow.

"Maybe a basement window," I suggested, but we soon discovered that they were all barred. The windows on the main level, on the other hand, were immense, of solid plate glass, and we recoiled at the prospect of shattering one except as a last resort.

"I think we'd better call the fire department right now," Gen said. "The firemen are also our paramedics, and they'll not only know the best way to break in but also how to take care of her."

"Wise idea," I said.

"Alonzo," she continued, "why don't you take Nathan's car and go down home right now to give them a call?"

"All right," he replied, and I handed him the keys. A minute or so later he was on his way, headlights playing out against the winding road below.

It was definitely the right move, but we were still apprehensive and frustrated, not knowing whether Melana was alive or dead and, if the former, whether every second might be crucial. "Maybe we'll just have to break out one of these windows," I said. "Costly, but nothing compared to a human life." With that, I began casting about for a rock or some other solid object.

"Hey, wait a minute, Dad," Dare said. "I've got an idea. See that little window up there?" He gestured. "Right up above where all these vines are growing."

"Yeah," I said a bit dubiously. Growing up the building's facade near the rear was a thick and tangled mass of trumpet vine. In the gathering moonlight we could see the profusion of orange blossoms with their deep, horn-shaped corollas, and we could smell their pungent fragrance. "But whether it will hold or not . . . "

"Well, only one way to find out," Dare replied. "There's got to be some sort of trellis for these vines to cling to." Already he was groping about among the foliage, laying hold of whatever he could beneath it. "Yeah . . . feels pretty solid. Basically just a big wide ladder." With that, he began to struggle upward, grasping the heavy, corded center of the vines like Jack climbing the beanstalk, simultaneously kicking and working for toeholds against the trellis.

"Oh, I hope it's strong enough to hold him," Gen fretted. The moon was shining upon her upturned face, revealing great motherly anxiety.

"Be careful," I warned, knowing that the warning was rather futile. If the trellis or vines collapsed, they would collapse. And in that event, the best I could hope for was to break his fall without breaking myself. He was progressing rapidly in any case, within only a minute or so about halfway to the window. "Dare," I called, "you may need something to knock out one of those panes."

"Got it," came the reply, "my shoe." He had on a pair of rubber-soled loafers that helped him retain a purchase against the trellis, yet were easy to slip off if necessary. Fortunately, he was not wearing his suit. We had both grabbed our casual togs in the interest of time. Again I glanced at Gen, who was clasping her hands and gazing upward, not only at Dare but beyond, it seemed, to the heavens.

One way or another, perhaps with her help, he made it to the top free of mishap, and by the time his hands had grasped the window ledge they were about thirty feet above the ground. "Try the window first," I advised, "in case it's already open."

"Gotcha," came the reply. I could see him groping at the window with one hand, heard him exhale and grunt with exertion. Then, distinctly, the sound of the window sliding up. "Yeah, you were right." Moments later he skirmished his way over the window sill. The last thing I saw were his size twelve loafers flailing slightly in the moonlight a bit like the fins of a scuba diver entering the depths. Another few moments and the window above filled with light. Shortly thereafter, those surrounding the living room were also aglow. Then we were gaining admittance at the front door.

"Maybe she's not even here," Dare said, a thought that hadn't occurred to me. "But there're medicine bottles lying all over the bathroom floor."

I turned to Gen. "Do you know where her bedroom is?"

"No," she said. For the first time in my experience, her round, amiable face was creased with lines, and her white hair seemed slightly electrified. "But I'm sure it's upstairs."

It was in a large room at the hallway's end that we found her—what appeared momentarily merely to be rumpled bedding, but a frail body lay beneath it all, hunched in a fetal position and motionless. Her hair splashed silver-gray across the pillow. The pale lips were waxen and parted as though the final sound from them had been a moan. Her eyes were barely slitted, revealing only the whites.

"Oh, my goodness!" Gen exclaimed, her voice curdled with dismay. "Oh, the poor, dear soul!" Hastening to the bedside, she gently laid a hand upon the pallid brow. Cautiously, she turned the covers down a little, exposing a dark purple dressing gown, so dark that it appeared black.

"Listen for her heart," I advised, feeling a strong sense of dread and sorrow. Spilling from the covers and scattered about upon the carpet were more of the tiny bottles Dare had noticed in her bathroom. Most were tan-colored plastic with prescription labels, their snap-on caps missing. Upon a large night table by her bed was a vase of white roses, several of them turning brown and losing their petals. Next to them was a pitcher of water, half full. An empty glass lay on its side next to it, ready to roll off onto the floor.

"Man, oh man!" Dare lamented. "It looks as if she's downed everything in her medicine cabinet."

"It does indeed." I shook my head.

"I can't hear any heartbeat," Gen lamented, and looked at me entreatingly as though I might refute her.

Taking Melana's wrist in my hand, I felt carefully for the faintest pulse but went unrewarded. Then I pressed my fingertips against her neck just beneath the angle of her jaw, checking the carotid artery. Nothing. In the process, I realized that the phone was there on her bed, half-covered by the pillow. The receiver was off the hook. Had I been the one to hear her final words?

It was a sad thought, and promptly deflected by something else. Leaning against the wall about ten feet away was a stack of paintings, one of which lay on its side and measured about two feet long by eighteen inches wide. For a second I stared, bemused, then I felt my skin writhe. I was looking at the original of our bizarre little Christmas card, the same one other of our missionaries had been receiving as well. The Morass, as I had chosen to call it. But there was no time to worry about it at the moment. By now, Alonzo had returned to announce that the firemen-paramedics were coming, and that he would wait for them below the driveway.

"Gen," I said, "it doesn't look as if there's much hope, but do you know how to give CPR?" I had read a booklet on the subject a few years earlier but was somewhat uncertain about up-to-date procedures.

"I think so," she replied tremulously. "We had some people from the Red Cross come and teach it in Relief Society a while back. They brought along one of those rubber dummies for us to practice on."

"Well, you have the real thing now," I said, then turned to my son. "Let's put her onto the floor, Dare—beds have too much give." I was surprised at Melana's lightness, almost as though we were holding a child, as we moved her from the bed to the carpet, and stretched her out upon her back. Gen tilted her head back, lifting the chin with two fingers to open the airway.

For a few moments Gen leaned over the parted lips, almost touching them with her ear. Then she straightened up, sighing. "No heartbeat and no respiration." For an instant she hesitated, then she began the CPR—four strong, measured breaths mouth-to-mouth before pausing to glance at me uncertainly. "I've forgotten how many chest compressions, but I know it's quite a few," she said.

"Fifteen," Dare told her. "Four mouth-to-mouth then fifteen compressions. That's what they taught us in my scuba diving class." Gen gave a quick nod and proceeded.

But again . . . no sign of life, merely the distant wail of a siren.

Dare had been watching somberly, squinting as if in pain. His white T-shirt was stretched and torn from his struggles up the trellis, and his blond hair was disheveled. "Pop," he said quietly, "I think there's one thing we should do for sure, no matter what." I watched him quizzically. "She asked us to give her a blessing, and I think that's what we should do—even if she's gone to the other side."

Until then I had been so engrossed in a sense of emergency that it had not occurred to me. Now, however, Dare's words seemed very appropriate. "You're right," I replied, "and what have we got to lose?" Simultaneously, I felt my faith diminish as if the depression that had overwhelmed Melana Gardner were contagious.

Meanwhile, Genevieve was repeating the CPR routine, so involved that she failed to respond for a few seconds. Then her face turned my way and she nodded. The siren was coming more loudly. "They're almost here, aren't they?" she said. "You haven't much time."

"Got the oil?" Dare asked.

I nodded and removed the tiny plastic bottle from my pocket, one I had carried with me for years on trips away from home. "Want me to anoint?" he inquired. For a second, I hesitated. As father and senior priesthood bearer, I might have logically assumed the responsibility of sealing which follows the anointing and involves the main blessing. On the other hand, my son was an officially appointed missionary; I myself, merely a self-styled junior companion. Those, however, were not the only considerations. All day, despite the trauma of a Dear John, Darren seemed to have been growing in strength and spirituality, and suddenly I had the distinct conviction that he should be the one.

"Thanks, son," I said, "but I think you should do it."

He looked me in the eye for a second to make certain, then he gave a slight nod. Moments later I anointed the crown of Melana Gardner's head with a tiny drop of oil and by the power of the Melchizedek Priesthood blessed her "to the end that you might be restored." That was the best word I could think of—restored, the only one, in fact, that seemed correct. Yet I must reiterate that my faith at that moment was rather feeble.

Then, the siren keening in the drive below and dying, both of us laid our hands upon Melana's head, and Darren sealed the anointing by the same authority and in the same divine name. The blessing, of necessity, was brief, and his voice quavered at times. I could feel the tears welling among the three of us. Never in Dare's twenty-one years had I sensed such profound humility, and I will never forget his final words. "Melana Gardner . . . if it be our Father's will . . ." There was a long pause. "We summon you, by the authority in us vested, to return to mortality . . . to love and care for your children, who need you greatly." Again his voice broke, and for an instant my eyes flicked open. His cheeks glistened, and the Spirit was suddenly almost resonant. "Who need you so very greatly." Another pause. I could hear voices below. "And to use your marvelous talents as an artist to perform great works . . . unto our Savior, Jesus Christ, in the glorious light of the gospel."

They had ascended the stairs and were coming down the hall as he concluded.

30

The paramedics performed with great efficiency, asking all the right questions. Then they inserted a plastic tube into Melana's trachea, one attached to a small bag that worked like a bellows pumping air into her lungs. One of them, a tall, lanky fellow with a bristling moustache, checked her heart with a cardiac monitor while another gathered the scattered medicine bottles and examined their labels. Watching the green line on the screen, I realized that it was not quite flat, emanating along its length the faintest, slightly irregular vibration.

Meanwhile, one of the paramedics, a short sturdy woman with carrot-colored hair, was conversing via her bio-com phone with the hospital. "Yes, we have a fine V-fib," she said, looking at the screen. "Okay—we'll proceed with the defibrillation." Next they were placing the "paddles" on Melana's chest, circular devices shaped like spotlights and attached by cords to a portable defibrillator. Three shocks were then administered, only seconds apart, and with each one her body was seized with an intense spasm. But there was no change, either with that procedure or with the medications administered intravenously afterward as another means of stimulating heart activity. Nor did a repetition of the entire routine produce any better results.

Thus nothing remained but to transport Melana to the waiting ambulance, and soon we were following its fleeing red lights to the hospital. Dare was driving as usual, and I was next to him, the Pedersons with us in the back seat. "Man, what a wild day!" Dare sighed and shook his head.

"Yes," I replied, "and it's not over yet."

Dare whooshed the air between his lips, looking very solemn. "I dunno, Pop," he said glumly. "Maybe I called it wrong with that blessing. Maybe it was just wishful thinking."

"No, I don't believe that," I replied. "You had the Spirit if anybody did—I could feel it. You said exactly the right thing. If she can't remain here in this life . . . well, it's because the Lord has a special reason for keeping her."

"That's right," Genevieve said.

Dare heaved another sigh, blinking rapidly. "I sure hope so." He angled a glance my way. "I guess you saw the painting?"

I nodded. "Yes—looked as if someone had stomped on it, right in the middle of that main face." Directly in the center of that awful mouth, forever frozen in its combined leer, snarl, and lament—an expression that made my skin crawl merely thinking about it.

"So what's it doing there?" he wondered.

"I'm not sure," I said. I had a theory, something that actually began that night two weeks or so earlier when I was examining the little duplicate postcard. Now was not the time to dwell upon it, though, or even think about it. Time instead for silent prayer.

Already the hospital was looming just ahead—a large, two-story building flanked by palms and slender, conical Italian cypress, the white facade illuminated by spotlights. We continued our pursuit of the ambulance. The siren now silent, it turned left at a half-street, passed along one side of the building, and stopped at a circular drive in the rear. The entrance was clearly marked in gleaming red letters that read: EMERGENCY.

Seconds later Melana was inside one of the small curtain-lined resuscitation rooms, being attended to by the physician on duty and two nurses. Although hospital rules prohibited having anyone but a single next of kin in the same room, Gen was allowed to be there as a kind of surrogate mother. The rest of us were stationed in a nearby waiting room.

It was apparent from what we had been told that they were repeating some of the earlier procedures, and the acoustics were good enough that we—even I, with only one good ear—could hear what was happening. Once a voice warned, "Clear!" meaning, as we had noted earlier, to stand back and avoid getting shocked. Then there was a lurching sound as Melana's body took the charge. The procedure was repeated several times, and at length we heard the doctor saying, "Okay, we're getting a rhythm; let's proceed with the lavage. I knew the general definition—a French term meaning to wash out, with particular reference to a hollow organ.

There followed a long silence, punctuated only by indistinct exchanges, but I could visualize all too clearly what was happening: the insertion of a narrow plastic tube through one nostril, all the way down the throat to her stomach in order to flush out its deadly contents. Dare was pacing restlessly about the waiting room. "Pumping her out?" he asked.

I nodded. "Like the time Robbie drank all that paint when he was only two years old." No further explanation was necessary; that was when we learned about the fine art of lavage. "Luckily, the paint had a latex rather than a lead base or we'd have lost him."

"Life's mighty fragile, isn't it?" Alonzo mused. He was leaning forward, elbows on knees, hands locked together, large hands with knobby joints inflamed from arthritis.

"It is that," Dare replied, and continued his pacing. Then came more waiting for perhaps ten minutes, during which time I was either praying or reflecting upon life's immense fragility, its mind-boggling unpredictability.

Finally, unable to remain seated any longer, I arose and

wandered partway into the emergency room, past the desk with its sleepy looking night clerk, an elderly woman with a narrow face and thick-lensed glasses. Seconds later I heard a voice saying, "It's stopped; we're not getting anything." For a moment I wondered if they meant anything from Melana's stomach. Then I realized that the statement referred to her heart. "Afraid not," another voice said, sounding rather objective, studious. "Nothing—asystole." I knew that word too; it meant that the heart was now completely nonfunctional.

Unable to resist, I approached the curtained room, peered inside, and saw the doctor and nurses bending over Melana's body. Her bare toes projected from beneath the sheet covering her, and somehow the toes themselves seemed very pathetic. As I looked on, the doctor straightened up—a young man with a round, ruddy face and receding hair the same color. He shook his head resignedly, and there was a fine spray of sweat on his brow. "Well—it looks like we've lost her." Gen was sitting there in a chair far enough away to avoid hampering their activity. Her glance shot my way tragically. Tears glistened on her cheeks, and she was wiping her eyes with her fingertips.

For some time they continued to work with Melana, adjusting the tube in her trachea and once again administering shock to a body that now appeared totally lifeless. There was no result whatsoever. The green line on the heart monitor was completely flat. The doctor shook his head, muttered something under his breath, then passed a hand over his sweating brow. "Well," he said, "that's it. Let's call it." He sounded angry, at whom I wasn't sure. Fate perhaps.

At that same instant, Gen's eyes widened in astonishment. "No, no—wait!" We all stared at her, nonplussed. "I saw her toe move—her little toe!" She reached out, touching it. "Right here on her left foot. It sort of trembled!"

"Probably just muscle contractions," one of the nurses said.

"No, no—look!" Her hand withdrew a few inches, poised, the fingertips tremulous as if evoking life. The toes—all but the big one—trembled in what seemed a kind of sympathetic vibration.

"You see?"

"They did, definitely," one of the nurses agreed.

I stood there dumbfounded, but my eyes flashed automatically to the heart monitor. The flat, green line was growing fuzzy and vibrant. Even as I watched, the line began developing little blips—tiny, green stalagmites about a centimeter apart, all flowing along quite steadily. I stared at the doctor. "Spontaneous heartbeat?"

"Yeah," he said, drawing the word out profoundly, squinting in disbelief. "Getting strong!" By now, having heard what was happening, Dare and Alonzo had joined me, peering over my shoulder in wonderment. Melana's breath whistled in the tube within her trachea. The respiratory therapist had begun to disconnect it a short time before, but now she reattached it to the airbag, and Melana's chest commenced to rise and fall. Her eyelids remained closed, her arms and legs inert, yet she was steadily taking on life; her lips, and steadily her entire countenance, acquiring normal color.

A brief time later in the intensive care unit, the tube was removed and Melana continued to breathe on her own. Within a short while, her eyes had opened, and she was able to speak a little. Speak enough to ask for my son. "Darren?" Her eyes were scarcely open as he approached her bed.

"Yeah, I'm right here, Melana," he said as she reached for his hand.

Gradually her eyes opened, exploring his face as if it were a miracle. "I've been away," she sighed. "It was hard coming back." Her eyes closed, and there was a long silence, so long that he became fearful. Then they opened, giving off in his words, "this beautiful kind of silvery light."

The lips moved again, the voice gaining strength. "But I had to, had to come back." Again she drifted, as if each phrase demanded an energy beyond her. "Because of your blessing, Darren. Because it was the Lord's will."

31

It was ten o'clock on December 23, and I was journeying almost due north across the Arizona desert on a brightly sunlit morning, cruising along alone in my little red Chevette. The highway stretched in a long straight line, materializing endlessly through arid dun-colored landscapes occupied by little but mesquite and saguaro cacti. The radio was still tuned to what had become Dare's favorite station, one that featured classical music. At the moment, it was playing strains of Mozart.

December 23 . . . birthday, I recalled, of the Prophet Joseph Smith, only two days from the time we commemorate the greatest birthday of all. I was leaving a full forty-eight hours later than planned, Dare and I having spent much of the preceding day visiting with Melana Gardner at the Pedersons' following her release from the hospital. It was not that she needed supervision; rather, it was simply clear to everyone, Melana especially, that their warm, abiding company would be good for her. Alonzo and Genevieve were old enough to be her parents and were beginning to treat her accordingly without the slightest presumption or fanfare.

It was there that Melana related the details of her own near-death experience, one to rival any of those recorded in the works of Raymond Moody, whom we had discussed earlier. It had been a combination of things that drove her over the brink, as she explained to us afterward. First, a pronounced low in her periodic mood swings. "'In a dark night of the soul,'" she had said, referring to my previous Fitzgerald allusion, "'It is always three o'clock in the morning.'" Melana had merely reached her own "three o'clock" shortly before midnight, at the time we received her call.

At that point, badly demoralized by her husband's fiendish pestering and the growing fear that she might not be granted custody of her children, Melana had begun sorting through the canvasses of her so-called Goya period, all of which were painted in times of despair, quite masochistically on the one hand, but also in the hope of somehow exorcising her misery and the powerful sense of evil that seemed to invade her. Instead, however, the paintings had greatly magnified her problem, both in their earlier creation and their later contemplation.

One of those paintings, above all—completed after the death of her son Lance—had dominated her attention, and she had taken it to her bedroom in a kind of trance almost as though directed by some awesome force beyond herself. The painting, as I had realized earlier, was a self-portrait. It actually symbolized, we learned later, the real and beautiful Melana suffocating under the assault of self-doubt, despair, and malevolence, reflecting, above all, her conviction at the time, that death was the end. Nothing beyond but the great, dark abyss.

It was the same painting we had seen upon her bedroom floor, the central mouth, or whatever it might be, caved in. The same painting that had been replicated photographically on all those sinister little Christmas hate messages: "Death and destruction to all Mormon Missionaries." As her overdose started taking hold, Melana had grown increasingly irrational and had begun hallucinating. For a time she had sat upon her bed, staring at it, both captivated and horrified. Then she had arisen and placed it upon her dresser beside the mirror. Gazing into the mirror, it seemed to her that her face and the painting were becoming one. In a sudden fit of hysteria, she had flung the painting upon the floor, shrieking, and stamped on it.

After that she had turned off the lamp on the nightstand and groped her way into bed, resigned to her fate. Though not quite. Before Melana had fully blanked out, something prompted her to pick up the phone on the night table and dial our number. Mere survival instinct? Prompting of the Spirit? That I can't say. Fortunately, however, the receiver with its numbered buttons was illuminated; otherwise she might never have dialed it. Fortunately also, perhaps miraculously, considering her state of mind, she could remember our number.

Driving across the lonely expanse of desert, I continued to relive our special moments with her that preceding afternoon. Dare and I were on hand, along with our Sister missionaries, in the Pederson living room, and Melana was sitting beside the grand piano with its little white-flocked Christmas tree and skeins of twinkling colored lights. Her attire, in fact, blended well with that of the tree—white slacks and blouse, small red earrings. She was smiling sweetly with that lovely light in her eyes. "So I'm here today to tell you . . . " She paused for a moment, and her words were quiet, measured, and even cautious, yet somehow beautifully assured. "To confirm all you have taught me. The spirit world is very close . . . and very real—right here with us—and that our loved ones are there waiting." The silver-gray eyes glistened. "Because I met many of my own there, including all four grandparents . . . and my son Lance."

For a moment, she pressed her hands to her sternum. As she had told us earlier, her chest and entire torso ached from the rigorous CPR treatment. "They all told me not to worry about them because they were engaged in important undertakings, learning and growing, and remarkably *happy*." For a few seconds, she closed her eyes as though drifting into the veil. "And it was so *beautiful* there—trees and flowers that I've never seen before, so alive that it seemed as if they could see and hear you, feel your touch.

And the colors! There's no way I can duplicate them on canvas, but . . . " She looked directly at me for an instant and smiled as though we shared a special secret. "But my painting with sunlight techniques sort of gets at some of the texture and blending."

I nodded. "And were your son's eyes as blue as those in the portrait you made?"

"Yes, yes!" The thought seemed to enthrall her. "Bluer than the bluest sky or lake, blue as sparks from an emery wheel."

"And he actually talked to you?" Gen asked gently.

Melana nodded, half closing her eyes in recollection, and even if she had said nothing further, her expression itself would have confirmed the reality of that experience for me. It was the kind one only sees upon the faces of certain sensitive, adoring mothers. The kind I had often seen on my wife's face.

"And I'll never, never forget how he put his arms around me, then took my hands and looked into my eyes." She paused briefly, biting her lips, fighting back the tears. "And spoke to me." Another pause. "'Lanie,' he told me— that was always his special pet name for me—almost as if he were the dad at times, and I the little girl. 'Lanie, we'd all love to keep you here with us more than you'll ever dream, and I know how much you want to stay.' And oh, how right he was! Already, I had fallen so in *love* with the place—the richness of it all, the *serenity*, the sense of hope and purpose!"

She shook her head, nonplussed. "The *love!*" The entire thing is simply indescribable; it really can't be expressed in words. But here's what Lance told me: 'Lanie . . . we know you want to stay, but some tremendous challenges and opportunities remain for you in mortality. Things that will truly help you realize your destiny.' Then he went on to tell me that his father would have to undergo many painful trials, perhaps even in the next life, because of his personality and attitudes, but that I didn't have to worry about Aaron and Amber, that they would be entrusted to me fairly soon."

We sat in silence for a time, pondering the matter, all of us convinced, I'm sure, that no comment from anyone at the moment could be fully appropriate. "And I knew that he spoke the truth," she continued, "because I was only a short distance from my body when I received the blessing." She glanced at me, then lingeringly at Darren with the same smile that had graced her face as she spoke of her own son. "So . . . " she smiled a bit helplessly, a bit mischievously. "I came *back*! And you'd better watch out!" Her eyes shifted, glancing about the room as if she expected to see others there. "I came back because of my children, yes, and because the Lord has a mission for me here in this life. Exactly what it is I don't know, but I'll find out. I'll know."

"I'm sure you will," Alonzo said.

"I hope this isn't too personal," Sister Bronson said. Her bright, cheery face looked uncertain, a bit importunate. "But—well, did you actually encounter a being of light?"

Melana shook her head slowly. "No, but it seemed as though I felt . . . oh, how can I describe it? A presence. As if at any moment, someone magnificent might be there in our midst." Again her eyes scanned the room, lifting toward the ceiling. Each time she did so, I could almost feel the veil dissolving. "Yet in another sense, they were *all* beings of light. My son, grandparents, other relatives and friends. Their faces, in fact, their entire bodies seemed radiant, like . . . " She held out her hands and gave a little smile, almost a grimace, of frustration. "Again, mere words just don't do it." She squinted. "Have you ever seen the glow—well, of course you have—of a holiday sparkler? It was almost like that with the people I met over there. It even hurts my eyes a little just remembering. And yet, it didn't hurt the eyes of my spirit, if that makes any sense."

"Makes perfect sense," I said.

Melana's spirit had apparently been absent from her body for nearly an hour—from the time of its departure in her room until she re-entered it in the hospital, where she had actually seen the medical personnel at work upon her prostrate form and heard the doctor say, "Let's call it," in effect pronouncing her dead. And she told us many other things about the other side, all of which I exhorted her to record soon in her journal. Indeed, also to commence writing her personal history promptly, because I had the strong conviction that she would acquire great enlightenment in the process, and that the undertaking would prove therapeutic. "Just don't dwell on the negative aspects too much," I cautioned. I definitely did not want another *Morass*, this time in a verbal form. "Just be guided by what truly feels right, and pray often for the Spirit."

"That's sound advice," she said. "Thank you."

"There's one thing I have to ask, though," I added. It was a question about which I felt hesitant, and yet a clear answer seemed imperative. "It's about the painting . . . Are you aware that some of our missionaries have been receiving post card versions of it in the mail?" Melana stared at me, her face a total blank. "Each one with little hate messages?"

Her eyes were riddled with disbelief. "Hate messages?" I nodded. "What did they say?"

"'Death and destruction to Mormon Missionaries,'" Dare replied. He also appeared reluctant, and for a moment it appeared that she might faint. Then her face began filling with comprehension. "Oh, no! Oh, that *mad* man!" We all stared at her. "Court—my husband. He must have made a photocopy of it when we were together in Mesa. He often photographs my art before I sell it, in fact." She shook her head slowly, eyes narrowed. "It's just his kind of fiendish prank."

"But *why*?" Sister Keller asked. "What did he hope to accomplish?"

"Nothing practical," Melana replied. She closed her eyes, shaking her head as though the very thought of her former husband were beyond toleration. "He just loves playing these weird, sadistic, little mind games with people—me above all." She was pressing her chest gently with one hand, massaging the back of her neck with the other. "I told Aaron and Amber a while back that I was meeting with the missionaries, and I'm sure Court wormed it out of them. It's his own warped way of protesting. Maybe he even had some notion that people would think I was responsible. He literally abhors the slightest thing I ever do to gain independence, especially in the religious vein, and this breakup has the man insane."

"But how would he get hold of so many of our addresses?" Sister Bronson wondered.

Melana shook her head. "I don't know, but he's diabolically cunning. Maybe he . . ." She shrugged. "He's a wizard with computers, as I said before. Maybe he found some way of tapping into the system at your missionary headquarters. He *has* done it with other organizations; I know that much." She glanced at me. "Like the time he sent letters to all those people in that other firm telling them they were fired."

"Yes," I said, and glanced at Darren. "Be a good idea to check with President Linford and see if there's any way that he might have gotten hold of their computer codes."

"Yeah, right."

"Well, I hope he isn't going to give you any more harassment," Alonzo said.

"Oh, he definitely will," Melana reassured him, "but I'm going to get an answering machine, as Nathan suggested, and not even pick up the phone until I seine out the messages. I may record some of those from Court, just in case I ever need any more legal ammunition."

"Good idea," Alonzo said. "But what about the children? Are they in any kind of danger?"

"Probably not physically," she replied, "or I'd never have left them to complete the present term in school. No, it's all pretty much mental and verbal. Anyway . . . he's lost his grip on me. Not that all my problems have fled, but

I'm a different woman now, believe me. And I'm going to have my children on hand soon; I'm sure of it."

Shortly afterward we were preparing to leave, and I was saying farewell to everyone, thanking the Pedersons for their continuing goodness and generosity, wishing our young Sisters well in their work. Melana followed us out onto the porch and gave Dare a motherly hug, gingerly because of her sore abdomen. "You remind me a great deal of someone else," she said, "someone I just visited on the other side." There was a tear in her eye, and her face filled with love and light.

He looked down at her, chin tucked in, his expression one of great empathy, free of all embarrassment. "You remind me of someone else, too," he said, and he began to smile. "She lives in Ogden, Utah, and has eleven kids." Nearby, several yellow warblers were flitting about a large bird feeder attached to the porch railing. For some reason, that little scene warmed me, generating happiness and hope.

Turning, Melana extended her hand to me in a gesture that was utterly spontaneous yet delightfully graceful and gracious. "I won't forget you, Nathan Connors."

"Nor I you, Melana Gardner," I replied. For a moment, I hesitated, than made the plunge. "There is one final thing I'd better tell you. It started coming to me a little while ago when we were talking about writing your journal and personal history. Now I feel it even more strongly." Her gaze was very intent and sweet; it touched me considerably. "Part, *much*, of your mission here in life is to continue your painting." I glanced at my son. "A fundamental part of your blessing, right?"

"Oh yes," she said. "Absolutely."

"And in addition . . . " I smiled, not wishing to be presumptuous, yet knowing it was essential. "I have some assignments for you."

The eyes widened, the brows arched eloquently. "Really?"

"Yes, really. First of all, to complete *The Phoenix Rising*."

Her face brightened more than ever. "Oh yes, I definitely intend to."

"Good—it's a remarkable creation, full of uplift, and rich in symbolism. And remember my saying I'd try to help you find the personal application?" She nodded. "Do you know what it is now?"

"Maybe," she said cautiously, "but tell me."

"Well, to me it seems very clear indeed." I paused for full effect. "It symbolizes, above all, your new life as you rise in the light of the gospel."

"Yes, oh yes!" Her face was radiant, never more lovely.

"Next . . . " Again the pause. "At least one painting—eventually, perhaps, a whole series—depicting your experiences in the spirit world."

"Oh, my!" She pressed a slender hand to her cheek. "Wow!" For an instant she sounded like a high schooler; I could almost see the girl she had been, say, thirty years before. "You *scare* me!"

I laughed. "Great challenges are always scary." Everyone was listening and smiling, taking it all in. "And third . . . " I had been holding up one finger with each assignment. Now there were three of them, which I playfully shook at her yet intended very seriously. In all the assignments I had given my students at Weber State, my children, or anyone else over the long years, I had never felt a more profound sense of correctness. "And finally—symbolically, straight realism, whatever . . . your future encounter with the Being of Light. The next time you go to the other side—hopefully at a ripe old age."

"Oh, no, no!" Melana Gardner shook her head and began to cry a little. "I'm not capable of it, Nathan—not *worthy!*"

"Oh yes you are." I reached out and squeezed her arm, struggling to keep my voice steady. "The Being of Light himself will help you. Through the Holy Spirit. He intends it."

215

32

The gray highway, with its bright yellow line, unfurled before me and fled hummingly backward beneath the tires. Mirages simmered ahead, expanded alluringly into tiny silver-blue lakes that evaporated within seconds. A dented white pickup bearing two young Navajos with crow-colored hair reamed by, spewing exhaust from its tail pipe, heading back the way I had come and reminding me of Dare's absentee companion Elder Begay. We had called President Linford the preceding day, given him the story on Melana Gardner, and learned, in the process, that Elder Begay would be back in the missionary saddle two days hence.

I hadn't informed the good president of my final words to Melana, fearing in retrospect that perhaps I had been presumptuous. And yet . . . the feeling of rightness, the "burning in the bosom," had been very keen, and after all, wasn't it our right, indeed constant responsibility, to discover the will of the Lord, especially in some of life's most critical situations? So maybe I had been right on target, I told myself; maybe I had been sent to the Arizona Phoenix Mission in large measure for that very reason.

Ahead, sunlight poured between a few passing clouds, cascading along the highway. I could see the sun riding high in the blue, a constant, blinding explosion of white-gold light—that mighty star that gives our world its life, without which it would not only be dead but might never have existed. Suddenly its significance, its power, and symbolism virtually roared in my mind. What greater natural symbol of the divine could one ever find? What greater natural extension of our Maker himself, the source of all light, who had ordained and created it.

Yes, all Melana's art would somehow celebrate light now, the light of God. What would become of her "works of darkness" I wasn't sure. I had an idea she might burn them, and for a moment I felt very conflicting emotions. On the one hand, I hated to think of such genius being destroyed. On the other, they all—The Morass in particular—literally seemed to emanate evil. Their consignment to the ash heap would probably prove very sound psychologically and spiritually for their creator.

For a time I reflected upon other things, one matter especially that also gladdened the heart considerably. The previous evening, after our good-byes that afternoon at the Pedersons, we received another special phone call. Dare had answered with the usual LDS missionary salutation. Then there was a long pause as his smile broadened. "Hey, that's great! I'm really glad to hear it." He continued to listen for some time with occasional little uh-huhs, rights, and more greats. "Okay, very good. I'll be there with one of the other Elders." A pause. "Yeah, my dad's heading back to Ogden in the morning. Yes . . . hey, that's wonderful. I'll be sure to tell him." Another pause. "Yes, absolutely; we'll be there!"

Moments later he hung up and favored me with a smile that was almost conspiratorial. "Three guesses."

I smiled back, vaguely realizing that I was mirroring his own expression. "The Williamses?"

He nodded vigorously, strode my way, and gave the winner's clap. It was a moment of grand rapport. "That was Allie. She told me they've really been talking it over and praying a lot—and they want to start studying again right away, maybe even be baptized New Year's Day if we think they're ready."

"Beautiful!" I exclaimed. "Incredible!" And truly I felt a thrill of delight.

"She said they'd been wrestling with it for a couple of days. But then your letter came along, and Pop—it really helped. It answered a lot of their questions and sort of put the whole thing into perspective."

"Praise be and hallelujah!" I truly meant it, because I felt very certain that anything of worth in that letter had come from the Spirit.

"'Course they'll have to be interviewed and everything, and we'll have to make real sure they're right on track. But . . ." He grinned and tossed out his hands. "Sounds like a winner."

So morning unfurled into noon, carrying me upward through the snowy mountains of Flagstaff, and by 3:00 P.M. I was crossing the big dam at Lake Powell, now in virtual summer. Even then, though, my heart was still in Arizona, reliving over and over the events of the past three-plus weeks. As a going-away present, I had taken my three young missionaries out for supper. Afterward, we deposited Mac and Hud at their apartment and pulled up into the parking lot outside our own. The classical music station was playing Beethoven's *Choral Symphony*, one of my favorite works, one resounding with glorious voices full of uplift and rejoicing. Full of light.

Dare yawned and stretched. "You know somethin', Pop? Back before my mission I couldn't have cared less for this stuff, but the pres said we could listen to it, any really good classical, along with the Tabernacle Choir. So I took him up on it, and you know somethin', Pop?" he repeated.

"What?"

"It's really been terrif. I mean, I always liked the Choir, but learning to groove on this great classical stuff . . . it's sort of like getting a testimony. Know what I mean?"

"Very similar," I replied, "a nice analogy, in fact."

"Sometimes I just . . . " For a few seconds, he merely bobbed his head a little from side to side as though weighing the matter. "Oh, like right this minute—I sit and listen to these great old guys, and I can't believe it. They're so *neat*, so incredible. Like, well, take Beethoven. Here he is, back two hundred years ago, sitting down out in the woods or whatever puttin' all these little marks on paper—even after he's stone deaf, like *hearing* the whole thing right inside his mind."

"Yes, isn't that fantastic?"

"And now, here we are listening to the results. I mean, think of all the *miracles* that it took to put it all together and bring it here, right now, two centuries later!"

"Verily," I said quietly. I must have been casting a small glow.

"And you wanna know something else?"

"Lay it on me."

"I'm really starting to tune in on what we were talking about a while back—what Alma said about *all things* proving there's a God. I can't really explain it all, but I believe it."

"I likewise," I said and gave the back of his neck a little squeeze. His final words alone had been worth my whole "December mission." That's what I was beginning to call it in my own mind. Then, uncertain as to whether I should raise the issue, I said casually, "So how goes the war?"

He shot me a glance, reflecting a gleam from the nearby street light. "The war?"

I shrugged, flipped up my thumbs. "The Cindy business—the infamous Dear John."

"Hmmm . . . oh, yes—the Cindy business. The Dear John." He took a deep breath and expelled it between his lips in a long silent whistle. "I really don't know; I'm still sort of shell-shocked or something. Like I can't quite make it compute. Ya know?"

"Yes, I really do," I said.

"And so much has been happening right on top of it, I've hardly had time to *think* about it."

"Maybe that's the secret to most of our woes," I said, "to be 'anxiously engaged in a good cause' all the time."

"Yeah. But ya know, Pop . . . " A slight twist of the head, the faintest snort of a laugh. "It's sort of like somebody you were really counting on has died. Except that the person who died dumped you for somebody else first."

"I hear you," I said.

"But . . . " He sighed, opening the door halfway, hesitating. "I guess my little problem's pretty small-time compared to what people like Melana have gone through."

"Not as bad, maybe," I said, "but not small-time either—even if it's traditional to make a big joke of the Dear John for some reason." I clapped my hand on his back. "No, old buddy, it's very significant, no small deal, not by any means. But . . . and I'm not going to give you a sermon or a bunch of the usual about other fishes in the sea. I'm just going to tell you one thing: you'll handle it, and you'll win. Okay? By carrying on the work. Because you're that kind of guy."

Night was settling as I reached Panguitch, Utah, and just beyond I angled left, heading west along a lonely little road that wound for twenty miles through the mountains. It was solid black within their folds, sans any illumination (except my headlights) even from the sky. For a time I felt a kind of superstitious anxiety, a childish yet also real wondering as to what was lying out there in all that darkness.

At length, however, I descried a pinpoint of light in the distance, and ere long I had attained the broad, welcoming expanse of the freeway, I-15. At that point a thought surfaced, not entirely new, certainly, but from a special perspective. "All the darkness in the universe," the words came, "cannot extinguish the smallest light . . . but the smallest light can always extinguish some of the darkness." At that precise moment, for a mere instant, I glimpsed a tiny star above a dark shoulder of mountain and felt a

220

pleasant tingling that gradually increased, full of truth and exhilaration.

My friendly little Chevette purred onward, its tank full of gas from a recent stop, running more smoothly and confidently the farther it went, passing the little towns of Kanosh, Holden, and Scipio, each marked by long stretches of amber highway lights. Again I was entering real Christmas country—fields skiffed with snow, periodic flakes sifting down, occasional farm homes in the distance atwinkle with colored lights, and I was listening again to the Roger Wagner Chorale and the Mormon Tabernacle Choir singing Christmas songs on the tapes I had brought from home. At Santaquin I hit heavy patches of fog and had to creep for long stretches at twenty mph, still reflecting upon the recent past—and now . . . about the future as well.

Now, finally, with Salt Lake City behind and Ogden itself approaching, I was reliving my farewell with Dare at nine that morning. I had deposited him for safekeeping with Mac and Hud down the street and thanked them for "putting up with an old interloper from another generation." We even exchanged vigorous hugs; already they were much like my own sons. Then Dare accompanied me out to the car, where I opened the door ready to climb in. "Well, Pop . . ." He grinned.

"Well, yourself," I said. "Give me a hug, pal—a good big one for the road." And that's what we did, a good, hard, combined rib-cruncher along with hefty pats on the back. "I sure do love ya, Darry Boy," I said as we released each other. It was the name I had used when he was just a little guy, and now used only on very special occasions.

"I love you too, Pop," he said. Did I detect a trace of moisture in one eye? Maybe, maybe not, but I felt something suspicious there in my own. The old tear ducts were certainly getting a workout lately—for quite a few of us. "It's really been terrif!"

"My sentiments exactly," I said. He was standing there with a quizzical little smile, looking a "titch," as he might put it, homesick, as if also the reality of his recent unattachment were taking hold a little. But now was not the time to talk about it. "Take care of my kid . . . and stay sober." He tossed his head, laughing, unleashing that familiar, empathic grin. Then he held up his palm vertically for me to give it the winner's clap, and we reversed the process with my own extended horizontally.

"Have a merry Christmas," I said. "Put in a kick on the finish, and get yourself home by jolly old St. Valentine's." Then, unable to resist, I turned back for an instant. "One final thing—something I just have to say." I placed a hand on his shoulder and looked him in the eye. "I'm so downright *proud* of you I'm about ready to do backflips."

"Thanks, Pop," he said. "Same to you."

He was still smiling that smile, standing there in the morning sunlight, and again there was that element of growing handsomeness, manliness—the facial features assuming their adult permanence, the cheekbones and brow more pronounced, the jaw a bit heavier, and jutting, with a slight cleft I had never noticed before. The beard roots were even denser and heavier, permanent "five o'clock shadow" despite the morning shave. Hair immensely blonde, almost halo-like in the sunlight, eyes a tan-gold with flecks of green, remarkably luminous.

"Drive with care, Pop."

"Will do." Then I was driving away—waving, catching a final glimpse of his white shirt as he tossed a jaunty little salute.

The lights of Ogden were emerging now. As I turned down the familiar street a short while later, it was beginning to snow again. Barely past midnight the day before Christmas. And there it was, my home on the edge of the great hollow at Polk's End. The golf course and the canyon mouth, below and beyond, lay steeped in enchantment and mystery. There in the far window was the lighted tree, casting pools of color through the darkness onto the white-mantled lawn.

Sally Girl and the kids were still up, waiting for me, just inside. I could feel it.